"Robert."

After four years the sound of her voice was still as familiar to him as his own. He could remember all its nuances, the clear musical sound with its husky undertones sliding like velvet over his skin.

But this rough voice, filled with shock and fear, was new. It cut through him like the blade of a knife. He wanted to draw her into his arms and promise her that this was nothing but a bad dream. He forced himself to stare out the window instead.

"Go," he muttered.

The terrorist came up from behind and pushed her forward. Marianne barely felt the shove. She stumbled, then took another step until she was even with Robert's row.

There her legs refused to obey. She could not walk past him as if he were a stranger. She could not leave him behind as if his fate did not matter.

Because it did matter.

She reached out and touched his shoulder.

Dear Reader:

Once again, Silhouette Intimate Moments has put together a very special month for you, with the sort of exciting yet always romantic plots you've come to expect from us.

A couple of books this month deserve special mention because their heroes are a bit different from the usual. In *Full Circle*, Paula Detmer Riggs gives us Trevor Markus, a man with a hidden past that threatens to destroy all his hopes for the future. I think your heart will beat a little faster and you may even find tears in your eyes as you discover the secret Trevor has spent years protecting—the secret that may separate him forever from the only woman he's ever loved.

New author Ann Williams brings us another very different hero in her first book, *Devil in Disguise*. "Nick" is a puzzle when he first appears, a mystery man with no memory of his past. Only two things about him are clear: he's the key to the troubles that have begun plaguing tiny Fate, Texas—and he's the most sensuous and appealing man rancher Caitlin Barratt has ever met.

I'd love to hear from you after you've read these books—or any of our other Intimate Moments, including this month's other selections, from Mary Anne Wilson and Sibylle Garrett. Please feel free to write to me with your comments at any time.

Sincerely,

Leslie J. Wainger
Senior Editor
Silhouette Books
300 E. 42nd Street
New York, NY 10017

Sibylle Garrett

Sullivan's Challenge

Silhouette Intimate Moments
Published by Silhouette Books New York
America's Publisher of Contemporary Romance

SILHOUETTE BOOKS
300 East 42nd St., New York, N.Y. 10017

ISBN: 0-373-07301-1

First Silhouette Books printing September 1989

SIBYLLE GARRETT

is a world traveler who finally settled down on Long Island with her husband of twenty-two years and their two children. Her love of books, her vivid imagination and a desire to share her many personal adventures eventually propelled her toward a career in writing. Writing romances satisfies the dreamer as well as the realist in her.

To Addie,
a wonderful friend.

And special thanks to my niece Tanya's husband, Mark Ford, for providing me with the detailed information about the Boeing 747.

Chapter 1

The intercom of the Boeing 747 crackled with static. "Ladies and gentlemen. We are now flying over the coast of France. We will be landing in Paris in approximately thirty minutes. Please return to your seats. The temperature at Orly airport is fifty-three degrees, and it's drizzling. The local time is 7:36."

In the first-class lounge on the upper deck, Robert Lewis Sullivan put down the empty brandy snifter he'd been twirling in his hand as the flight attendant began collecting empty glasses, peanut wrappers and ashtrays. Three years after his discharge from the State Department's anti-terrorist division, discipline was still as much a part of him as was his habit of observing and listening to conversations instead of joining them.

His hooded green eyes looked over the group of men and women still hovering at the bar. He shook his head. Only one other person, a slim, dark-haired man, was following the captain's instructions. The others continued their talk, leisurely finishing their drinks and their discussions of yesterday's market performance, the latest in spring fashions, and house parties to be given over the upcoming Easter holidays.

Robert had noticed the Mideastern businessman earlier. He'd nursed his glass of Perrier with an appreciation for the water that had reminded Robert of the Bedouins who roamed the desert beyond Omari. First he'd taken a mouthful, then had slowly swirled the liquid around in his glass, much like a connoisseur enjoying a great wine. Like Robert, the man hadn't taken part in any of the conversations and had also kept apart from the party crowd. Occasionally he studied the faces of the passengers who surrounded him. But Robert would have bet that he hadn't missed a single word of their conversations and that the passengers' faces were permanently imprinted in his mind.

Restlessly Robert uncoiled his lean long body from the comfortable seat. He watched as the man strode toward the staircase leading down to first class. Old habits die hard, he thought with a grimace. He'd observed people almost as long as he could remember. Only the reasons for his scrutiny had changed. At first it had been because of his desperate need to get away from foster homes, then it was to find the formula that made one man a failure and another a success. The formula he discovered had been simple: put in a lot of work, get to know the right people, and be ready when opportunity came along. Following that basic formula had gotten him into West Point and later into the elite anti-terrorist division, the ATD. There his objective had changed again. Observation had become a matter of survival in its truest meaning.

That had been a long time ago, Robert thought, straightening his green-and-gray striped tie and brushing a few peanut shells from his pale green shirt. Sometimes he still missed those days when he'd lived on the edge. The days before Marianne.

Not wanting to think about her, Robert fixed his attention again on the Arab. His eyes sharpened. Something about the slim straight figure clad in a dark mohair business suit jarred his senses. Perhaps it was the man's erect, almost military, carriage and the precise step, which did not fit the typical image of a travel-weary businessman. Or maybe it was the way he hesitated at the head of the stairs and looked back over his shoulder. That act reminded Robert of his own continuing compulsion to watch his back, another of his many habits that were so deeply ingrained they had survived his switch of careers.

When the man walked down the stairs without even glancing at the door leading to the cockpit, Robert's suspicions eased and he relaxed a little. But he reached for the attaché case that was now as much a part of him as was his gun during his field days, and followed the man.

He knew he was nervous and on edge. He had been ever since the leaks about the negotiations with Omari had begun. The news that the United States was planning to build a military base in that small Persian Gulf emirate had created a great deal of heat from student groups as well as demonstrators who were financed by Shiite terrorists. Iran wanted to prevent the establishment of another outpost of the "Satanic" U.S. so close to its borders and had threatened more violent actions. Robert's fingers tightened around the handle of the leather case. He'd love to get his hands on the person responsible for the leak that had put a great many lives at risk.

When he reached the top of the stairs, the man had disappeared.

Uneasily Robert shot another look at the closed door to the flight deck, then swiftly went down the steps. In the first class compartment his glance flew past a mother collecting

Lego blocks and a gray-haired woman buckling a three-foot-high pink Easter bunny into the seat next to hers. For a moment his eyes lingered on the pink monstrosity. Marianne, he thought, would have loved its long satiny ears and its cheeky grin. She'd had a weakness for whimsical toys. Briefly he wondered if she still collected teddy bears, then returned to his objective. Where was that man? Many passengers were still in the aisles, searching the overhead storage bins for their wool coats and mink jackets. But the man was nowhere in sight.

Robert turned back to go to the galley where the man might have stopped for a word with one of the flight attendants. But a steady stream of passengers returning from the rest rooms blocked his path.

"Sir, please sit down." The brunette flight attendant who had served him his meals asked him with a polite, if slightly strained, smile.

Robert hesitated, uneasily turning to her. "Did you see..." Then he checked himself and proceeded to his seat. This mission was important to him, for personal as well as professional reasons, but that was no excuse to suspect every Mideastern male of terrorism. Suspicion was another habit that died hard, he told himself, trying to shake his uneasiness. But that deep gut feeling had saved his life more than once.

Sliding into his aisle seat in the last row, he placed his briefcase beneath the seat in front, then once again examined the faces of his fellow passengers. Why not suspect the two men wearing army surplus jackets, who sat in the front row? With their unshaven faces and surly expressions they at least looked the part.

Suddenly the plane lurched sharply, freezing the grim smile on Robert's face. Before he could brace himself, he was tossed sideways, into the lean black-haired man sitting next to him. The plane straightened and Robert eased his

weight off his seatmate. "Sorry," he said, "I wasn't prepared for that."

"Funny maneuver." The man's soft drawl was barely
audible above the gasps and screams filling the cabin. "I
thought this plane was too big to drop into air pockets."

"I thought so, too." Robert bent down to retrieve his
briefcase, which had come to rest near the man's scuffed
leather boots. Then he watched the other passengers
scramble for their Hermès cases, Gucci purses and Saks
shopping bags now littering the aisle.

The 747 had veered off course as if to avoid a midair col-
lision and seemed to be climbing now. What the hell was
going on? Robert swore silently, feeling the back of his neck
bristle in anticipation of danger. His questions were answered almost instantly.

"Sit down. Everybody return to their seats."

Robert froze at the sound of the harsh guttural order
barked in heavily accented English. He shot a narrowed look
at the two men in their army surplus jackets. They now
stood back to back, kicking the bags at their feet out of the
way. They did not fit into this setting of wealth and success. Their faces showed a different kind of arrogance—a
mixture of raw power, contemptuous superiority and fanatical sneers. Robert was utterly familiar with their kind.
He had dealt with them for years. But the knowledge that
his instincts were just as sharp as they'd always been had
come too late. "Damn!" he swore softly.

This was a hijacking.

Anger shot through him. Strong. Boiling hot. For a moment he crouched in his chair, every muscle in his lean body
tensing against the threat. His hard eyes glittered as he considered jumping them before they could draw the weapons
bulging their pockets.

But in midair the risk was too great.

Suddenly the flight attendant straightened up from helping to buckle a red-haired boy into his seat. With the child's stuffed tiger still clutched in her hand, she faced the two men. ''Gentlemen, I must ask you to return to your seats immediately.'' Her voice was slightly hoarse, as if she, too, sensed the gravity of the situation.

Robert was out of his seat before she'd finished the order, but not soon enough to prevent the man from slapping her. At her cry, the cabin fell silent, as if holding its breath. For a moment she stood her ground. Then she fell back.

''Easy now.'' Robert braced the slight, trembling body with his own while staring at the pear-shaped object the terrorist had withdrawn from his pocket.

And then the loudspeaker crackled over their heads.

''Ladies and gentlemen. This is your captain. Please remain seated and don't panic. The plane has been hijacked by members of the Holy Islamic Brigade. I have been assured that no one will be harmed in any way as long as we follow their instructions. Please be assured that the Trans Atlantic Airlines officials will do everything in their power to resolve this situation as soon as possible. In the meantime, please be patient.''

Marianne Lloyd Sullivan stared blankly at the two men as if they were a nightmare she expected to fade.

Hijacked!

So this is what a hand grenade looks like, she thought, still trying to grasp the harsh reality of the situation. It seemed so small, smaller than a Fourth of July sky rocket. Too small to threaten hundreds of lives and reroute a plane in midair. It didn't seem real. This was a joke.

Paris was only twenty minutes away. The plane had to land on time or she'd miss her connection to Chamonix. Her travel agent had warned her that she was cutting it close when she'd made the reservation. Marianne could still hear her laughing response, that she'd never missed a flight in her life, that planes seemed to have a habit of waiting for her.

Now the commuter plane would leave without her. Would someone warn her father before he made the long drive into Chamonix? She stared at the grenade once again. In the dim light of the cabin it looked black.

With a shaky hand she pushed a swath of her chin-length blond hair behind her ear. Only minutes ago the cabin had rung with laughter and eager anticipation. Then the swift, brutal attack on the stewardess had stunned them all. Now the only sounds she heard were those of the terrorists walking up and down the aisle and their harsh guttural orders to the passengers to fasten seat belts and keep their hands in sight. The red-haired toddler who had played so intently with his Lego blocks earlier sobbed "Mommy, I'm scared. I want Daddy."

The boy's cry for help tightened Marianne's throat. *Thank God, Bobby and my parents are okay.* Her mind repeated those words over and over again, as if drawing strength from her loved ones' safety. She had been reluctant to take her son out of school a week before Easter recess. Now she thanked God that she had given in to her parents' suggestion to let them take him off her hands while she dealt with the ever-growing mountain of tax returns piling up on her desk. Bobby was with them at her mother's family house near Chamonix. That was something to be grateful for.

"Oh, why did I let my kids persuade me to fly?" Mrs. Rafferty, Marianne's flight companion from Paris, Texas, whispered shakily. "I wanted to take a cruise to London and from there the boat-train to France. But my kids thought it would be safer to avoid England." She swallowed, then added with a ghost of a smile, "I guess violence can explode anywhere, any time."

Marianne nodded. While she did not share the older woman's fear, she, too, preferred the sea. The sound of groaning boards and snapping sails was as familiar to her as the creaking of her own brass bed. It was this deadly silence that terrified her, the smell of fear instead of salt air. She reached for the gnarled, blue-veined hand clawing the armrest as if it were a life preserver. Like her own, it was cold.

But still there was comfort in touching another human being.

"I almost missed the flight because of an accident on Grand Central Parkway," Marianne said. "Now I wish I was still stuck in that traffic jam. I arrived at the ticket counter so late that they'd already given my seat to a passenger on standby. This place in first class was the only one left." Her voice cracked as she became aware of the hijacker stopping next to Mrs. Rafferty's seat.

Marianne could feel his dark liquid eyes burning into her skin. Even before the hijacking he had made this trip misery. From the moment he'd sat down in the seat behind her, he had watched her every move with an almost fanatical intensity that had made her skin crawl. When his whispers to her had started she'd been tempted to ask the flight attendant for the empty seat next to the gray-haired woman with the Easter bunny. But she'd refused to let the obtuse imbecile chase her out of her seat and away from a woman whose company she enjoyed. That same stubborn pride made her ignore him now. And after a few more breathless seconds, he turned away.

Cautiously Marianne watched him walk down the aisle to meet the other terrorist. Listening to their words, she wished she could understand what they were discussing so heatedly. Robert would have understood every word of it, she thought. Bobby's father spoke Arabic as fluently as Marianne spoke French.

Her ex-husband worked for the State Department and would probably hear the news long before her parents did. The knowledge that Robert was somewhere out there was oddly comforting. At least, she thought with rising panic, Bobby had one parent to turn to if things went wrong.

"What time is it?" asked Mrs. Rafferty. With shaking fingers, she had pushed back the sleeve of her flowered blue silk dress and was squinting at the small diamond-studded wristwatch as if time was the only reality in her world gone mad. "My glasses are in my purse."

"It's ten after eight," Marianne whispered with a glance at the pink-and-white Swatch watch her parents had given her for Christmas. Only forty-five minutes until her flight left for Chamonix.

She still could not quite grasp the harsh reality. That would take hours yet. But the practical part of her still seemed to function. After the seven-hour flight the plane must be running low on fuel, she thought. They would have to land somewhere soon. But where?

And what would happen to them when they did?

Again she reached for Mrs. Rafferty's hand. She had never felt so alone before, so isolated, shipwrecked. All her life she had been surrounded by her family, her parents and her brother Colin, and enough aunts, uncles and cousins to form two football teams.

Robert had once said that. She remembered that day so well. July 4, 1979, two weeks after she'd run into Robert with her bicycle. It had been a warm, breezy day, perfect for the annual family picnic. But even if it had poured, she would have thought the day was great. She'd done well on her finals. The fall semester had been a carefree summer away. She'd been nineteen and deliriously happy. She had been in love with the most gorgeous man she'd ever met.

"In Texas it's only one o'clock in the morning," Mrs. Rafferty whispered with a convulsive squeeze on Marianne's hand. "My kids couldn't have heard the news yet. My husband and I always planned to go and see the old Paris. But he died last year. We would have been married fifty years this month." She blinked and waited until strength had returned to her voice. "I didn't want to make this trip without him. And then my children gave me this ticket." Her voice broke.

"Perhaps we'll be free by the time they wake up," Marianne whispered back with some of her old optimism. Things rarely turned out to be as bad as they seemed. Once she'd thought she'd die if she ever lost the man she loved. Now she knew that pain faded and wounds healed if one was determined to look at the bright side of life.

Why then did Robert come to mind so insistently now?

Marianne closed her eyes, willing herself to think of her family. She could see them almost as clearly as if she were there. Her father and Bobby would slide into the boots she had given them both for Christmas, green ones for her son and brown ones for her Dad. In her mind she followed them through her grandmother's house, from the big blue- and white-tiled kitchen where they'd just finished their café au lait to the long narrow foyer. Her father would duck his head to avoid knocking into the braids of garlic and onions hanging from the dark beams while Bobby would jump to touch them, sending a shower of dry skins down on him. She could hear her mother's "Stop that, Bobby" followed by her grandmother Marie's chuckling reminder that as a girl she'd done the same thing.

Panic rushed through her as she realized that she might never hug her father and son again. She pushed herself up on her armrests and twisted to stare at the exit door at the back of the cabin. Would it ever open for her again? Would she ever see her family again? Or Robert?

"Marianne, sit down," Mrs. Rafferty whispered, tugging at her pleated gray flannel skirt. "We are going to be fine, my dear. Please, just sit down. You are going to attract that man's attention again.''

The older woman's voice penetrated her panic. Marianne shook her head, her eyes sliding apprehensively over the passengers and toward the terrorist who had walked up the aisle to meet his friend. That's when she saw the tall, dark-haired man wearing a gray tweed jacket. The same man who had helped the flight attendant back to her seat. She hadn't seen him clearly then. Now she did, and she braced herself against the shock.

He sat with his head tilted back, his forearms propped on the armrests, his long fingers loosely cupping the ends. He looked as relaxed as if he were sitting in one of her mother's patio chairs, lulled into sleep by the gently breaking waves of Long Island Sound.

Seeing Robert brought back a flood of memories about her failed marriage. At first she'd blamed her youth for her inability to reach Robert. At nineteen, she'd been too young and inexperienced to stir more than desire in a man nine years older. It had taken four years of heartbreak to realize that her sheltered innocence and his street-wise experience had been only two of the stumbling blocks in their marriage. Eventually the growing mountain of stumbling blocks had become irreconcilable differences.

She still winced at those words.

He had changed so little, she thought, trying to stem the sudden surge of seething emotions. The two dimples bracketing his mouth had deepened into slashes accentuating his lean, tough looks. He had a rawboned, sharp-edged look to him that even the thick, unruly dark hair did not soften.

Suddenly she noticed a slight twitch of his square jaw and realized that his attention was totally fixed on the two terrorists. She couldn't see his cool green eyes because they were masked by thick lashes, but she remembered them well.

They were sharp and intense, and not always entirely comfortable to look into.

And then, as if sensing her stare, he raised his lids.

Before Marianne could sink back into her chair, their eyes clashed. He blinked, as if he did not trust his vision, then focused on her again. His firm mouth flattened into a straight line of denial as if she was an unwelcome vision he wanted to fade. Then his eyes probed the seat next to hers, where Mrs. Rafferty was bending down to take her glasses out of her purse. His lips moved in silent question. "Bobby?"

Marianne shook her head. *How could you forget Bobby flew to Chamonix last week with Mom and Dad? Your son didn't talk about anything else the last time he called you. But then you rarely remember dates.*

Her sudden bitterness startled her. She'd thought she'd come to terms with her pain long ago. She had been rather proud of her state of detachment whenever Robert's name cropped up. Bobby loved his father and talked about him frequently. Her parents were fond of him and still saw him occasionally. Robert had become a persistent shadow at the fringe of her life. She'd learned to live with it gracefully, and without bitterness. Now she realized that she had merely deluded herself. There was still pain and anger and a feeling of inadequacy that she had tried so hard to overcome.

She wondered how she could have missed him before. She distinctly remembered that the aisle seat in the last row had been vacant when she'd entered the cabin in New York. She'd mistakenly assumed that it was hers.

Then why hadn't she noticed him on her way to the rest room? She'd had to walk right past his seat. Frowning, she remembered that two hours ago the lights in the cabin had been dimmed and that she'd had to pick her way over sprawling legs, a three-foot pink Easter bunny and a car made out of Lego blocks. Also, she'd been afraid that the man sitting behind her would follow her. Still, she would have noticed Robert. She was certain of it. She couldn't imagine walking right past his seat and not recognizing the man she'd once loved beyond everything. . . .

Marianne was on this plane! Alone. Robert shut his eyes, thanking fate for small mercies, then opened them again. What the hell was she doing on this flight? She was supposed to have left for France a week ago. But even as his body absorbed the shock, he realized that as an accountant she could hardly have gone on vacation the week before April 15. Had his son mentioned that he was flying ahead with his grandparents and that Marianne would follow them?

He couldn't remember. He'd been swamped with meetings and paperwork, trying to tie up all the loose ends of the treaty with Omari before Easter.

Marianne's hair was darker than he remembered. And definitely shorter. The new style was sophisticated, accentuating her large gray eyes and the flawless structure of her oval face. He guessed the new style was more practical than the thick long mane that had once rippled through his fingers like heavy silk. Still, there was a vague sense of loss, much the same as he felt every time he saw his son after long months of separation and was confronted with his changes.

Whenever he thought of Marianne, he always envisioned her as he had seen her on the day they'd met: coasting down the hill in front of her parents' house in Stony Brook, her white T-shirt clinging to her breasts, her long brown legs revealed by skimpy red shorts. She'd been the embodiment of laughter, warmth and youth. Perhaps because his life had always lacked those qualities, he had been drawn to her instantly. Somehow that first impression had always stayed with him. She'd been carefree, a little reckless. Young.

And he had felt too old, too experienced and far too cynical for her.

They had been worlds apart. And now they were together again on a flight into hell.

Her face was so pale, shocked, her large gray eyes dark with fear. He wanted to jump up, take her in his arms and promise her that she would be safe, that she had nothing to fear. They usually released the women and children. It was men like himself they kept as hostages.

And then her first, incredulous shock of recognition passed, and a wave of bitterness rolled toward him. Bitterness for what? he demanded, staring back at her. *She* had walked out on *him*.

But not without good reason, he reminded himself. It had taken him years to admit his full share of the blame for their divorce. At the time he'd felt furious, betrayed—and in some ways relieved, because deep down he had always felt guilty about getting her pregnant and robbing her of her youth.

He tore his eyes loose and gave the briefcase beneath his seat a swift, sideways kick.

The sudden, angry motion startled his seatmate, who looked at him sharply. "Watch out," he warned softly, studying Robert's taut features. "Don't want to attract their interest without a good reason."

Robert bent down and retrieved his brown leather case. He'd needed to hit out at something, but the stranger was right. The momentary release of tension hadn't been worth the risk of drawing attention to himself again. Once had been more than enough.

"I've wanted to do that a couple of times myself," the man next to him admitted beneath his breath. "But I prefer a different target." His light brown eyes strayed to the terrorists. "Any idea how many more are on the plane?"

"Your guess is as good as mine," Robert said evasively, probing the harsh, deeply bronzed face with sudden interest. The man's high cheekbones, beaked nose and blue-black hair fairly shouted his Indian warrior heritage. The more Robert looked beneath the surface, the better he liked what he saw. He leaned back in his chair and said softly, "My name's Robert."

"Rafe."

The fact that Rafe did not mention his last name only strengthened Robert's conviction that he once had lived in a world where names changed with each new assignment.

Because their lives might depend on each other, Robert tested his seatmate's tactical knowledge. "About twelve, I suspect. They need at least three to guard the larger business and coach sections, and about four for the upper lounge and flight deck."

The man looked at Robert with the deadpan expression of the poker player who knew his opponent was bluffing. "Eight's their lucky number, I would say," he drawled, revealing his knowledge one card at a time. With a gleam in his eyes, he turned over a second card. "Two well-trained soldiers with automatics are enough to hold a hundred or so frightened passengers in check."

Robert's thoughts returned to the Arab businessman with his military carriage and nodded his agreement. "Any idea where we're going to land?"

Rafe shook his head. "Beirut seems like the most obvious choice, but they can't make Lebanon on what's left in the fuel tanks. My bet is they'll try to first land in Paris. We've been flying in circles ever since the takeover."

Robert listened to the confirmation of his own thoughts with a nod of relief. He infinitely preferred Paris to Rome or Athens, and especially to Libya. In Paris, when the women and children were released—at this moment he refused to consider the alternative—Marianne wouldn't be alone, stranded in a foreign country with only strangers to turn to for help. The thought was reassuring.

He didn't have any illusions about his own release. He was the wrong sex and the wrong age. In addition, both his present mission and his past occupation made him a prime target. For a moment he wished he still carried a gun instead of a diplomatic passport.

He allowed himself another glance at the top of Marianne's head, barely visible above the high back of the seat. It would have to be the last glance, he thought. He did not want her connected to himself in any way. Her release and his survival depended on it. If the terrorists found out who he was and who Marianne was, they would use her to persuade him to cooperate. The thought made his blood freeze.

He saw her half rise out of her seat and turn to look at him again. *Sit down and pretend I'm a stranger,* he wanted to shout. But his lips never formed the silent words. They froze when he saw the terrorist stop at her row and stare at her as he had done several times before.

Robert did not like the looks of the man. He was volatile, unpredictable. A defective fuse that could blow at any time. He'd noticed the man's interest in her earlier, before he had seen who she was. He'd felt pity for her then. Now anger shot through him.

Marianne noticed the terrorist only after his fingers began scratching at the cushion above Mrs. Rafferty's head, wrinkling the starched blue doily, then smoothing it out again, while Mrs. Rafferty shrank further into her seat and her tanned skin faded into a yellowish parchment white.

Marianne held her breath, wishing she hadn't dared another look at Robert's face. After sweeping a glance over the other passenger's faces to mask her real interest, she sank back into her seat, trying to ignore the terrorist's presence. But her mouth was dry with fear.

"You do not like Hamid?" The guttural voice was heavily accented and hoarse, like the voices nightmares were made of.

So his name was Hamid. The knowledge did not ease her fear. It increased it instead. That he revealed his name only emphasized just how safe he felt, and how vulnerable she was. She became aware of his fingers tearing at the fabric, like a boy cruelly tearing out a fly's legs. That made her angry. She hated needless destruction. Fear receded and her backbone stiffened.

She was a fighter, not a simple fly caught in a spider's web, but she realized that it would be stupid to enrage him further with her silence. Coolly she turned to answer him. "I don't know you." She pitched her voice low and soothing, the way she did when she tried to calm an enraged client who had just received an audit from the IRS. For a moment it seemed to work because the plucking motion stilled. Then it started again.

"You be nice to Hamid and nothing happen to you."

It took all of Marianne's control not to shiver with loathing at the suggestion. Then the other hijacker snapped something in what Marianne suspected was Arabic. Hamid's answer was an angry tug at the doily, finally tearing the fabric from its Velcro fastening. He stared at the light blue linen in his hand for a moment, then crushed it in his fist. He dropped it and, looking at her pointedly, ground it under his heel. Only then did he join his friend.

Robert slowly let out the breath he'd been holding and unclenched his fists, but a fury boiled beneath his tautly stretched skin.

"She handled that rather well," Rafe commented with a sharp look at Robert's face. "*You* had me worried, though. I was all prepared to tackle you. That bastard is so nervous, he'd have pulled the pin if you'd jumped him."

"I wouldn't have been that stupid," Robert said. He willed his body to relax, but his pulse still beat unevenly.

"If that woman had been my wife or my girlfriend, I'd have felt like killing him," Rafe said softly.

Robert shot him a bland look. "I'm single and unattached."

"Then she must be one of the ghosts from your past. Sometimes they are more disturbing than the real thing."

Robert neither confirmed nor denied Rafe's suspicions. But he did agree with him that Marianne had handled the situation well. If she'd tried to ignore the man, he would have pushed until he'd gotten a response. And Marianne's pent-up responses had always erupted with the fierce, swift rage of a summer thunderstorm. Pride swelled within him when he thought of her control, the mature way she had defused the potentially explosive situation. With that pride came the realization that once she was released he need not worry about her ever again.

And with the realization came pain and disorientation. He had expected to feel regret at this final severance, much like a father feels when his daughter strikes out on her own. But he had not expected the pain nor this feeling of disorientation, as if he were the one cutting loose.

Then the captain's voice came over the loudspeaker.

"Ladies and gentlemen. We have received permission to land at Orly airport. We are in contact with the French authorities and hope to negotiate your freedom soon. Please, stay in your seats and remain calm even after the engines are shut down. And thank you for your cooperation."

Robert slowly expelled a sigh of relief. He couldn't wait for Marianne to get off this plane.

Chapter 2

How much longer do we have to wait?" Mrs. Rafferty shifted anxiously in her seat.

"The fuel truck just left," Marianne said quietly, slipping her seatmate a concerned look. They had been sitting in this plane for close to twelve hours, and Mrs. Rafferty's feet had swollen to twice their normal size. Since the fuel truck had arrived, the exit door had been wide open, and cool, damp air was seeping into their bones. She noticed that Mrs. Rafferty was shivering in her thin silk dress, so she shrugged out of her blazer and draped it across the older woman's lap. "That should keep you a little warmer," she said, firmly dismissing Mrs. Rafferty's gratitude.

She ran her hands over the white silk of her blouse. She'd been numb for hours, watching a seemingly endless stream of ambulances, military vehicles and diplomatic limousines surround the plane. The thick ground fog that had swirled around them earlier had lifted, and now she could see the flashing red- and-blue lights clearly. Beacons of hope so close, and yet so far away.

Marianne dreaded the moment when they'd be told who would be released and who would stay. Not only for herself. Usually they freed the women and children, and some of the elderly and sick. Her chances were fairly good. The ones to stay behind would be men in their prime. Those with money, power and influence.

Men like Robert Sullivan.

Her hands clenched at the thought.

She turned for another glance at Robert's face, willing him to look at her. Since that first startled recognition, he had ignored her completely. Occasionally he'd talked with the man sitting next to him. But mostly his attention had been focused on the two terrorists. Perhaps it was his way of showing her that he hated her still, that he hadn't forgiven her for walking out on him. But under these circumstances his attitude seemed petty and unnecessarily cruel. And unlike anything she had expected from the father of her son.

Mrs. Rafferty shifted uneasily and tugged one of her blue-gray curls into place. "I wonder why they took our passports. We won't be able to fly back home without them."

"Don't worry about that," Marianne said soothingly. "Our embassy officials will take care of us."

Marianne thought ruefully that she seemed to have all the right answers to keep up Mrs. Rafferty's flagging spirits. But her own were sagging. Without her papers, she felt stripped of her identity. Vulnerable, and lost. Which was one of the reasons the terrorists had taken them, she supposed grimly. In the last few hours she'd found out that the men holding them hostage were a well-trained and disciplined group who knew how to instill fear while resorting to very little real violence. If only Robert had smiled at her, even once, or sent her some other silent message of support, the hours of waiting would be much easier to bear.

Suddenly the loudspeaker crackled to life. Mrs. Rafferty stopped her nervous fidgeting and sat up straight. Marianne bit her lip and slanted another look at Robert's cold, remote face.

"The Holy Islamic Brigade does not make war on women and children. You will be allowed to leave. As your names are called, you will walk *slowly* to the front exit. Leave everything behind. Your shoes, glasses and purses could puncture the plastic of the emergency chute." The slightly accented voice was cold and controlled. Without pausing, it went on to call out the names of the first passengers to be released.

"Arron, Barbarcon, Carter..."

A woman with black curls topping an olive-green turtleneck sweater jumped to her feet and flew into the aisle.

"Take your boots off," the terrorist patrolling the rear of the cabin ordered sharply.

Robert watched the woman yank off her black leather boots, walk to the exit door, then hesitate at the yellow plastic chute. *Move, damn it,* he thought with an impatience that had been growing for hours. *It looks flimsy, but the plastic will hold. About two hundred people are waiting to slide to freedom, and you're holding them up.* As if she'd heard him, the woman squatted down and suddenly disappeared. Another took her place. The second woman didn't hesitate, but plunged down swiftly.

"You think they'll keep all the men?" Rafe's eyes slid to a white-haired passenger mopping his pallid brow with a shaky hand.

"Not unless they plan to hold us all on this plane. It would be a little difficult to hide over a hundred hostages in Beirut." Robert knew he wouldn't be freed, no matter how many others were. An American diplomat was too big a prize to let slip through their fingers.

But he wasted few thoughts on what lay ahead. He would have plenty of time to prepare for captivity. Right now, Marianne's freedom was top priority. "My guess is that they'll hold about twenty of us here."

Rafe's hard mouth twisted. "Depends on the reason for the hijacking. Any idea?"

"Several. How about an independent Palestinian state? Or retaliation for bringing the two terrorists we caught to trial? Or perhaps the treaty with Omari. Take your pick."

Robert watched the gray-haired woman with the Easter bunny get to her feet. As she began to carry the stuffed toy down the aisle, the terrorist ordered, "Leave it," snatched it out of her hands and tossed it back into the seat. The woman swallowed, then raised her head regally and sailed past the terrorist and down the chute.

"I bet it's that proposed base in Omari," Rafe muttered.

"Are you against it?" Robert gave Rafe a penetrating look.

Rafe shook his head. "I thought it was a good solution to the Gulf War. Until now," he added roughly.

"They may let you go."

Rafe shook his head. "I have a visa for Jordan in my passport. I was planning to look at and possibly buy an Arabian mare I've had my eyes on for months." His eyes narrowed. "How deeply involved are you in this deal with Omari?"

Robert's first reaction was to deny any knowledge outright. But Rafe was too sharp to be deceived easily. "Deep enough," he said quietly. "Prince Jamal of Omari and I have been friends for years. You two have something in common. Jamal owns an Arabian stud in Arizona. Ever heard of him?"

"Yeah—" Rafe broke off abruptly as the terrorist stopped at their seats.

''No talking,'' he snarled, pointing his gun at Robert's head, his finger curling around the trigger threateningly. Robert stared back with eyes narrowed to silver-green slits, watching, waiting, trying to keep his mind blank, but it wasn't easy with Marianne sitting only a few feet away. Seconds later, the gun wavered, then dropped. With a cruel grin the terrorist turned away.

Robert's eyes flew to Marianne's head. Damn, he thought, she had witnessed the whole scene. Her eyes were wide and nearly black with fear. Don't do anything stupid, he warned with a slight shake of his head. When she sank back into her seat he breathed easy again, wishing that the exodus was over and he needn't worry about her anymore.

During his days in the field he had faced death more times than he liked to remember. He knew what to expect. The thought of solitary confinement, beatings, degradation and possible torture scared the hell out of him. But as long as he knew that Marianne was safe and that Bobby would have his mother, he'd survive.

Restlessly he shifted in his seat. He hated the inactivity, the waiting. Patience had never been one of his strong points. If he'd been the type to sit back and pray for miracles to drop into his lap, he'd still be only one step away from the foster homes he'd been placed in after his parents' deaths. Being tied to this damn chair with nothing to do sorely tested his self control.

He slid a hard, cold look at the terrorist named Hamid, who was leaning against the movie screen. Even now, with the passengers waiting like docile sheep for their release, he was nervously stroking the barrel of the snub-nosed automatic he had exchanged for the hand grenade. But at least he wasn't undressing Marianne with his eyes as he had done repeatedly during the dragging hours of waiting.

Fortunately Hamid was not in command. Like everyone else, he followed the clipped orders of that faceless, slightly accented voice now droning on, "M. Conway, R. Conway, Durant..."

Robert was almost certain that it belonged to the businessman. That bastard knew his job, he thought grimly. This assault was better organized than most of the ones Robert had investigated in his time. Which made him question why the man had used someone as unstable and unreliable as Hamid. Maybe he was a last-minute replacement for a more capable man.

"It's moving pretty fast. If I'm lucky I can call my children before they hear the news," Mrs. Rafferty whispered, her faded blue eyes bright with hope. "Perhaps in an hour you will be able to talk to your son."

"Yes." For the woman's sake, Marianne forced a smile on her lips. Her hands were still shaking. It wouldn't be easy to tell Bobby about his father's fate—she felt certain he wouldn't be released. She might hide the news from him if Robert were freed after only a few days. But what if his father disappeared for weeks, or a few months or even a year? What if he never came back?

The vision of Robert with the gun pointed at his head closed in on her like a dark wave, pounding at the wall of detachment she'd built so carefully over the years, tearing it down piece by piece until she could no longer lie to herself. She did care. More than she wanted to. A divorce decree could separate a son from his father and divide a household into his and hers; it limited their future relationship to child support and visiting rights. But it could not change the past.

There had been good times. Happy times.

She had fallen in love with him instantly. From the moment her brake had failed and she'd run into him with her bicycle, she had been lost. She remembered scrambling to her feet, staring at his strikingly handsome face. He'd worn a starched blue chambray shirt and sharply creased jeans. She'd noticed those because they had made her feel self-conscious about the way her damp T-shirt clung to her breasts and how her brief French shorts revealed so much of her legs....

"Are you all right?" he had asked her.

She nodded. For the first time in her life she was speechless. He had a marvelous voice—deep, vibrant, mesmerizing. Hers was a humiliating croak when she finally managed to form the words, "How about you?"

"Not a scratch. But your knee needs attention." Leaning the bike against the white picket fence behind him, he pulled a handkerchief from his jeans pocket and squatted in front of her. Gently he wiped away the blood that had run down her leg, then bandaged the wound. "My car's over there. I'll drive you home."

Marianne followed his glance to a white BMW parked about twenty feet away. "I live in the house over the hill. I can easily walk those two hundred yards. There's no need to mess up your car."

With a catlike movement he rose to his feet. He was a head taller than her five foot five, with broad shoulders and a lean build that spoke of power and speed. She had to tilt her head back to look into his face. "If you give me your address I'll send your handkerchief back to you."

He stared at her with eyes that were a silvery green, like the sea on a bright sunny day. "You can't walk ten yards on that leg." He didn't wait for her protest. He simply lifted her as if she were a child. She struggled in his strong arms. "I can't leave my bike. Someone will steal it."

"Good. That thing is a health hazard."

She bristled. "Not everyone can afford a BMW."

His eyes assessed the houses in the historic part of Stony Brook, set on manicured lawns on either side of the road. "What kind of car do you drive?" he asked.

· Marianne felt an irrational urge to trace the two dimples bracketing his mouth. "A Camaro. Only my brother borrowed it. Without my bike I'll be stranded." She struggled as he strode toward his car.

"I'll put the bike in my trunk," he offered.

Normally she would have scoffed at being carried. But since she seemed to have no choice, she decided to enjoy the novel sensation of his fluid muscles supporting her effortlessly.

She could have hugged her mother when she invited him to lunch. Over a light meal consisting of a French onion-tomato tart and a fresh garden salad, eaten on the terrace overlooking Long Island Sound, she learned that he lived in Washington and was visiting a friend at the university hospital here in Stony Brook.

"I've never been on Long Island before. It's beautiful," he said, his eyes sweeping the calm ocean dotted with sailboats and power cruisers.

"Do you sail?" Marianne asked, watching the breeze ruffle his dark hair, giving him a rakish air.

He shook his head. "I've always wanted to learn, but I never seem to have the time."

All during their lunch Marianne had searched for an excuse to see him again. Returning the handkerchief in person had seemed too tacky. Now he'd handed her the perfect opportunity, and she jumped at it instantly. "I'll teach you," she said in an offhand way, then steeled herself for a polite refusal.

He was a mature man in his late twenties, and she felt all arms and legs. He looked at her thoughtfully, as if searching for a polite refusal, and she gnawed at her lip to keep herself from pressing.

"I'd like that," he said finally and turned to her mother, a petite brunette, "that is, if you have no objection."

Cecile Lloyd shrugged her tanned shoulders in typical French fashion and teased in her charmingly accented voice, "It's your life you're taking into your hands."

"Mother!" Marianne sent an exasperated look across the table.

"She knows how to handle the sloop," Cecile capitulated with a laugh. "In fact, she's won several races. Have fun."

Teaching Robert to sail bridged the age gap, and Marianne's self-confidence bounced back. Out on the water the breeze picked up and she headed almost straight into the wind. The sun was warm on their faces and saltwater sprayed their clothes. She couldn't take her eyes off him for more than a few seconds, watching how the damp shirt clung to his body, molding every sinew and muscle, and how the breeze played with his thick, dark brown hair. "Your pants are wrinkled now, and there's no starch left in your shirt," she teased.

Looking at her with a lazy smile that stilled the laughter on her lips, he took one hand off the tiller and caught a handful of her hair.

"Don't play with fire," he warned her huskily, his eyes flaring with awareness. "I'm not one of your college boys you can tease and tie into knots." His hand tightened on the light blond strands, drawing her head closer to his. "You're very beautiful. Disturbingly so." He studied her upturned face with a somber intensity, before, with a wry twist of his firm mouth, he freed her. "But you're too young and innocent for a man like me." He used the word innocent as if it were something precious and rare, as if it were something he could not remember in his own youth.

Marianne felt a frisson of apprehension, as if the wind had suddenly shifted from the south to the north. She thought of the many times she had wanted to be older.

Perhaps if she'd listened to the warning then, she could have saved herself a lot of heartbreak. But at the time, she had been touched by his loneliness. And a little piqued, she admitted with a rueful twist of her lips. At nineteen, she had not wanted to hear that she was too young or too innocent. She'd much preferred words like gorgeous and sexy.

For two days, he managed to keep his distance, treating her with an amused tolerance that had her fuming and gritting her teeth in frustration. On the third morning she woke up late for their early morning sail. She jumped into her clothes. Then she found that Colin had borrowed her car because his wouldn't start. Again. Since she was almost an hour late she grabbed the bicycle. Halfway down the hill she met Robert's BMW. That was when she remembered that the brake didn't work, but this time she managed to stop without falling or running into his car.

"That damn thing belongs in the garbage." Robert climbed out of the car and slammed the door. His voice was clipped, controlled, but his eyes were burning with fury when he lifted her off the seat. His hard hands bit into her waist as if they wanted to shake some sense into her. He kicked the bicycle instead. "If your father won't throw it out, I will."

Her youth was already a sore point, but to be treated like a child was intolerable. The fact that he was right only made her angrier. Her temper flared like a summer squall—swift, hot, out of control. She threw her head back and taunted him. "You can try."

"You could have broken your neck."

He was losing his control, and she egged him on. "It's my neck. So what do you care?"

"Grow up, Marianne," he snapped, his hands clamping on her shoulders, his fingers biting into her skin.

Up close, she could see the white line around his mouth and realized that he was more shaken than angry, and her anger eased. "I am grown-up, only you don't want to notice it," she said softly, splaying her hands on his chest.

He'd always been careful to keep some distance between them, as if he hadn't trusted himself to touch her before. Now she stood within the circle of his arms, with her hands caressing his chest. Beneath her fingertips she could feel his heart pound. That gave her the courage to touch his face. "I am nineteen, not nine," she added, outlining his firm mouth with the tip of her finger.

"I'd prefer nine," he said wryly, catching her wrist and drawing her hand down. They were so close that she could read the hunger in his eyes, the desire to take what she offered so willingly. Then he released her hand and stepped back. "I came to say goodbye. I'm leaving this afternoon."

She did not wince, or protest, or blanch. She had too much pride to let him see her pain. Perhaps if she had tried to change his mind he would have walked away and never come back. But she squared her shoulders and turned away with a casual grin. She was proud of the seemingly careless way she managed to toss over her shoulder, "So long, mate. Have a good trip. Look us up, if you ever come this way again."

He came up behind her, spinning her around so swiftly she fell against him. "That's no way to say goodbye." He bent his head and kissed her right on her protesting mouth.

The heat springing up between them fused their lips. Her response, and his, startled him. She could see it in the widening of his eyes. And suddenly she was glad that he would not be able to forget her with the change of the tides. She kissed him again with all her heart.

And when the tides changed, he was still there.

He spent the whole two weeks of his vacation with her....

"Lamar, Lipcomb, Luisette." Marianne was pulled back to the present.

A woman's hoarse scream from the business section tore at Marianne's heart. She couldn't see the woman but her words were loud and clear. "No. I'm not leaving without my husband. Oh, please—"

"Get up." The snarled order was emphasized by an ominous click.

In the terrifying silence that followed, the husband's voice was quiet and controlled. "Go, love. I'll be all right." But even her husband's plea would not make his wife budge. She began sobbing wildly, desperately pleading with the hijackers to let her stay.

Marianne's hands clenched. She felt so useless, sitting here, listening to the poor woman cry her heart out without being able to help. As Hamid rushed into the business section, she wondered if that was how Robert felt; frustrated and angry. She turned her head and saw a reflection of her feelings in the taut line of his mouth. As the screaming woman was dragged to the exit and shoved down the emergency chute, she saw him wince. His head turned back to her and their eyes clashed.

Thank God it's almost over, Robert thought, watching a tear run down her cheek. It was torture sitting there, denying her the comfort she asked of him, letting her down as he had so many times before.

He hadn't done so deliberately, not then. If she had been older and more self-controlled, he might have explained the frequent absences that had taken him away from her at odd hours during the night, sometimes for days. She'd been too soft and too impulsive for him to burden with his secrets, with the dangers and ugly side of his job. He had tried to understand her frustration. But he'd felt trapped, faced with the choice of giving up work he loved or losing the only family he'd ever known.

Had she really believed that he hadn't cared about missing his son's birth and her own graduation from college?

Did she really believe that he didn't give a damn about her now, that he was breaking eye contact because he couldn't stand the sight of her?

But that was exactly what was going through her mind. He could see it in the straight line of her lips, in the angry way she wiped away the tears and the proud tilt of her head.

What kind of bastard did she think he was? Angry frustration flared, making his jaw clench. She was twenty-eight now, not nineteen. The woman he'd watched handle Hamid so expertly should be able to put two and two together and come out with four, and not jump to the wrong conclusion that he didn't care, that he had never given a damn about anything but his job. It hadn't been true then and it wasn't true now.

His hands flexed with the need to shake some sense into her, to convey his frustration, to make her feel this need curling inside him to touch her, to hold her, to kiss that disapproving mouth.

And that, he thought grimly, was exactly what he would do. If he got out of this mess alive, he'd set the record straight.

Marianne was shaking. Not with cold or fear. She was angry, furious enough to brush past Robert without a backward glance.

"I'll wait outside for you," Mrs. Rafferty said as her name was called. She shrugged out of the blazer and handed it back to Marianne. Bending down, she reached for her purse and took two books of traveler's checks out of the zippered side pocket and hid them inside her dress. Then she kicked off shoes and folded her glasses. "Thank God Hamid hasn't come back. Your name is so close to mine that you won't have long to wait."

Hugging Mrs. Rafferty, Marianne whispered, "Be careful on that slide. And—" sudden fear made her stop, then continue swiftly "—if I don't make it, please give my father and my son a hug. My father's name is Don Lloyd. He's staying in Chamonix. And tell him that—'' she briefly hesitated again ''—tell him that Robert is also on the plane.''

"Robert?"

"He'll understand," Marianne said swiftly before the woman could ask more questions.

"You'll be able to tell him yourself," Mrs. Rafferty said.

And then she was gone, walking down the aisle, waiting at the slide for a bald, heavyset man to take his turn. Apparently they were letting some of the men go, too. When she had disappeared, Marianne took her billfold from her purse and extracted her credit cards, driver's license, insurance cards, money and traveler's checks and put them inside her bra. Then she buttoned her blazer to hide the bulges.

"Soulange, M. Sullivan, Sutter."

Marianne kicked off her shoes and jumped to her feet. They'd bypassed Robert's name. It wasn't easy to go down the aisle past the many empty seats, knowing that some of the men still sitting there would not be freed. And how could she walk past Robert?

The closer she came to him, the more difficult it became to place one foot in front of the other. He tried to make it easy for her, she guessed. He did not turn his head, but stared out of the window. Beneath his gray tweed jacket she could sense his coiled impatience, his tightly leashed power and restless energy.

It took all of his willpower not to turn his head and look at her. Gritting his teeth, he willed her to ignore him, to walk past him and slide down to safety. *Think of our son. He needs you more than he needs me.*

Instead, she did the stupidest thing she'd ever done in her life. She stopped in front of him and whispered his name.

"Robert."

After four years the sound of her voice was still as familiar to him as his own. He could remember all its nuances, the clear musical sound with its husky undertones sliding like velvet over his skin.

But this rough voice, filled with shock and fear, was new. It cut through him like the blade of a knife. He wanted to draw her into his arms and promise her that this was nothing but a bad dream. He forced himself to stare out of the window and count the scratches on the plastic instead. "Go," he muttered.

"Move." The terrorist came up behind her and pushed her forward. Marianne barely felt the shove. She stumbled, took another step until she was level with Robert's row. There her legs refused to obey. She could not walk past him as if he were a stranger. She could not leave him behind as if his fate did not matter. Because it did matter. They had shared four years of their lives. They had a child. Their love for Bobby would always tie them together. How could she face their son with the thought that she had walked past his father without a gesture of support?

She reached out and touched his shoulder. Beneath his jacket she could feel his muscles tense, rejecting her. Look at me, please. Her grasp tightened. Say something. Anything.

Another hard shove between her shoulder blades made her stumble past his seat. She could already see the bright yellow plastic of the inflated slide and a piece of gray sky through the open door.

Freedom.

She had prayed for it for hours. Another few steps, a swift ride and she would walk behind the line of flashing lights into the arms of her father and son.

Another second and she might never see Robert again.

She stopped for one last look.

Watching her lagging steps, Robert swore silently. His fists clenched tightly, as if the strength of his balled hands could push her the last few steps and down the slide. *"Go, damn it,"* he whispered beneath his breath. *"You walked away from me once without looking back. I didn't stop you then. And I sure as hell won't stop you now. Keep walking."* When he saw her stop, he did something he hadn't done since he was six years old. He begged roughly. *"Please."*

And like the last time he had pleaded, his prayer remained unanswered. She turned around, her gray eyes dark, huge pools of anguish in a chalk-white face.

Prayers had never worked for him. Anger had helped him claw his way out of poverty, away from foster homes and above minimum wage. Anger and the driving need to succeed. His hard, cold voice thundered above the guard's shouts. "Go, damn it."

Marianne heard him swear, saw the blazing fury on his face, but even at nineteen she hadn't run from him. Now his anger slid off her like rain off oiled skin. She couldn't move, shock and anguish rooting her to the floor. She did not feel the rough hands biting into her arms. She did not hear the crude curses as she was half led, half dragged to the exit. She did not taste the tears running down her face. All she saw was Robert's lean, hard face and the green fire blazing in her heart.

The terrorists' rough hands and crude language unleashed a primitive fury in Robert, though. His body coiled with cold rage.

"Don't do anything stupid," Rafe warned urgently and placed one hand on the tweed jacket to restrain Robert. "You can't help her," he reasoned. "You'll only make things worse. Let it go. Another few moments and she'll be safe."

The voice of reason penetrated his rage. Control seeped back, dulling the edge of his fury. With his hands clenched over the armrests, he watched her legs dangle over the slide. He tore his eyes away from her face, still turned toward him. Another moment and she would be free.

And then Hamid came into view and began shouting in Arabic. "Not this one. I told you, she's staying."

With the sharp reflexes of a man who ran five miles every day, Robert's powerful body unleashed himself. Slipping through Rafe's restraining hands, he lunged for her, pushing her. "Get out of here. Bobby needs you."

Thrown off balance, Marianne instinctively grasped the rough tweed of his jacket to save herself from falling down the slide head first. She wasn't aware that she was clinging to Robert until he shouted, "Don't fight me. Let go."

His harsh words penetrated her shock and she went limp. As her legs touched the plastic and her grasp on his shoulders eased, she thought how close they were to freedom. Freedom for both of them.

"Stop. Hold your fire!" A sharp, staccato voice cut through the shouts and the warning shots being fired into the air. Robert was hauled to his feet while rough hands closed on Marianne's arms and dragged her back inside the plane. There she was dumped back on her feet with her arms twisted behind her back.

Black mist swirled before her eyes. She was gasping for breath, and her knees refused to lock into place. When the fog lifted, she saw the flash of blue- and-red lights reflected on the wet pavement below. "Dear God, what have I done," she thought. Then she straightened her back, locked her knees and turned her back to the blinking lights.

It was too late for regrets.

Chapter 3

Marianne stared at the man who had ordered them back inside.

He had a narrow face, an olive complexion and a thin, neat, military mustache. His dark business suit and snow-white shirt spoke of success and control. His eyes were liquid black pools, showing neither curiosity nor hate. He's a man without a soul, Marianne thought with a sinking feeling in the pit of her stomach. They could expect no mercy from him.

He stared at them for what seemed like several minutes. But it was really mere seconds. The look was cold, clinical. Terrifying.

"What's going on?" The clipped question was addressed to his men.

"She struggled..."

Hamid explained heatedly in Arabic, "I want to keep her. That man doesn't like it. He's the troublemaker I told you about. He interfered once before with the stewardess."

With an irritated frown the man faced Robert. "Your name, Boy Scout?"

Robert fixed the man with an unblinking stare. Something in the man's voice warned him that he already knew his identity. It seemed a logical assumption. How many other passengers on board carried diplomatic passports?

"Sullivan," Robert said calmly.

The man's hooded eyes slide from Robert's expressionless face to Marianne, pouncing on the weaker link. "And who are you? What's your name?"

It took all of Robert's iron self-control not to draw the man's attention back to himself. He'd never allowed himself to become dependent on anyone else. Now he had no choice.

Illogically Marianne wished for her shoes. The extra two inches would have put her eyes on the same level with those cold, dark pools. With her free hand she swept her hair off her face. She hated the fact that her voice was still shaky and hoarse. Why couldn't she be cool and in control, facing the man with the same courage Robert showed? "Marianne Lloyd—"

"Sullivan." Hamid's guttural voice almost drowned out Marianne's response. She remembered how intensely he had studied her passport when he'd collected it.

The man's eyes narrowed. "Quite a coincidence," he sneered. "You are related?"

"The name Sullivan is about as common as Smith," Robert answered for her smoothly. For the first time he was glad that they were divorced, that their passports showed different addresses. If only Marianne kept her head.

"Maybe so. That still doesn't explain why you risked your life for a stranger."

"No red-blooded American would idly watch defenseless women being beaten and harassed. I was just the closest one in both instances." Robert's lip curled with a sneer.

"Didn't you say that the Holy Islamic Brigade does not make war on women?" He looked at Marianne's frozen face. "She looks like a woman to me."

The man shot a furious look at Hamid, who was still holding Marianne's arms behind her back. Then his eyes returned to Robert's face, probing, questioning, until Robert wondered if he'd allowed too much emotion to enter into his voice.

So he switched tactics. "Or is it Hamid who makes the final decisions here?" The trick to pitch one man against another was as old as mankind itself. But it still worked. The man shot Hamid another quelling look, then ordered abruptly, "Let her go."

"Sullivan's lying," Hamid protested furiously in Arabic. His hands tightened around Marianne's wrists like steel manacles, pressing the watch into her flesh. "I caught her looking at him more than once. Would she do that if they were strangers?"

With a cold, sick feeling in his gut, Robert saw the leader's eyes narrow suspiciously. How long would it take to get the truth out of Marianne? he speculated grimly. She was no match for their brand of interrogation.

Anger shot through him, mingling with his fear. Why hadn't she followed his clues? She should've guessed that he had damn good reasons for his behavior.

But emotional blindness was typical of her. She had always needed feelings spelled out for her. And pretty words had never come easy for him. When he had been unable to explain his absences she'd always assumed the worst: that he didn't care, that he preferred sleeping in flea-infested huts to making love to her and playing with their son.

Abruptly he caught himself before he lost control. But how could she have known that he'd been burning with need, counting the days, hours, minutes until he could hold her again? One thing his new job had taught him was that words were necessary to prevent misunderstandings and to clear them up.

Marianne felt Hamid's hold on her arms loosen a fraction, then tighten again. It was this action rather than the heated rush of foreign words that told her that the tide had changed. For a moment she felt nothing, neither despair nor pain, not even when her arms were jerked higher up her back.

"She stopped at his chair. I had to push her," Hamid's friend added in a rush of Arabic, prodding Robert in the side with the nose of his automatic. "And he cried, 'Bobby needs you.'"

She didn't have to understand their words. Their meaning was frightening clear—and so now were Robert's actions since the beginning of the hijacking.

Why hadn't she searched for good reasons for Robert's behavior instead of just assuming the worst? With her senses now sharpened by fear, she realized that his ignoring her was uncharacteristic for a man who had unselfishly placed his body between the flight attendant and the terrorist. His action had been instinctive, without thought to possible retribution, hardly the action of an uncaring man.

Then why hadn't she questioned his motives instead of instantly condemning him? Why had it been easier to see him as a cold and uncaring man? Was it because seeing him had opened the old wounds and old longings, and she'd needed a shield to hide behind? The thought shook her almost as much as the leader's voice, snapping at her, "Who is Bobby?"

"How should I know?" Marianne dissembled smoothly, staring unblinkingly into the black eyes.

"I am certain Hamid will enjoy forcing the truth out of you, Miss Sullivan," the man threatened with menacing softness, his eyes raking her slender form pointedly. He turned his attention back to Robert's stony face and snapped, "Take them upstairs. Get the rest off the plane while I question them."

Marianne sent a swift, frightened look at Robert. His profile was hard and unyielding, his eyes fixed steadily on the man walking up the stairs ahead of them. His dark wavy hair fell onto his forehead, and a long scratch on his jaw was beginning to bleed. With his six-foot-two frame of leashed power, he looked tough and dangerous, making the hijackers look like toy soldiers.

But the gun barrel pressed into Robert's back was no toy. It was as real as the pain Hamid's hands caused as he wrenched her arms a little tighter and a little higher up her back.

Her involuntary groan made Robert stiffen. He stopped and slowly turned. "Release her," he ordered with chilling softness. There was an indefinable assurance about him. He did not move. He did not bluster. He simply stood and waited with menacing patience.

Marianne stared at him, caught by the color of his eyes, a blazing silver-green that was startling against the sun-bronzed skin. She'd always sensed a ruthless, barely contained violence in him, but she'd never witnessed it before.

Hamid's grasp on her arms weakened, and she felt him take an involuntary step back. Drawing a shaky breath, Marianne took her cue from Robert, squaring her shoulders and angling her chin.

"That's it," he said approvingly. She'd always had courage, but it had been the reckless, youthful kind. Now her classic profile showed the quiet dignity and spirit of maturity. Robert gave her a quick look of approval and support, then took command and turned toward the stairs. "Let's go."

Marianne shook her head at the ease with which he seemed to have reversed the roles of hostages and terrorists. The absurdity of the situation brought a faint smile to her eyes. She nodded and stepped past Robert with Hamid following her.

Her smile faded as they climbed the softly carpeted spiral stairs. The intercom began calling out names again. With every step, with every name, her fear increased.

They were ordered to stop at the top of the stairs, facing the door leading to the flight deck. When it opened, Marianne caught a glimpse of the crew held in check by another terrorist with a submachine gun. Then the leader walked toward them, a smug look on his face. Her eyes widened when she saw their passports in his hand. Her body tensed.

"Marianne Lloyd Sullivan," he read, stopping a few feet in front of her. Flipping back a page, he continued, "In case of accident or death notify the nearest American diplomatic or consular office and the individual named below." He paused for effect, then continued with a sneer in his voice, "Robert Sullivan. State Department, Washington, D.C." Then he closed the passport gently. "So, now tell me the truth. What's the connection between you and Sullivan?" he demanded softly, dangerously.

Marianne couldn't breathe. For one instant she stopped fighting the wave of despair dragging her down; but for only an instant. Her instinct for survival was too strong. There was always another chance, another hope. She squared her shoulders, hid her trembling hands in her blazer pockets and raised her chin. "Okay. We were divorced four years ago, and I haven't seen him since. I stared at him out of curiosity to see if he'd changed." She forced her stiff lips to curl with a pretense of disgust. "He's still the same."

A damn good try, Robert thought, watching doubt flicker across the man's swarthy face. But not good enough, he added, when the man shot the next question at her. "Who is this Bobby that needs you?" Marianne stubbornly bit her lip. "Your son?" he demanded. She shook her head.

With a cruel, knowing smile, the man pounced on Robert. "I'm going to get the truth out of both of you. But that will have to wait until later." He turned to Hamid. "Put them in the galley up here. You watch Sullivan closely. He's not your average diplomat. And keep your hands off the woman."

The galley was at the end of the deserted upper lounge. Robert motioned Marianne ahead of him, then followed her past the bar and the seat he'd relaxed in earlier. His empty brandy snifter lay on the blue carpet a few feet away. Around the bar the floor was littered with shards of highball glasses and stained with drink. A whole arsenal of weapons was spread out over the seats. So much for airport security, Robert thought grimly.

In the small stainless-steel kitchen the smell of coffee still lingered. Marianne walked to the end of the narrow space, then leaned against the counter for support. Robert followed her, blocking the entrance with his body.

She was one of the hostages now. It was still difficult to accept that for Robert and herself freedom was beyond reach. Above their heads the loudspeaker announced another set of names. Soon the voice calling out freedom would fall silent, and the steady stream of passengers running toward the red-and-blue lights would stop. What would happen to those left behind? Don't think about it, she told herself, gripping the cold steel of the counter pressing into her back. Take one minute at a time.

Her eyes went to Robert's grim face. Even up close he hadn't changed much. She wished he had aged. She wished he showed some sign that he had missed her, had suffered some part of the pain and bitterness she had gone through. No, that wasn't fair, she thought, remembering their last meeting in court and the way he had winced when the question of custody had come up. To relinquish most of a father's rights hadn't been easy for him. He loved his son.

But he hadn't loved her.

She remembered also how she'd hoped that even at that last, final meeting, he'd tell her that he needed her too much to let her go. And how much it had hurt to accept, irrevocably, that he had only married her for Bobby's sake.

She hid her hands in her pockets and clenched them against the pain. She had expected to feel bitterness, but not this sharp knife-edge ripping through her. A few minutes ago he had risked his life to get her off this plane. Again for Bobby. Whatever softness and desire he'd once felt for her had died years ago. She couldn't hate him for that. Not anymore. But pain was understandable. And a little bitterness was human, too.

Robert wondered where her thoughts had gone. She was staring through him as if he didn't exist. Why couldn't she have walked past him as if he were a stranger instead of wasting those precious seconds that would have put her beyond Hamid's reach? He looked at her, his green eyes glacier-cold, his mouth hard. "That was one of the dumbest kid stunts you've ever pulled."

Nothing could have fanned her anger swifter than his reference to her youth. In response, her eyes flashed like bright steel. "Just what are you referring to? Your name in my passport? I put it there for Bobby. If something happened to me, he'd need his father more than anyone else." She felt tears pricking her eyes and went on angrily, "And I stopped at your seat because *I'm* human enough to care. And I won't apologize for that, either."

Robert's mouth tightened at the implication that he didn't give a damn. More than once during their marriage she'd thrown that accusation at him, and in some ways she had been justified. It was true that he hadn't loved her. At least not the way she'd deserved to be loved, with a young man's romantic passion. He did not believe in romantic love and the blissful "forever after." But he'd given her all he'd been capable of: solid, honest emotions, like passion, loyalty and commitment. Only those hadn't been sentimental enough for the young girl with stars in her eyes.

But there were no stars now, only fear and despair. His angry frustration eased. God, how he hated to see her this way.

He didn't blame her for expecting more from him than he'd been able to give. At nineteen she'd had every right to dream. He had known that he was the wrong man for her, but he had taken her anyway. The cutting words he'd wanted to hurl at her died on his lips. "It's too late for apologies," he said instead, with grim weariness.

Involuntarily his gaze slid from her angry face down to her slender throat. The sudden tightening of his body shook him. Damn it. He shouldn't want her. She looked a wreck. Her hair was disheveled, the sleeve of her blazer had been ripped at the seam, and one brass button had been torn off. But she held her head high, and her eyes still flashed. Suddenly he wished that she had written his name into her passport because she still cared enough for him to want him at her side in case of an emergency, and not just because of Bobby. "We're in this together whether we like it or not," he said.

Marianne nodded. "You're right." The hours of waiting couldn't have been easy for him. Suddenly, the reason why he had looked through her seemed important.

"Why did you pretend we were strangers?" she asked softly, so that Hamid could not hear them. The terrorist had retreated to the other side of the aisle. An unlit cigarette dangled between his lips as he searched his shirt pockets for a match or a lighter with one hand. The other was holding the gun.

Robert did not respond immediately. His face was bland, in that subtle way of his, as if a sheet of lightly frosted glass had slid down between them. Marianne prepared herself for another rebuff, another evasion, the way he'd responded to most of her questions in the past.

She'd known little about his work. Most of it had been classified, so he hadn't been able to talk much about it. And she'd respected that. But he'd also rarely talked about the people close to him. During their four years of marriage she had only met one of Robert's friends. Prince Jamal of Omari had been best man at their wedding and a guest at Bobby's christening.

His silence fueled her bitterness once again.

Why should there be another reason for his behavior? They were strangers, had always been strangers. That hadn't changed. She'd been a fool to ask and leave herself open for more pain. She wouldn't demean herself by showing how much he still had the power to hurt her. "Forget that I asked," she said tightly and stared down at her feet.

It was still easy to read her face: the hurt, the bitterness, the pride. That hadn't changed, Robert thought. But his need to make her understand was new. He'd long wanted to set the record straight, and now was his chance. He stepped closer and said softly, "I was trying to keep you out of this mess. I still don't know the reason for the hijacking, but our treaty with Omari could be one of them."

With her head still bent, her hair had parted at the nape, exposing her slender, vulnerable neck. She still used the same perfume, a very subtle fresh floral scent that he'd had created especially for her in one of the perfume factories in Grasse, France. The sight and smell triggered other memories.

He remembered threading his fingers through her thick hair, lifting it to rain light, teasing kisses on her skin, and how she'd responded by leaning back against him and pulling his head down to hers. His body stiffened with the need to touch her once again, to feel, to taste. The flick of Hamid's lighter brought him back to the present. "I'm part of the team negotiating the treaty with Emir Yussuf," he explained, his voice husky.

Marianne felt his breath fan her neck, sending familiar shivers down her spine. She almost swayed to lean against him, but his unexpected explanation made her raise her head and stare at him. "You wanted to protect me. I didn't know. I thought..." Her eyes focused on the cut on his jaw and the small red stain on the collar of his shirt. Her fingers curled around the handkerchief in her pocket, but she didn't have the nerve to touch him.

"That I didn't give a damn?" Robert finished her sentence with an edge in his voice. "You never did look beneath the surface," he said tightly, then added on a softer note, "Perhaps it was too much to expect. You were so young."

Her eyes flared, shooting silver darts at him. "Yes, I was young, but I was not insensitive," she objected quietly, trying to control the temper rising at the familiar words. "Communication is a two-way street." She stopped and wearily shook her head. "There's no point rehashing the past."

Robert wanted to point out that the past was not dead as long as they still felt bitter about it, but she edged sideways to put a small distance between them, and the moment was lost.

"I always wondered if you and Jamal were involved in the deal. You two discussed the idea years ago. Before you switched to the foreign service." Her voice was cool, showing none of the anger she'd felt when she'd first found out about Robert's shift of careers. So many times she had pleaded with him to look for a post with more regular hours and fewer trips. If he'd changed careers before the divorce their marriage might have survived. But he had always cared more for his job than he had for her and it was time she accepted it.

Robert had been watching Hamid and missed the bitterness flashing across her face. "Yes. But old Yussuf wasn't interested then. It took a few missile attacks on Omari's harbor to change his mind." His face set determinedly. "The deal must go through. At this point a base within missile range of Iran is vital for peace in the Persian Gulf. Without it the war will continue for years."

Marianne understood the political necessity and the dangers involved. For weeks the pros and cons of the treaty had been discussed on the television news. Terrorist organizations had threatened a new wave of death to stop the treaty. Was this hijacking their first act of retribution?

A shiver went through her at the thought. "Do they know that you've been involved in the negotiations?" she asked, her voice tight with fear.

Robert shrugged. "I'm not sure."

"Do you think that they hijacked this plane because of you?"

"I hope not." He'd taken the usual precautions, picking Thursday evening for his departure date, when politicians would leave Washington for the Easter holidays. He'd called the airline directly to order his ticket and had boarded at the last minute. That was how he must have missed her, he realized.

Only three people knew of his travel plans: Jamal, Howard Barton, the Secretary of State, and Hank, his own personal secretary. Robert trusted each one of them implicitly. If there had been a leak, where the hell had it come from?

"If I'd waited until Tuesday to fly to Omari with the rest of the team, we wouldn't be in this fix," he said with grim self-recrimination.

She hated to see this self-assured man look so bitter and weary. "It could have happened on any domestic flight," she argued firmly.

At that moment the loudspeaker clicked into silence. Marianne's smile froze. Robert moved to the entrance to see what was going on. His movements alerted Hamid. He got to his feet, pointed the barrel of his gun at Robert's chest and ordered sharply, "Do not move another step."

From somewhere below muffled orders drifted upstairs, followed by odd shuffling sounds. Then silence descended once again, eerie, frightening in its intensity.

The exodus was over, Marianne thought. Only those passengers to be kept as hostages remained on board. At that thought, the blood drained out of her face. The galley began spinning in front of her eyes. She gripped the steel counter, taking deep breaths. She wasn't going to fall apart, she told herself sternly. Robert had enough on his hands. He needed support—not someone draining his strength.

When Robert turned back to her, her fear was under control. "The *bastard* is coming back," he said, studying her pale face intently. She looked as white as a sheet. "Ready for another battle of wits? That's all it is," he said, trying to bring some color back into her cheeks. "You used to be good at outwitting your cousins."

Marianne smiled wanly and moved closer to Robert. "I'm sorry I got you into this mess. I'll try not to let you down again," she promised with quiet determination. And then her hand slid into his with the same trust she had given him on their wedding day.

The simple gesture was poignant. It reached across the barriers that had separated them for four years. Startled, Robert's face softened for an instant. Her large gray eyes were filled with regret, but they remained steady despite the fear lurking in their depths. His fingers closed over hers in a brief, hard, reassuring response.

With their hands still linked, Robert turned his attention back to the leader. Who was he? What made him tick?

Robert concentrated on each of his movements, the sharp, militarylike step, the arrogant bearing, the meticulous business suit he wore like a uniform. He stopped a few feet in front of them, legs planted apart, hands clasped behind his back, in a position the military call "at ease." Was the man still on active duty? Or was he the leader of one of the many guerrilla factions that terrorized the Western world for either ideological or mercenary reasons?

He'd soon find out, Robert thought.

"I see you've decided on a united front," the man jeered, looking at their linked hands. Then he flashed a photo in front of their eyes. "This is Bobby, I believe."

For one long aching moment Marianne stared at an eight-by-ten, the school photograph Bobby had sent his father as a Christmas present. Even at the age of eight, with his face still softened by youth, he was the image of his father. They shared the same dark unruly hair, dimples, the same grin. Tears pressed behind her eyes, and a lump formed in her throat. Would she ever hold him again? Would she ever see his gray eyes sparkle with mischief and hear him scoff, "Oh, Mom."

Instinctively her hand went to the stickpin he had given her for Christmas, a two-inch teddy bear with a red bow tie and plaid pants. He had raked ten bags of leaves last fall to pay for it. Marianne had worn it ever since.

"Nothing to say?" the man mocked. "Let me jog your memory a little then. The back is signed 'To Dad, Merry Christmas, with love, Bobby and Mom.'"

She hadn't been aware of the fact that Bobby added "Mom" to every photo, letter or postcard, Robert realized with a sinking feeling as he saw Marianne's shocked expression. He'd hoped differently. Sometimes he had seen it as an olive branch, but he'd never been certain enough to pick up the phone and call her. But she was here right now, with her hand curled into his. Gently he tightened his hold.

Marianne felt the squeeze, warning, yet oddly comforting at the same time. She inched closer to him, realizing and accepting that for as long as this nightmare lasted their fates would be linked together. For Bobby's sake.

Confronted with two deadpan faces, irritation flickered in the man's eyes. "I know your kind, Sullivan," he said, this time deliberately insulting Robert. "You are a selfish bastard who wouldn't risk his skin for a woman you threw out of your house years ago."

Robert did not even blink. He'd been called worse. "I didn't care for your men's rough methods," he said flatly, the expression in his eyes as bland as the tone of his voice. He was too good a poker player to reveal a single card too early at what promised to be a long, frustrating game. Fate, Robert thought grimly, had dealt him some lousy cards before, but this was one of the worst hands he'd ever held. "You seem to know a great deal about me," he drawled.

The man adjusted the white cuffs that showed beneath the sleeves of his dark business suit.

A vain man and more nervous than he'd like to show, Robert interpreted the gesture.

"Apparently not enough. We knew nothing about your marriage or your son." As he frowned, his dark eyes swerved back to Marianne and he studied her intently. Then he smiled. "Luck is truly with us today."

"Lady Luck is fickle," Robert said calmly, shifting subtly until his body almost shielded Marianne. "Keeping my former wife here is a big mistake. You'll regret it soon enough."

The man made a swift cutting motion with his hand. "That remains to be seen. I may not have known about your private life, Sullivan, but the rest is an open book. We've made it our business to keep tabs on everyone even remotely connected to the Emir of Omari. You've had close personal ties with him for years. You are deeply involved in the negotiations." His eyes flashed angrily. "We won't tolerate another American outpost at our front door. We will do everything in our power to prevent such a deal."

Robert wished he knew who was behind the "we." "You flatter me. I'm a member of the American foreign service, but hardly in a position of power. And the Emir does not approve of my friendship with his son." The difference between Emir Yussuf and Jamal were well known. Born and educated in the States, Jamal had for years supported a pact with the U.S., while old Yussuf had kept up trade relations with anyone willing to pay. His oldest son, Muhrad, opposed the treaty still, which was one of the reasons why the negotiations had been so difficult. Almost as an afterthought, Robert asked, "And who is 'we'?"

"You may call me Major," the man said smoothly.

The thin smile told Robert that he had recognized the trap but was too experienced a player to fall for it. For what stakes would the major be willing to play? What would it take to get Marianne released? "Major who?" he asked, softly challenging the man. "Are you afraid to reveal your name?"

Marianne drew a sharp breath, her body stiffening with apprehension. What was Robert trying to accomplish by insulting the man? Why test the limits of his patience? Why see how far he could push him? For a moment it seemed that he had pushed too hard and too far. The major's face darkened and his eyes flashed.

Then he shook his head, and his thin mustache lifted at the corners. "I'm not afraid. I call it caution. You see, Sullivan, all the trump cards are in my hand," he said smoothly. "You, your wife, and eleven other hostages—all of them Americans. And if your government refuses to negotiate, I'll kill you one by one. Then I'll hand that pretty little wife of yours over to my man Hamid. He's been hot for her since the beginning of this trip."

The same primitive rage that had pushed Robert to interfere before boiled like hot lava in his veins. Marianne winced as his hand clamped down on hers. His face was frozen; only his green eyes blazed. "I wouldn't if I were you," he said with such soft, deadly calm the major's smile wavered then disappeared.

The man straightened his slim shoulders and tilted his head up to Robert who towered above him by about four inches. "I think I've just found your Achilles' heel."

"Touch it and you'll sign your death warrant," Robert warned.

"That's a dangerous and empty threat to make." The major shrugged his shoulders, but his smile did not return. "Perhaps I will shoot you now."

"Shoot your biggest trump card?" Robert countered calmly. For a moment he hesitated, wondering if the timing was right to make the next move. Trying to bribe the major was a calculated risk. Still, the opportunity might never present itself again. "What would it take to set us free?"

"Are you trying to bribe me?" the major asked with narrowed eyes.

Robert shrugged his shoulders. "As a diplomat I call it a compromise. You are an intelligent man, Major. You know what your chances are of getting away free. I'm offering you a way to save your skin. What you do with that offer is up to you."

With an appreciative gleam, the major shook his head. "You're smooth, Sullivan. But if your offer is money, I don't like it. I'll make you an offer in return. If you can convince your government to withdraw from their deal with Omari, I will consider releasing all of you."

"I agree with my government's stand on terrorism. You haven't a chance in hell to prevent a treaty with Omari. On the contrary, this hijacking may push old Yussuf into an agreement that much sooner."

Until now Marianne had shared Robert's views. But it was easy to support a theory from the safety of your own home. Now, threatened with harsh reality, she found it difficult to stick to it. Her admiration for Robert soared.

"A pity," the major drawled, stroking his neat mustache. "You may be prepared to die for a principle." Then he shifted his attention to Marianne. "I wonder if your wife feels the same."

There was so much more than a principle separating them, Marianne thought. But they had shelved those differences already. Together they might have a chance to get out of this alive. Pitched against each other they would be lost. The pressure of her fingers increased as they curled in Robert's hand. "I do," she said with her eyes steady and her voice firm.

But inside she was shaking with fear.

Chapter 4

As Marianne walked down the stairs she noticed that the drizzle outside had turned into a steady downpour. Rain slanted through the still-open exit door. Drawing her jacket tightly around her, she descended the last two steps. An eerie silence echoed around her. The first-class cabin looked deserted. Shopping bags, blankets and pillows littered the aisle. Nearby, the three-foot Easter bunny lay on its side. One of its long, satiny ears had been torn off and foam stuffing had spilled out.

The wanton destruction pierced her numbness. Marianne picked up the bunny and gently tried to close the gap.

"Give me that." With a snarl, Hamid tore the rabbit from her hand and tossed it through the door. "Move." He shoved her forward, then waved with his gun for Robert to follow her.

A gust of wind almost raised the hem of her skirt. Holding it down, Marianne stopped at the exit and stared down into empty space. The yellow slide was gone. Hope, she thought, had become a few pieces of shredded plastic fluttering in the wind. How would Bobby react to the news that both of his parents were on the hijacked plane? She knew that her family would do everything to support and to shield him, but how long could they keep reporters at bay?

"I said, move," Hamid shouted.

She lingered for one last anguished second. "I wonder if Mother and Dad will tie yellow ribbons on their front door," she whispered, turning away from the gaping hole.

"Don't," Robert said roughly. Following close behind her, he could see small tremors shaking her. He wanted to promise her that she would be safe. But he'd never given Marianne empty promises, and he had never lied to her. He wanted to now, but the words stuck in his throat.

"Wait." Hamid pressed his gun into Robert's back. Robert stopped and so did Marianne. "You stay here."

Over his shoulder Robert watched the terrorist push the button to close the door. His gray silk tie suddenly seemed like a tight band constricting his throat, and he jerked it off. Stuffing it into his pocket, he moved closer to Marianne until their bodies almost touched. She seemed so alone and distant.

He knew all about loneliness. He'd been alone most of his life, ever since that night over thirty years ago when he'd been awakened by flashing lights and a policewoman had told him that his parents had gone away. He had taught himself not to need anyone, to rely totally on himself. Then he'd met Marianne and he suddenly realized that he had been lying to himself for years.

But the one person he needed desperately had closed herself off from him years ago.

He wanted to tear down the barrier she had erected around herself, touch her, make her turn to him. He was good at taking what he wanted, but for the first time in his life he was afraid. Afraid that she would stare straight through him, that she would turn away from him as she had four years ago. So he watched and waited, but she did not shift and lean against him.

Robert raised his hands, hesitated, then dropped one of them; the other went to his neck as he opened the top buttons of his shirt. "Don't worry about Bobby," he said, because words came easier than gestures. "He's going to be fine."

Behind him he could hear Hamid kick the door, curse because it refused to lock, then push it down.

Marianne hunched her shoulders and wrapped her arms around herself. "He has such a vivid imagination. He used to have terrible nightmares."

Robert frowned. "Every child has bad dreams once in a while. I remember a nightmare or two myself."

"He had them often. But in the past year there have been fewer of them." She'd sometimes wondered if Robert's return to the States had actually had a calming effect on Bobby or if he had simply outgrown that stage.

"No one told me. I had a right to know."

Marianne turned and faced him, tilting her head back. "You didn't ask," she countered quietly. "I thought you didn't want to know."

His lips twisted in wry acknowledgement. He'd always made it a point to ask Bobby about his school grades and to discuss his social life and sports activities. Those were a father's responsibilities. But he hadn't worried about Bobby's health. His son looked perfectly fit; and deep down he had always known that Marianne would contact him in the event of an emergency. Now he wondered if she would have talked to him if he'd swallowed his pride and made the first move. "It was rather difficult while I lived in Europe."

The Atlantic Ocean had never kept her mother from keeping in touch with her family, Marianne thought. Calls were expensive, especially those made from Europe to the

U.S., but Robert wasn't a poor man. He could easily have afforded the extra charges. Still, she did not want to regress to accusations and bitterness again. "The time difference does cause problems," she agreed softly.

Behind them Hamid swore loudly. Both Marianne and Robert turned, watching the terrorist hammer at the lock with the butt of his gun. Their eyes met in smiling satisfaction and held even when Hamid yelled for help at the top of his lungs.

The warm feeling was so intense it left no room for words. She stared while heat pulsed through her as if she had never seen him before, as if she didn't know what kind of man he was. And perhaps she had never seen past the defenses he had erected so early in life. Because their son was now almost the same age as Robert had been then, she could better understand what the loss of his parents must have done to him.

But could she accept that there were places inside him no one would ever touch?

It would be so easy to fall in love with him all over again. She couldn't afford that kind of madness, not again. The first time she had been too young to know better. This time she was forewarned. She took a step back, bumping into a seat.

Hamid's angry shouts had brought the major downstairs. "Sullivan, don't try anything funny while I have a look at this door," he warned.

Robert watched the major pull up his pants before he squatted down and examined the lock. If he had been alone, he'd have shoved Hamid outside the moment he'd reached for the door. Alone, he would have taken the chance and jumped down the twenty-foot drop. But he doubted that Hamid would have been so careless then. "Do you mind if we get out of the wind?"

"Shut up, Sullivan. And stay where I can see you," the major said over his shoulder while he examined and tested the lock.

"Sure. How far could I go?" Robert asked with a gleam in his eyes. If the door wouldn't lock, the plane would be grounded here in France. He preferred Paris to Beirut any day. "Want me to have a look at it?"

The major cursed viciously.

With a small, satisfied grin, Robert joined Marianne.

As Marianne listened to the exchange, she traced the blue cloth that covered the top of the seat with a fingertip and tried to control the smile tugging at the corners of her mouth. She wondered how she could find anything amusing in Robert's attempt to annoy the man. It was foolish, and dangerous—and satisfying. It was a little like sailing before a storm, she thought, as she met his gleaming eyes.

He was still more attractive to her than any other man, and still capable of making her heart skip a beat. Her hands itched to touch him, to hold on to his solid frame until her world had stopped spinning. She needed him in ways she had never wanted him before.

That was the greatest danger of all, she thought.

She was an independent person and proud of it, but her family had always stood behind her through laughter and tears. Now, for the first time in her life, she was truly alone. And she was more vulnerable than she'd ever been.

The shock of meeting Robert here among the passengers had ripped away the layers of detachment she had so carefully erected around herself. He still had the power to hurt her. She shivered as another gust of wind blew through the door.

"You're freezing." Before she could stop him, Robert took her hands and held them between his warm palms, gently chafing her skin to increase the flow of blood.

She was burning, and with every small circle of his fingertips the heat grew. But she wasn't going to tell him so. She tried to snatch her hands away, but his fingers held, sensitizing every nerve call, not giving an inch. Since she couldn't stop him, she looked for a distraction. "Who was the man sitting beside you? Did they let him go?"

His eyes narrowed and the movement stilled. He'd never been a possessive man. But it surprised him how much he disliked her sudden interest in another man. "I don't know his last name. He could have been released after we went upstairs. But my guess is we'll find him in the coach section at the rear of the plane."

His grip loosened, and she snatched her hands away. "Mrs. Rafferty, the woman who sat next to me, promised to talk to Dad. I told her that you were on the plane." She put her hands into her pockets. "I should have asked for her telephone number. I want to call her if—when we get back home."

"I'll get the number for you," Robert offered calmly, as if their freedom was a certainty and their release only a matter of time.

When she looked at the spread of his shoulders and his firm, jutting jaw, she could almost believe in their freedom and safety. "I may take you up on that offer," she said. It was easier to make plans for the more distant future than to speculate on what lay directly ahead.

Robert noticed her evasion and turned away to hide the frustration he felt. He did not know why he had offered to get the number for her. Perhaps he had done it because it would provide him with a reason to call her, like keeping one foot in the door.

Warily he glanced over his shoulder. Apparently the lock still refused to snap into place. Both terrorists were squatting down, examining it, raising the handle bar up and down, testing.

Marianne followed his glance, then focused on Robert. The cut along his jawline had stopped bleeding. Dried blood stained his neck and the collar of his shirt. This time she did not hesitate, "You've got a scratch," she said, and tilting his head, gently wiped away the traces of blood. "I didn't even thank you for trying to save me."

He could have been killed. Her hand shook with delayed reaction. With a deep breath she tried to control the fear welling up in her. The nightmare wasn't over yet. The storm was only beginning.

"You can thank me when we're free." Robert shrugged off her gratitude. He had *tried* to get her out, but the bottom line was that he had failed, and to him a failed try was only a notch above no try at all. This miscalculation wasn't as easy as usual to dismiss and chalk up to experience.

He clenched his teeth. The sheer magnitude of the stakes was staggering. So much higher than any he'd faced before: Marianne's life; his own, their son's happiness. Bobby was only two years older than he had been when the accident had taken his parents. He didn't want his son to go through the loneliness, bitterness and rage that had shadowed his own childhood. If there was a way to get out of here, he would find it no matter what the cost.

Grimly he wondered what price he placed on his honor and integrity. His breaking point had never been tested before. He'd been shot at, but never been hit. After five years out in the field, he'd walked away without one serious injury, earning himself the nickname Lucky Sullivan.

But his luck had just run out.

He wanted to hit something, to slam his fist into the wall, to seek a physical release for the anger, the frustration and, yes, the fear raging inside him. For the first time in his adult life he was afraid. The tough Robert Sullivan was as vulnerable as anyone else on this plane.

Then he looked into Marianne's pale face. Concern darkened her eyes and he felt the heat of her touch scorching through the layers of clothes. Memories he had sealed tightly and locked away four years ago flashed open. For one unguarded moment his eyes flared with a mixture of passion and need. "Thank me with a kiss," he said roughly, covering her hand.

Marianne caught her breath, and her hand squirmed beneath his. He made her feel defenseless, exposed, threatened. She was afraid of being drawn into a whirlpool of memories, afraid of opening old wounds, of being hurt again. The defenses she had built so carefully weren't ready to come down. Would they ever be?

She leaned sideways to catch a glimpse of the terrorists. The major was raising the heavy door and slamming it down again. "You're crazy," she whispered. She took a step backward.

Robert turned and watched as the major pushed the door shut and pulled on it. He almost grinned when it opened again beneath the pressure. "Perhaps the fickle Lady Luck has changed sides once again."

Marianne's gaze was glued to Robert's dark head. At nineteen, she had loved him with the intense emotional fervor only the young are capable of. Her experience from high school proms and college dates and from watching her parents' interactions had not prepared her for Robert. She had been raised in a house filled with love, and no timidity toward showing that love. Her father still brought her mother flowers, and her mother still saved him the choicest selections when he was late for a meal.

That was the kind of marriage she'd believed she would have when she met Robert. Even the knowledge that Robert had not loved her had not deterred her, then. It was enough that he had wanted her. She had been too young to understand that passion took but gave little in return. Not enough to build a happy marriage on.

She was wiser now. More cautious. Even wary. She needed time to recover from the shock of this unexpected reunion before she tested the strength of her defenses. But still her heart skipped crazily as she stared at him.

"Sullivan, I want you both to go to the rear," the major ordered sharply.

"Having trouble?" Robert asked, not hiding the satisfaction in his voice.

The major raised his voice threateningly. "Start walking past the movie screen and up the aisle to your left."

Taking Marianne's hand, Robert drew her past the center row of seats. Once they were hidden from the major's view, he stopped and framed her face. "A kiss," he repeated huskily.

"You're crazy," Marianne repeated in turn, but her voice was softer. The need to taste and to feel pulsed through her veins, and some of her old recklessness surfaced. Surely one chaste kiss would not topple the wall she had so painfully erected over the years. And if it did begin to crumble, wasn't it better to know just how vulnerable she still was?

She stood on her toes and splayed her fingers on his lean, hard cheek. Beneath the tips she felt the tiny bristles of his strong beard. He must have shaved at some point on this trip because the bristles were still short. His skin smelled fresh and faintly of the soap he always used.

She remembered so many details. Too many. "Thank you, Robert," she whispered. Brushing his lips with a butterfly's touch, she swiftly withdrew. The hammering of her blood drowned out the banging noise coming from the door.

"That wasn't a kiss." The brief touch had been an enticement, a teasing whisper that left him aching for more. Robert's arms clamped around her waist, holding her close to him. "I know you can do better than that."

"This isn't wise," Marianne cautioned, glancing past him nervously. "They might follow us at any moment."

"True." Robert's eyes glinted recklessly. He knew that this might be their only chance to be alone, and he was determined not to waste the opportunity. He took a step sideways, pulling her along until they were hidden by the coat closet that doubled as a movie screen. "I think we both need to get this out of the way before we join the others."

His fingers slid into her hair, caressing her cheeks with his hard palms. The need to find out if there was more than possessiveness and fading memories between them was a driving force. He watched her clear gray eyes darken and her black pupils widen until they were dark pools. Her fear shot through him, gentling him. "Don't be afraid of me," he whispered hoarsely against her lips. "Don't ever be afraid of me."

Marianne shook her head. She wasn't afraid of Robert, but of the sudden surge of need almost swamping her. Sensations, desires she had locked away for years, shivered through her. She stared into the silver-green depths of his eyes and watched as his thick lashes came down. The tip of his tongue teased her lips apart until she opened to him. He took her lips with a devastating mixture of gentleness and hunger that made her forget everything: the terrorists, the dangers. She clung to him.

Robert had not known just how much he had hungered for the taste of her, how much he had yearned for her passion and how starved he had been for the sweetness of her response. If he had, he would not have touched her.

He knew he should stop, but it was too late. She was in his blood. He had guessed it the moment he'd seen her again. He had known it when she had faced the major and she had slid her hand into his. This was one hell of a time to discover how much she still meant to him. Reluctantly he raised his head and asked gently, "That wasn't so bad, was it?"

It was worse than she had expected, Marianne realized. Much, much worse. Her whole body was pulsing with desire, and her lips could barely form the word no. She stared at him, remembering other kisses and the promises and dreams she had read into them. She had been wrong then, she reminded herself, and stepped back. She could be wrong again. She didn't want to fall in love with him all over again.

As his arms fell away, she reached for her pride and wrapped it around her like armor. "It wasn't bad," she said, "but it wasn't nearly as good as my memories."

The moment she uttered the words, she regretted them. She had not forgotten how he tasted and smelled or felt. But she had forgotten that he never refused a challenge, and he was accepting this one now with all his heart, body and soul. His eyes gleamed brighter and his lips curved, deepening the creases in his lean cheeks. Groaning, she turned and fled down the aisle.

There was something ghostly about shoes standing at odd angles, attaché cases peeking from beneath the seats, and the case of Matchbox cars spilling over the upholstery onto the floor. Marianne's face froze at the sight. No kiss was worth the risk they had just taken.

Bending down, she picked up a bright blue dune buggy and twisted it in her hand. Her mind flew back to the space station she had helped Bobby build two months ago.

"Dad would know what the lunar landing module really looks like," her son had muttered at one point, studying the *half-completed structure in his hand.*

"Why don't you call him. Perhaps he can explain it to you over the phone."

"He's in Arizona." Bobby's voice had been matter-of-fact. *"He said he needed to see Jamal."* Then he had gotten up and searched among his books. *"But he bought me a book about NASA when we visited the space station last year. Maybe there's a picture of the module in it."* Later

he'd added, "Dad said that he might not have much time for me this summer and asked if I wanted to go to the space camp for two weeks. Can I, Mom?"

Marianne could sense Robert right behind her. He hadn't changed. But she had. She had grown up and away from him. It had been a slow and often painful process. There had been times when she'd picked up the phone to call him with the same need an alcoholic felt for a drink, only to drop the receiver at the last moment.

She was still thirsty for his kisses, she still ached for his touch. Perhaps a part of her would always crave him. That wasn't love. That was lust. She'd left him because she'd needed more out of life than what Robert had been willing to give. Regretting her biting remark about his kiss, she apologized. "I shouldn't have said what I did. Hell, I shouldn't even have kissed you."

Robert's dark brows rose sharply at the curse. He knew she had a sailor's vocabulary but she rarely used it, unless she was facing a storm. He remembered the first time he'd heard her swear. They had been on her father's sailboat, and she had discovered her brother had forgotten to refill the gas tank of the outboard motor. He had laughed and teased her then. Now he was wary. "It was only a kiss," Robert said quietly. "And understandable under the circumstances."

"Perhaps." She pounced on the excuse he had just handed her. "Perhaps we did need to release the tension. It shouldn't happen again, though. We have enough problems already."

Robert looked at her pale, drawn face and at the shadows beneath her eyes. It wasn't only the stress of the last few hours that had etched those lines of weariness, he guessed. She must have been pushing herself for weeks. How many hours of sleep had she averaged during those last days before April 15?

Gently he brushed his knuckles across her skin. "You're right," he said quietly, his baritone voice deep and reassuring. "No complications." He could wait. What was another few days when he'd already spent years marking time?

And that was exactly what he had been doing, he realized.

He'd told himself that he'd switched to the foreign service for his son's sake, because at the ATD his hours had been too irregular and the job too dangerous. There had always been the chance that someone would recognize him and use him for target practice. But instead of staying close, he'd packed up and moved overseas. There was only one explanation for the contradiction. Subconsciously he had never quite accepted their divorce as final. He had removed himself from temptation to give her time to heal, to forget the bad memories and remember the good times. Since his return to Washington he'd hesitated to knock on her door. How much longer would he have waited before taking the shuttle to New York?

Taking her by the shoulders, he turned her around. "We'll have plenty of time to sort out our lives. Later. After this is over."

Behind them the door banged and snapped shut. Turning, they watched both the major and Hamid put their full weight against it and held their breath. It wouldn't budge, even when the terrorists kicked and banged to test its hold.

Marianne bit her lips, and Robert muttered a heartfelt "damn."

Their faces were pale when they turned away.

The passengers had been crowded together into the window aisle in the rear of the cabin with two terrorists guarding them. When Marianne and Robert entered, they were greeted with a collective sigh of relief. Walking ahead, Marianne counted eleven heads, among them a distinguished-looking blond giant and Robert's black-haired travel companion.

"Sit over there." A terrorist with a crooked nose pointed at the two empty window seats next to the man with the coal-black hair. Then he pulled a pack of cigarettes from his pocket, extracted one, struck a match and lit it. With slow deliberation, he drew the nicotine into his body, then exhaled, fixing Marianne with a hostile stare through the swirling blue smoke. "Sit," he ordered again, tossing the match on the floor.

"Glad to see you in one piece. I'd almost given up on you." Robert's former seatmate got to his feet with the fluid movements of an athlete, placing himself between the hijacker and Marianne. "The name's Rafe, ma'am," he said, holding out his hand.

His grip was firm and hard, like the man himself. In his light-colored Western suit and shirt he looked like a successful businessman. But a turquoise-studded scorpion bola around his neck added a dangerous touch. She liked what she saw and smiled at him. "Mine's Marianne."

Still holding her hand, Rafe looked at Robert. "You look a little battered," he said lightly, pointing at the scratch. "You two had me worried. I'm glad you're all right."

Robert nodded stiffly, then watched with narrowed eyes as Rafe helped Marianne into the seat next to him. The sight of any man but him touching her, even casually, made his blood heat. Did she have to smile at the man and thank him so sweetly? His hands were clenched at his side. He wasn't going to stand for it. He did not like the seating arrangements, with Marianne sandwiched between them. "Marianne, move over," he ordered briskly.

Marianne's smile faded abruptly. It had been years since anyone had ordered her around. She swallowed an angry retort, but refused to move. "You'll be more comfortable here," she said calmly, patting the empty window seat.

Robert wanted to insist, but at that moment the guard lost his patience and said threateningly, "Sit down." Robert stepped past Rafe, bent over and fastened his hard hands around Marianne's waist. Before she could protest, Robert had shifted her into the window seat. "This is the safest place," he muttered out loud.

"You're going to be very uncomfortable." Though she smiled, her eyes were stormy and two bright spots of anger appeared on her skin. Glaring, she watched Robert squeeze his bulk into the narrow center space.

Robert ignored the sarcastic edge in her voice. Gingerly he stretched his legs until his shins hit the seat in front of him. His knees were still bent at a sixty-degree angle. The spread of his shoulders was wider than the backrest, and he hunched them forward by crossing his arms in front of him.

It had been years since he'd traveled coach, and he'd forgotten just how small the spaces were, but he wasn't going to admit how caged-in he felt. He pushed down the armrest between himself and Rafe's seat and leaned on it, then shifted his legs into Marianne's space. "That's better," he said softly, and slowly smiled at her.

The small, satisfied smile was so much like Bobby's when he thought he had outsmarted her that her face softened and her anger fled. "I'm glad *you* are comfortable now," she said with honeyed sweetness. "But I am not." The hard strength of his thighs pressed against hers and his ankles rubbing her shins warmed her until her skin felt on fire with wanting him.

"Then put your legs on top of mine," Robert suggested smoothly. The gleam in his eyes told her that he knew exactly what he was doing to her. Then, abruptly, the teasing light vanished. "I think you should try to get some sleep," he said quietly. "You look as if you haven't seen a bed since Bobby went to France."

"It wasn't quite that bad," she protested ruefully. "I managed at least five hours every night." But despite her protests, she felt weariness dragging her down like lead weights. She was tempted to put her head on Robert's shoulder and rest. She wished he'd take her hand and draw her against him. But she wasn't a child to be coddled and soothed. She was a woman who had learned to face storms alone.

"Later, perhaps," she said, leaning against the outside wall.

"Do you play poker, Marianne?" Rafe asked, leaning forward to look past Robert.

"I used to, a long time ago. But I was always lousy at it."

Robert raised one dark brow. She had beaten him on more than one occasion, he remembered. But looking back, he realized that he had been so fascinated by the tip of her tongue moistening her lips that he had been quite unable to pay close attention to the game. "She used to be quite a challenge," Robert told Rafe with a hard smile.

Marianne tried to hide the blush staining her cheeks and turned to look out the window. But even the gray sky and the pearly raindrops bouncing off the glass could not dispel the memories of how every game had ended. She could almost feel the weight of his hard body covering hers, his subtle skin sliding smoothly over her, pleasure expanding with every movement until she'd cried out and dissolved in his arms.

Wearily she wondered how she would survive these coming days of shared danger and fear and refreshed memories without falling in love all over again.

She turned back, challenged Robert with the tilt of her chin, and gave Rafe a brilliant smile. "Do you have cards?"

"Never travel without them, ma'am," he said and withdrew a pack from his jacket. As he was dealing, the major walked into the cabin.

Stopping at their row, the major scooped up the cards, then fixed them with hard, angry eyes. "Still think this is a game, Sullivan?" He dropped the cards from one hand to the other. "A few days in Beirut, and you'll change your mind." With a cruel twist of his thin lips, he picked up the top card and crumpled it pointedly.

Then he stared at each of the hostages. "I don't want to kill any of you, but I will if I have to. There will be no talking, no smoking, no getting up without permission from my men. Sullivan, for your wife's sake, I hope you'll be more cooperative the next time we talk."

Chapter 5

Bright sunlight flooded the cabin as the plane headed east. The heat and the smooth drone of the engines had spread lethargy among the hostages as they reclined in their seats. Some whispered while others read or wrote letters that would probably never be mailed. Still others had finally given up fighting exhaustion and were dozing fitfully. The terrorists were smoking and talking as they lounged in seats across the aisle. With their guns across their laps, they kept a close eye on their prisoners.

Robert was watching their every move. This bunch was less nervous than Hamid and his friend, especially since their smooth takeoff in Paris. The one sitting in the center seat was dark-haired, with a crooked nose and thick heavy brows. He smoked a Gauloise, a rough, filterless cigarette, inhaling the acrid smoke all the way down to his toes. He had shed his black corduroy jacket some time ago, revealing a gray T-shirt with SUNY written across it. That didn't mean that he was or ever had been a student at the State

University of New York, Robert admitted to himself, but it was a clue worth considering.

The terrorist sitting in the aisle seat had the slender build of a true Bedouin. His hair was brown, and his eyes, also brown, were creased at the corners, perhaps from constantly having to squint into the sun. He wore jeans and a khaki shirt that was much too large for him, as if he had only recently exchanged his loose desert garb for the tighter-fitting Western wear. He also smoked, but he puffed rather than inhaled, like a man who had only lately started smoking. For some time now his attention had been almost totally fixed on Rafe, who was immersed in a book about horses.

Not much to go on, Robert thought grimly. He had tried every way he knew how to make contact with them. He'd gone to the bathroom three times with the sole purpose of talking to his escort. But the only words he'd gotten out of either man had been, "Shut up. You have one minute."

Crossing his arms over his chest, Robert touched the dry roof of his mouth with his tongue, wishing for a glass of ice water, a workout, a cold shower, anything. Even a cigarette.

He hadn't smoked in ten years, but he needed something to keep his hands occupied and his mind alert. He guessed that the moment he closed his eyes, he'd be taken back to the major. If their roles were reversed that's what he would do; watch for signs of mental and physical fatigue, then pounce and squeeze.

Under different circumstances Robert would have faked sleep to precipitate another confrontation. But he was afraid that if he didn't cooperate, the major would send Hamid into the cabin to harass Marianne and tighten the screws.

Damn! He knew no more about the major now than he had five hours ago. Who did he work for? Who had paid for the operation? And who was responsible for the leak? Robert shifted into another but no more comfortable position—at least his discomfort kept him awake. Still, the inactivity was getting to him.

Checking his slim gold watch, he tried to predict when the major's patience would run out. Beirut was less than three hours away, and Robert was certain that he would make another move before they reached their destination. The *bastard* was probably sleeping right now. Or drinking another glass of Perrier—a *cold* glass of Perrier. Swearing beneath his breath, Robert sat up straight and looked at Marianne.

She had fallen asleep about halfway between Paris and Beirut. Her toes were almost touching his, and her body rested against the hard plastic of the wall. Robert would have been content if she'd used his shoulder for a pillow, but he hadn't suggested it. He wanted her to feel comfortable with him. He had promised her no added pressure, and he was going to stick to his word. He could wait, but it wasn't easy, not when he was forced to sit idly next to her, watching the sun burnish her hair with gold highlights.

And not when she wrinkled her nose and muttered something beneath her breath. When her tongue came out to moisten her dry lips, he almost groaned. Robert tore his eyes away and balled his hands into white-knuckled fists.

He was searching for control, and he would never find it while watching her. She was too beautiful, too soft, and much too desirable. He wanted to kiss her again. He needed to know that the kiss they had stolen was more than temporary insanity, more than the result of a rush of adrenaline. He wanted to believe that the special magic still existed somewhere, hidden beneath the bitterness and pain. He needed to believe in that as much as he needed to believe in their eventual escape. The bond that was tying him to her was too strong to break. He accepted that now, but he had not always felt this way.

There had been a time when he'd resented the hold she had on him. Until he'd met her, he'd gone through life without taking more than passing interest in women. He hadn't had the time for more. His life had been unsettled, exciting, unpredictable, and he had liked it that way.

All during that summer nine years ago, he had told himself that he could walk away from her any time he pleased, that he would miss her family more than he would miss her, and that the reason why he'd kept returning to Long Island after his vacation was to let her down gently. He'd already felt like a bastard kissing her, touching her. He didn't want to scar her permanently by callously abandoning her.

He remembered a Sunday morning when he had driven to Stony Brook on a Labor Day weekend. He'd just returned from hell, searching for one of his men who'd been missing. For the last two weeks he'd been combing bazaars, turning tents inside out, following a trail that got colder instead of warmer as he went on. Three days earlier he'd found Chuck—or what was left of him—and the stench and the nightmare had followed him all the way back to the States.

Chuck wasn't married, but he'd had a family. Parents, a brother and sister, and nephews and nieces, all of whose pictures had been in his wallet. Lately he'd talked about quitting field work. He wanted a "cushy" job like Robert's and a woman to come home to every night. Chuck would never know a woman's warmth again, Robert had thought as he grimly stuffed clothes into a bag for his visit to Marianne.

He'd grabbed his bag, locked the door to his studio apartment and made for his car. He could already smell the fresh scent of the sea, hear Marianne's laughter rising above the squawk of the sea gulls and feel the warm softness of her sun-kissed skin.

Marianne's brother, Colin, was beneath his '73 Corvette when Robert pulled up in the driveway. Marianne's car was gone.

"She's out fishing." Getting to his feet, Colin wiped his greasy hands on a rag. But even then he didn't offer Robert one of them. He raised his grease-streaked face and ground out angrily, "I think you have a hell of a lot of nerve showing up again."

Colin was a taller, masculine version of his sister, and two years older. For all his easygoing charm, he was very protective of her. Robert didn't blame him for wanting to punch him. As a brother he probably would have felt the same way. He said calmly, "I want to know how she is."

"Great. She's got a new boyfriend in tow."

He hadn't expected that. He had wanted her to be happy, but damn it, not going out with someone else. Still, he shrugged his shoulders and said lightly, "I'm glad. Where are your parents?"

"At the yacht club. I'll tell them you came by."

For a moment Robert considered leaving. The thought of spending the weekend watching Marianne with another man was not exactly what he'd had in mind. On the other hand, he did owe her parents an explanation of some sort. His honor demanded that. His chin jutted out. "Want me to help?"

Colin stared at him angrily. "Stop playing with my sister," he snapped, then crawled back under his car.

Robert calmly rolled up his sleeves and squatted down. "It was never a game," he said, handing him a wrench. If it had been, he would have paid up, counted his losses and walked away without looking back. But for the first time in his life he wanted to stay, he wanted to belong. He wanted to put down roots, have children, a home, the things that Chuck had planned and now would never have. At first, that thought had sent shock waves through him.

He wasn't ready yet to settle down, he had argued. In another few years perhaps, when Marianne had grown up and finished college, he thought, trying to talk himself out of it.

And he almost succeeded—until he saw Marianne that night.

He was sitting with Don and Cecile on the patio, drinking an ice cold beer, his eyes fixed on the sea, which stretched from the bottom of the sloping lawn to the horizon, like gold cloth rippling in the setting sun. She was wearing cutoff jeans and an open shirt tied below a yellow bikini top, and she was showing more golden skin than was decent, Robert thought. The tall blond stud following her as she carried two coolers could barely take his eyes off her long enough to say hello to him. He couldn't blame the poor guy for staring. Even smelling of fish and with her face screwed into a frown, she was beautiful.

"We caught about seventy pounds of flounder." Tossing her long, sun-bleached mane over her shoulder, Marianne turned to him and greeted him with polite friendliness, "Hi, Robert. Long time, no see." Then she turned back to David, splayed her fingers on his brawny arm and pulled him forward. "Robert, this is David. David, meet Robert Sullivan, a friend of my parents."

The hell I am, Robert thought grimly, acknowledging the younger man with a brief, taut smile. The challenge would have amused him weeks ago, but now it made him grit his teeth. At a guess, David was only three years younger than himself, easygoing, charming. Dull. Robert looked at Marianne and asked with dangerous softness, "How are you?"

"Fine." Her smile was polite, but her eyes flashed with defiance and pride. "David's parents suggested a fish fry. I'm going over to his place."

"Let's have it over here," Cecile suggested in her charmingly accented voice. With a mixture of exasperation and amusement, she pushed back her chair and got to her feet. "That is, if you've already cleaned the fish?"

"We did." With a toothpaste smile the blond giant grasped Marianne's hand. "May I use your phone and call my parents?"

It didn't seem to bother Marianne that David was pawing her. Robert placed the beer can on the glass-topped table, leaned back in his chair and laced his hands behind his back. It was either that or pull David's hands off her.

"I'll do it," Don said, a grin creasing his weathered, tanned face.

"Then I'll drive David home." Marianne shot Robert a furious look. But she was too well-mannered to voice her anger out loud. "Do you want me to pick up some salads and rolls at the village market?" she asked.

Cecile nodded, ran her fingers through her blond curls and gave her daughter a warning look. "I'll get the money," she said dryly, giving Robert an apologetic smile and following her husband.

Robert smoothly rose to his feet. He wasn't going to give David another chance to put his smelly hands on Marianne's golden skin. "I'll drive David home and stop at the store."

Marianne's eyes darkened angrily, like storm clouds gathering over the sea. Angling her chin, she leaned closer to David. "I'm coming with you. You don't know what to buy."

Robert raked her flesh with cold sea-green eyes. He knew he was reacting like a possessive Neanderthal. Caveman tactics weren't his style, but he seemed unable to stop from snapping, "Not dressed like that, you won't."

She compressed her lips and flashed her eyes. The look she gave Robert's clean sneakers, pressed jeans and ironed white shirt made him feel stuffy, overdressed and middle-aged. He would have to remember to leave a note for his cleaning woman not to iron his jeans anymore, he thought.

Then, to his surprise, Marianne capitulated. "You're right. I reek of fish." She threw her keys at David with the words, "You can take my car home, but bring it back in one piece."

Then she walked into the house to return minutes later, dressed in white shorts and a pink T-shirt showing a bear dressed in a bow tie and pants on the front and the logo Stuffy the Bear on the back.

Robert chuckled appreciatively. "Did you buy that with me in mind?" he asked, walking toward his car.

"You were rude," she flared at him. "There was nothing wrong with the way I was dressed."

"David couldn't keep his eyes or hands off you," Robert snapped, opening the car door for her.

She faced him with the door between them. "So what's it to you?" Her fingers gripped the top of the door and her lips tightened angrily, trying to keep the words from spilling out. But she was to hurt and they burst out anyway. "I haven't heard from you in four weeks. I thought you weren't coming back."

Robert's lips thinned into a narrow smile. He wished he could tell her where he'd been. But how could he trust her with secrets and the lives of his men when she couldn't even control her own emotions? It was too damn dangerous. "I was down south on business," he said.

"You could've called." She started to slide into the seat, but his hand covered her, keeping her from retreating.

The flame that was never quite under control when he was with her ignited. He wanted to kiss her and show her that he had dreamed of the smell of her skin, of making love to her every night. He wanted to explain that the nearest phone had been too far away and too dangerous to use. Besides, he doubted that he could've placed a call to the States from any one of them.

"It wasn't convenient," he said, removing his hand. He felt like a bastard when she slid into the seat without saying another word.

He shouldn't have come back, he thought with grim weariness, closing the door. She was too young for marriage, especially to a man like himself. If he wanted a family he should have looked for someone tougher, more independent, an asset instead of a liability. He walked around the car, telling himself that he would leave tomorrow morning.

But during the long, lonely night he found more reasons for staying than for leaving. Whatever it was that burned inside him, it was too compelling, too intense. He didn't have the strength to walk away. On that thought he finally fell asleep.

He awoke to the sound of car doors slamming in the driveway. He got up too late to escape Don's large, boisterous family gathering for the Labor Day picnic. When he came downstairs he found himself being paired off with Marianne to gather mussels for the clambake. But from the first moment he'd met her, it had been too late to leave. He was through fighting this need that twisted inside him day and night.

While they looked for mussels, they would come to an understanding of some sort, agree on a testing period. He'd have to tell her something about his job, enough to make her understand that he couldn't talk about that part of his life.

He was choosing his words carefully as their silver canoe silently slid through the shallow water of the marsh. Reeds stood high, isolating them from the occasional houses set back among oak and maple trees. The sun burned through his shirt as they rowed in silence. Sitting in front of him, Marianne occasionally raised her oar to examine clusters of shiny black shells clinging to rocks half buried in the sand. Then she'd grip the shaft and dip the blade, and the canoe would shoot forward again. She couldn't avoid him forever.

Eventually she dropped her oar into the canoe, jumped lightly into the shallow water, picked up a cluster of big mussels covered with seaweed, threw them into the first of the two buckets that had to be filled and turned her back to him again. "These look good. We'll stop right here," she called over her shoulder and bent down to pick another cluster.

She was dressed in her skimpy red French shorts and a T-shirt that fastened high at her neck. When she bent over, Robert's gaze followed her long slender legs to the edge of the yellow bikini bottom she wore underneath her shorts. Since his return he had thought of little else but how she would feel in his arms and how his body reacted when she smiled and how much brighter the world seemed when she laughed.

But she was still mad at him.

Robert rested his arms on his knees and decided to let her pick mussels until she'd worked her anger out of her system. His pride demanded that she make the first move. In the meantime, he would enjoy the view and wait for her to come to him.

She tugged at another bunch of the shiny shells clinging to a rock beneath the surface, putting all her frustration into prying them loose. Robert watched her struggle, tug and swear, waiting for the inevitable fall backward into the cold water. She needed to cool off.

Suddenly she sat down with a splash and an oath that startled the gulls nearby, then lost her balance again in the soft sand and fell back.

Grinning, Robert leaned over the side, caught her wrist and helped her back into a sitting position. "Since you're already wet, you can get the rest of the mussels. I'll hold the bucket," he offered calmly, watching her wipe her wet hair out of her face, waiting for the explosion. None came.

"Fine." She jumped to her feet and stared at him with narrowed eyes while she reached for a towel and dried her face. Then she spun around and, pushing against the side of the bow, tipped the canoe on its side. Only his swift reflexes saved Robert from landing among the reeds. By the time he'd straightened the canoe, he was as soaked as Marianne.

"Are you wet enough now to do your share of the work?" she challenged with her hands on her hips and a smirk on her face.

Robert shot her a dangerous grin that promised retaliation. He felt the sharp jagged edge of need shredding his control. So she wanted to fight, he thought, feeling desire burning through him. He took his time taking his dripping sneakers off, putting them side by side in the water at the bottom of the boat, but the action didn't cool him down. The way her wet T-shirt clung to every curve of her body didn't help, molding itself to the proud swell of her breasts, nipping in at her slender waist and stretching over narrow, rounded hips. He tried to ignore the desire that tied him into knots. Since his arrival, she'd alternately ignored or taunted him, and because she'd been hurt, he'd let her get away with it. Until now.

Now she was going to pay. If she hissed at him, he would kiss her until she had no strength left to defy him anymore. If she hurled mussels at him he'd duck and tackle her and strip that damn shirt off her body.... He caught his breath. He wanted to take her here among the reeds. He wanted to feel her small, strong hands slide over his body and hear her taunting lips whisper his name. He wanted—he'd wanted too passionately for too long. For months he'd kept his hands off her. Now his control had slipped its leash.

"There's something we should get out of the way first," he ground out and lithely jumped into the water, barely causing a splash. He reached for her before she could retreat and dragged her against him.

"Damn it, let me go." Angrily she shoved at his shoulders, but he didn't budge. "I wish you'd never come back."

He captured her wrists, pulled them down and behind her back, then drew her body forward until she fell against him. "So do I," he snapped, with his mouth inches away from her lips. He didn't like to feel out of control. "Would it solve anything? Would you stop wanting me?"

"Yes," she spat at him, defying him with her words and her body. But her eyes sent a different message. As he kissed her lightly, avoiding her lips, her body was beginning to tremble and her breath came out fast.

He transferred his grip, holding her slender wrists in one of his hands while the other cupped her chin to prevent her from turning her face away. "Liar," he groaned, his breath caressing her skin. "I've tried it. It doesn't work." He teased her with his lips, torturing himself by holding back. He wanted her to come to him; his pride and his conscience demanded it. "For months I've been telling myself that I'm the wrong man for you. That hasn't worked, either. You're like gambling fever in my blood. Right and wrong don't seem to matter anymore."

He could feel her weakening, so his hold on her wrists relaxed. The next instant she twisted away from him and ran, splashing through the water. A safe distance away from him, she turned, angled her chin and hissed, "I hope your arrogance chokes you." Then she read the purpose in his eyes, and she whispered in a voice that was barely audible above the rustling of the reed. "Don't touch me if you don't mean it."

Was it the raucous cry of the gulls circling above their heads that he heard? Or was it his conscience warning him?

Whatever it was, it had come too late. He wanted this sea nymph standing before him, calling to him in a language that was as old as time. He didn't understand the words but he felt its power, drawing him relentlessly, step-by-step, into her arms. He had no conscience, no defenses. There was only fire and need burning for the girl-woman standing before him. "I want you."

It couldn't be love that was coursing through his veins. He felt no gentleness, no sweetness, no warmth. His desire was wild, near breaking point. Every hour he'd spent with her had pushed him closer to the brink. He took one final, careful step, giving her a last chance to retreat. But she stood there, waiting.

When his mouth covered hers, she didn't pull away. Her hands were trembling slightly as they framed his face, but her lips parted, her tongue invited him, and the heat of her mouth pushed him over the edge. He pressed her against his body while her hands slid up to his neck, drawing his head down.

Robert made a sound of pleasure deep in his throat. He felt as if he could not hold her close enough and kiss her deeply enough. Wild passion ran through him, threatening to break free. With a last grab at sanity he whispered hoarsely, "Tell me to stop."

He wished that he still had illusions left, that he was still young enough to believe in love. "I want to give you roses, candlelight, romance."

Her answer was the most beautiful smile he had ever seen: misty, tender, heart-wrenching. "I love you," she whispered, turning her face into his palm. "I love you enough for both of us. I don't want you to give me roses or candlelight. Just show me that you want me. That's all I need."

Then she took a step back and pulled the T-shirt over her head, dropping it in the shallow water swirling around her feet.

Her bikini top followed. For a moment Robert stared at her pale, proud breasts, then with a groan he reached for what she offered, cupping the firm heavy mounds, feeling them swell into his hands with their nipples erect.

He had enough restraint left to lift her high in his arms and carry her through the reeds to a spot of grass at the water's edge. He had enough restraint left to shed his own clothes before touching her. But he did not have enough control left to walk away from her.

She smelled of saltwater and sun—cool and clean. Her skin was as smooth as velvet and tasted of fresh air and the sea. Suddenly it seemed right that they should make love here, in the morning sun, with the water lapping only inches away.

Touching her, Robert felt an aching tenderness well up in him, spreading a strange kind of need, a mixture of warmth and gentleness, a longing to cherish and to protect, a fiery hunger to take and to give. He entered her, giving her everything he had to give: passion and tenderness.

And a child . . .

The guilt had haunted him ever since, he thought grimly, watching Marianne stir in her sleep and shift her face away from the sun. Not because he hadn't wanted the child. He would always remember the exultation, the pride, the joy when she had told him that she was pregnant.

But he would never forget the knowledge that he had taken away her choices, that he had made her a mother before she had tested her own wings, had gnawed at him ever since.

This time, he promised himself, he was going to give her a choice. But first they had to get out of this mess.

Impatiently he shifted, bumping into Rafe's arms.

Taking one sharp look at him, Rafe snapped the book shut. "Another two hours to Beirut," he said quietly, opening the lid of the leather case resting on his knees. "I'll give them another fifteen minutes before they come for you again."

Smiling grimly, Robert shot another look at Marianne. "I'm ready," he muttered, flexing his hands like a player loosening up before dealing out cards.

Following his eyes, Rafe said quietly, "Don't worry about Marianne. I'll watch over her." His promise given, he placed his book into the briefcase.

Suddenly the guard stubbed out his cigarette and stepped into the aisle. With the barrel of his gun he stopped Rafe from closing the lid. "What you have in there?"

"Papers. Books." Rafe leaned back as the guard riffled through his papers and his checkbook. Robert could have sworn that behind that impassive facade, Rafe was grinning when he should have been furious.

Understanding dawned as he watched the Bedouin pick up the book and study the magnificent gray stallion gracing the cover. Hell, he almost grinned himself. How could he have missed the link when it had almost smacked him in the face? If there was one thing that could turn strangers into friends and get enemies talking, it was a shared obsession.

Horses.

The Bedouin tribesmen were as obsessed with their horses as they were with their religion. Muhammad had made the breeding of horses an integral part of his teachings. The Koran stated, for example, that *no evil spirt will dare to enter a tent where there is a purebred horse* and that *for every barley grain that is given to a horse, Allah will pardon one sin.*

"You like horses?" the Bedouin asked, opening the cover.

"Yeah." Rafe hid his excitement behind a deadpan face. "Do you?"

"My father, he grow horses like this." Proudly the terrorist pointed at a gray stallion racing through the desert hills. "He sell one like this to the king of Morocco."

"I also breed Arabians," Rafe explained with studied casualness. "I'm on my way to Jordan to buy a mare."

"From Hussein's stud?" the hijacker asked knowledgeably, again flipping through the pages until he found a photograph of the famous royal stables. "His horses very good. My father, he own better ones. Our horses live in the desert with much places to run. They are strong and fast as the wind."

"I can't afford a royal stud mare," Rafe said with just the right inflection of interest and regret. "They're too expensive for my checkbook. Your father must be a wealthy man if he sells horses to kings."

The Bedouin nodded. "He sell one to Prince Muhrad of Omari last month," he added, almost bursting with pride. "The prince come to the high desert because he hear about my father's famous stallion. My father, he not sell his best horse. Muhrad buy Sultan, the young son. He promise to buy more—" As if suddenly becoming aware of how much he was revealing to a man who was his enemy, he stopped, dropped the book and stepped back across the aisle.

Robert veiled the sudden gleam in his own eyes. Muhrad, Jamal's half brother, was running to fat and preferred his fleet of cars to horses. On the few occasions when his presence was required to settle disputes among the constantly warring desert tribes, he used a helicopter as transportation.

Why would a man who hadn't been near the stables in years suddenly display an interest in Arabians? Robert stroked his bristly chin, watching the Bedouin sit down and reach for another cigarette. For investment purposes? Muhrad was a shrewd businessman and generated more wealth in one hour on the phone than he would profit from a trip into the desert to buy a horse.

The stallion could have been meant as a present for his brother Jamal, but Robert doubted it. The half brothers were barely on speaking terms and tolerated each other's presence only for old Yussuf's sake. It was much more likely that Muhrad had bought the stallion *because* Jamal had had his eye on the horse. Still, it was worth looking into—once they were free.

Rafe seemed reluctant to let things slide. He extended the heavy volume across the aisle, a seemingly innocent gift from one horse-lover to another. "You want to borrow my book?"

Robert held his breath, willing the Bedouin to reach for it. But his young face closed up, once again becoming hostile and suspicious. He had been too well-trained to take bribes. He lit his cigarette, inhaled deeply, coughed, then chanced another look through the blue smoke. With satisfaction Robert noticed that while the man had not swallowed the bait he had taken a first nibbling bite.

"Do you have any idea who his father is?" Robert asked Rafe when he'd stored his briefcase beneath his seat.

"Can you identify an oasis in the desert if I mention palm trees?" Rafe countered dryly. "You tell me. You're the expert on Omari. I never heard of a Prince Muhrad. How is he connected to Jamal?"

"Muhrad is the emir's heir. Jamal is his half brother," Robert explained. "Have you met Jamal?"

Rafe wryly shook his head. "He's way out of my league, though I tour his stud farm every chance I get. God, I'd give five years of my life for one of his beauties. But I couldn't touch them anymore than I could a foal from Hussein's stable."

"That mare you considered buying would cost a fortune in transportation alone," Robert said, hesitating briefly because he respected Jamal's need for privacy. "If you haven't made a firm commitment yet, I suggest you talk to Jamal before you decide. He cares more about his horses than profits. He'll give you a fair deal."

As good a deal as Rafe's pride would allow him to accept, Robert added silently. If Jamal liked a man, he thought nothing of giving him the horse instead of selling it.

Rafe's eyes burned like polished onyx in his hard face, but his pride made him say offhandedly, "Perhaps I will. It's one hell of an inducement to get back home soon."

Marianne stirred and stretched. She had been awake long enough to observe the scene with the terrorist. Because she barely knew one end of a horse from another she'd missed some of its significance. She understood about obsessions, though. At her father's boat yard the talk centered around yachts, hulls, riggings and races. Like horses, boats were an obsession. Any man's passion was also his weakness.

What were Robert's weaknesses? she wondered, watching the fabric of his shirt stretch over his shoulders as he leaned toward Rafe. It was a strange question to ask herself after four years of marriage. Robert enjoyed riding and sailing, but it wasn't in his blood. He jogged every morning, sometimes five or six miles a day, but Marianne suspected that he did it more to keep himself fit and not because he was addicted to the surge of adrenaline. Was he afraid to allow things to become important to him? Afraid to wake up one day and find what he cared for had vanished like his parents, his home, his friends?

Perhaps he'd never really believed their marriage would last. Was that why he hadn't allowed himself to love her? Was that why he had spent so little time at the home she had tried to make for him? And then she really had left him. She bit her trembling lip and blinked the moisture from her eyes. How could she have been so blind?

She wanted to apologize for hurting him, and for separating him from the only person he truly loved. But there had been mistakes on both sides. After all, she may have been young, selfish and too blind to understand, but she had loved him. And she had tried to make their marriage work. Robert had married her because she had been pregnant. Not because he had loved her.

No, she thought, she couldn't apologize for leaving him. That had been an act of desperation. If he had cared for her at all, he would have tried to change her mind. Instead, he had packed the things she had deliberately left behind to give him a reason to contact her and had handed them to her parents.

Swinging her legs to the floor, she straightened her skirt with shaking hands, ran her fingers through her hair and tucked her blouse back into her waistband. She was falling in love with him all over again. And she was scared.

She'd watched his interaction with the other hostages each time he'd left his seat. He was more open than she remembered, reaching out instead of waiting to be drawn into a circle. Just now he'd opened a door that would enable Rafe to fulfill his dream. It gave her hope that they could become friends, which they never had been before. But friendship wasn't enough for her.

How long had she been awake? Robert turned and studied her face. Her skin was flushed and her eyes were guarded. "Sleep well?" he asked casually.

She nodded. He needed a shave. "You didn't rest."

"I never sleep on planes."

"You used to fall asleep out on the water. What's so different about planes?" Before she could stop herself she ran her fingers over the bristles as she had done on those warm, lazy summer days.

"You."

His answer shook her. Her fingers stilled, but when she tried to snatch them away, he held them in place. "Why should that surprise you?" he asked gently. "When I was with you, I could relax."

"I thought you were bored." The old insecurities surfaced before she could suppress them. "Stony Brook is hardly as exciting as Washington," she added quickly, trying to cover up her feelings.

"I felt comfortable," he corrected her quietly, "and safe. I didn't have to watch my back." His mouth twisted ruefully. "Except for that one memorable occasion in the marsh."

Marianne blushed and snatched her hand away. She had always looked back on that day with mixed emotions. He had been patient, tender and passionate, and she had gloried in the knowledge that he had wanted her. Her pregnancy had changed all that. How could he remember the day without a dash of resentment?

"How can you smile about that day?" She gripped her hands and twisted them, wishing the subject had never come up. But she wasn't a person to run away from problems. She raised her eyes and said, "I didn't mean to trap you into marriage, but that was exactly what I did. I always wanted to apologize for my stupidity—but it seemed so futile afterward."

"Good God." Marianne wondered why her words had shaken him. He covered her hands and muttered, "I wish I had known. It never occurred to me that you would blame yourself." He paused and his face softened. "I was twenty-eight, old enough and certainly experienced enough to know better than to take such risks." He leaned closer until his face filled her vision and she had to look at him. "I had already decided to ask you to marry me, only I'd planned on a long engagement." His rueful smile returned. "But you drove sanity from my mind."

She stared at him as if a great weight had been lifted from her shoulders. He'd considered marriage *before* they had made love—*before* she'd become pregnant. How many other misunderstandings had festered and finally torn their marriage apart? It would take time to unravel their mistakes, she thought, blinking back the moisture in her eyes. "What did you mean about not having to watch your back?"

Robert leaned back in his seat, but he didn't release her hands. He wanted to explain about his work with the ATD, and he would—after they were safe. It wasn't that he didn't trust her—the knowledge was simply too dangerous. "Forget that I said that," he said softly.

It was as if he'd slapped her, and she retreated against the wall. "You don't owe me any explanation," she said coolly.

Frustration made his own temper flare. "That's right," he snapped. "I don't owe you anything. But when we get out of here, you're damn well going to listen to me."

"And I say to hell with you."

"Hey, kids, stop your squabbling," Rafe suddenly intervened from the sidelines. "We're about to have company."

Chapter 6

The upstairs lounge looked like a pigsty.

Robert viewed the candy and peanut wrappers, empty cola bottles and cigarette packages with disgust. Paper cases had been torn from pillows, and blankets were stained. The bar top was sticky with the residue from spilled soft drinks, and a ball of chewing gum was stuck beneath the edge. The major's tightly run, militarylike discipline seemed to be deteriorating.

"Now that you've had time to assess the situation, are you willing to cooperate?" The major opened a bottle of Perrier, half filled two highball glasses and pushed one in front of Robert. He threw the bottle cap dead center into the trash container on the other side of the bar.

Robert noted that the major sat on the same stool he'd used before. He added to the mental file he was compiling about his enemy: the man was a creature of habit. That should make it easier to trace him later.

Robert also noticed that he looked more like a player on a losing streak than a man who had everything under control. The major was nervous, tired and on edge. His movements were impatient, his steps were becoming shorter, and his black hair was slightly out of place, as if he'd speared his fingers through it repeatedly, then smoothed it out with his hands.

Nervous, edgy men make mistakes.

Calmly Robert ran his finger lightly over the edge of the bar, found a clean spot and leaned against it. Ignoring the water, he asked, "What exactly do you want from me?"

"I'm coming to that." The major stared at his glass. "What stage have the negotiations with Omari reached?"

"I don't know."

"You are a member of the negotiating team."

"I'm on vacation."

The major picked a slice of lime from the plate in front of him and squeezed the juice into the glass. "My informants tell me that the base was your idea and that you first discussed the plans with Emir Yussuf three years ago."

"If you paid for that information, you should ask for your money back," Robert suggested evenly. The idea for a military base in Omari had actually formed during the Iranian hostage crisis eight years ago, when they'd needed a base close to the Iranian border from which to launch their helicopters. But, at that time, Emir Yussuf had refused even to consider changing his country's neutral status. With Iran in chaos, Omari's oil revenues had risen to astronomical heights. Then, five years later, after several missile attacks on Omari's harbor, the Emir had been more receptive. Robert remembered their discussions in Yussaf's private apartments with Jamal and Muhrad and remembered too that Muhrad had angrily opposed the move. He still did.

Watching the major swirl the water in his glass, Robert thought that he didn't like the way Muhrad's name kept leaping into his mind.

The major set his glass down with a thud. His voice was sharper and his accent thicker when he snapped, "I'm running out of patience, Sullivan. The West is not going to get another foothold in our part of the world. You are vultures. You suck us dry. You ruin our land. You sneer at our customs. We will blow up this plane if that's what it takes to stop you from destroying our way of life. With the help of their neighbors, the people of Omari will fight your Western greed and corruption." Jerkily he twisted the cap off another bottle of Perrier. This time his aim was off center, hitting the edge of the bin.

Robert hid his satisfaction at the signs of agitation and egged the major on. "Are these the same neighbors who bombed Omari's harbor and killed innocent people?" he asked with a sneer.

The major's eyes narrowed. "When we land in Beirut, we will give a press conference. You will tell your government to make a public withdrawal from the negotiations. We also demand a statement from Yussuf."

He was losing his cool, Robert thought, and pushed a little more. "Anything else?"

"Yes. You have thirty minutes to compose the speech you will read out loud at the taping session tonight." When there was no reaction from Robert, his lip curled. "There are ways to make you more amenable."

Robert waited for the "inducement," the first turn of the screw. The major could have him beaten, but Robert doubted he would. It would take a lot of pain to make him cooperate.

"Your wife will prepare our meals."

There was a flat, dangerous look in Robert's eyes when he said, "My wife is no maid." The thought of Marianne serving their meals was repugnant.

"All women are maids. Allah created them for the sole purpose of serving men." He slid from the bar stool. "You Westerners are fools. You've given your women so much freedom you can't control them anymore." He adjusted his white cuffs, then raised his head again. "Did I forget to mention that Hamid will see to it that my orders are obeyed?"

"You better make damn certain that he keeps his eyes closed, his mouth shut and his hands in his pockets. If he insults her or touches her, there will be hell to pay."

The major met Robert's eyes with cold dislike. "I think I'm going to kill you before this is finished."

"The world is not big enough for both of us," Robert agreed. His voice was very calm, emotionless and matter-of-fact.

With a fatalistic shrug the major turned. Passing the two terrorists who had escorted Robert to the upper lounge, he ordered them to take their prisoner back downstairs. Halfway to the flight deck, he threw over his shoulder. "Start working on that speech, Sullivan."

The moment the major turned his back, Robert slid a bottle of Perrier into his coat pocket. "Major," he called. When the major turned with an almost eager look on his face, Robert asked, "Do you like horses?"

"You try my patience, Sullivan," the major snapped, opening the door to the cockpit.

"Do you?"

"Like women, horses have their uses," the major replied and closed the door behind him with a bang.

Robert's face looked grim. The major's words so accurately reflected Muhrad's philosophy that he wondered how much else the two men had in common.

Marianne tore her eyes away from the entrance to the business class, brushed specks of lint off the dark blue blazer, then ran her fingers through her hair. She longed for a comb and a toothbrush. It had been more than twenty-four hours since she'd washed her face and brushed her teeth. A shower now seemed the ultimate luxury. A long warm shower with a fresh pine-scented gel. Clean clothes. Shoes. She would never take any of them for granted again, she thought, taking another anxious sidelong glance down the aisle.

"He should have been back by now," she muttered, twisting the plastic strap of her watch, listening for steps. But all she heard was the hissing of forced air rushing out of the vents, whispers and the occasional chuckle from the seats behind her.

The chuckles grated on her nerves. Didn't anyone care that Robert had been gone for twenty-three minutes and fifteen seconds?

Rafe covered Marianne's hand, stilling her nervous tugging and twisting before she broke the strap. "Robert's going to be fine. He can take care of himself," he reassured her.

Marianne smiled tightly, her stomach knotted in fear. "I wish I hadn't argued with him."

"Arguments are like thunderstorms. They clear the air." He paused, then added, "Robert is too experienced a man to let a little spat like this spoil his concentration."

The cabin felt hot and the air seemed to have sucked every drop of moisture from her skin. Marianne's apprehension grew. Where was Robert? Why were they keeping him so long?

She saw Rafe glance down the aisle where the two terrorists were stretching their legs. "Marianne, I wouldn't worry about Robert. You know, I used to do the same thing he did, although I wasn't in his league. I only gathered intelligence," he said. When his statement was followed by silence, he turned back to Marianne. Seeing the mixture of dawning understanding and shock, he said quietly, "You didn't know. Hell, I should've kept my mouth shut."

She shook her head. Could Robert have been an agent? The idea seemed preposterous, outrageous—and so utterly plausible that she wondered why she had never considered it before. The danger, the challenge and the vagabond life would have suited him perfectly. The comical look of self-disgust on Rafe's face made her smile. "I'm glad you told me," she said quietly.

"How long were you two married? I know it's none of my business, but how did he explain his absences?"

Again she cast a worried look down the aisle. If he isn't back in five minutes, I'm going to look for him, she thought. Turning back to Rafe, she said, "We were married for four years. I was young and, I guess, slightly in awe of him and didn't ask many questions."

"That must have been tough," Rafe said quietly. "There must have been a lot of commitment on both sides to keep the marriage going."

"Did I forget to mention that I am also tenacious and stubborn?" Marianne asked, watching the Bedouin guard walk toward them.

The Bedouin stopped next to Rafe and asked, "How many horses you have?"

"Two stallions and seventeen mares." Rafe stroked his chin. "I'll bet your father has many more."

Marianne checked her watch. Twenty-seven minutes and forty seconds, she thought. Her mind returned to Rafe's revelation. Looking back now, Robert's prolonged absences and his long, erratic working schedule made sense. She had never known when to expect Robert. Sometimes he would arrive in the middle of the night, and at other times she'd found him asleep on the living room couch when she returned from class.

Once when he had come home, he had interrupted a study session before finals. Marianne had never forgotten that particular night. Later, she had always thought of it as the beginning of the end of their marriage.

It had been past ten when Robert suddenly stood in the door of the living room, where Marianne was sitting with Ann, her friend since she had transferred to NYU three years before and Ben, Cal and Dan, the math wizards. They had ordered in pizza and were taking a break, listening to music while eating. Ann suddenly nudged Marianne so hard that she almost dropped her slice of pizza on the cream carpet.

"Robert." For a moment Marianne simply feasted her eyes on him. He hadn't taken the time to change before catching the shuttle and still wore his uniform. He looked strikingly handsome. Devastatingly so. And weary, she thought, noticing how tautly the skin was stretched over the hollows beneath his cheekbones. She scrambled to her feet, her eyes bright with joy. "I didn't expect you tonight," she said, cautiously picking her way through Styrofoam cups, books and paper plates.

She wanted to fling herself into his arms, but she looked a mess. She still held the pizza in one hand and the other was greasy. There was a stain on her blue NYU sweatshirt where the anchovy had landed in the middle of the Y. Her jeans were patched at the knee and her hair was pulled back in a ponytail. Robert's sardonic smile made her painfully aware of the fact that she looked more like Bobby's older sister than his wife. "I didn't hear you come in," she said, stopping in front of him.

"I could hear the music the moment I stepped off the elevator." Robert swept the room with a look that made her friends squirm. "Good evening. I trust I'm not interrupting anything?"

Marianne's eyes narrowed angrily. "We were studying for the math final."

"So I see." His eyes went to the half-gallon jug of Gallo Burgundy. "Don't let me keep you," he said, turning away.

"Don't you want to join us? There's some pizza left."

He shook his head. "I'm not hungry." Meeting her angry gaze, his own softened. "I'll see you later," he said, brushing his knuckles over her cheek as he went toward the bedroom.

Her friends left almost immediately. Still angry, Marianne returned to the living room to straighten it. The room looked as if a tornado had whirled through it. Swiftly she stacked the paper plates, cups and pizza boxes in paper sacks and carried them into the foyer. Then she rearranged the white leather furniture she had moved out of the way earlier to allow more room in the center. This is my home, she muttered to herself, punching a pillow, and I can damn well invite my friends over if I want to.

By the time everything was neat she had worked off her anger.

Robert had looked so weary, she thought, turning off the lights. Walking down the hall, she heard the water running in the bathroom.

She stopped to check on Bobby. His room reeked of the pungent ointment she had spread on his chest. Bobby had been running a fever for the past two days. He was always catching colds at the day-care center he attended while she went to class.

Brushing his damp hair from his forehead, she noticed that he was breathing easier. She'd considered taking night classes so that she could be with him all day. She sighed. Robert's erratic work schedule made planning difficult. Night classes would cut short the few hours they had to themselves. Sometimes, Marianne thought, tucking the quilt tightly around her son, she hated Robert's job as liaison officer between the Pentagon and the State Department. His hours were a joke. Whatever had happened to forty-hour work weeks?

Placing a kiss on Bobby's flushed cheek, she wondered how long Robert would be able to stay. One night? Two? Or would he remain a whole week? She had two finals coming up and a term paper wasn't finished yet.

Then she heard the shower stop and forgot about tests and the last bit of research she still had to do. Somehow she'd juggle things around. Leaving Bobby's door ajar, she went into their bedroom.

After graduation, she promised herself she would visit her parents and sleep for a whole week. Then she would look for a job in Washington, with or without Robert's approval. She was tired of being alone, of living separate lives, of feeling like a mistress instead of a wife.

Opening the door, she had to bite back an oath when she found him on the phone. He had a towel wrapped around his waist and his bronzed skin still glistened with water drops. She'd often wondered when he found the time to be outdoors. He wasn't the type to visit tanning salons, yet his tan never seemed to fade.

"Call me if there's some new development," Robert said into the phone, looking over his shoulder and waving her in. "I'll be here for the next thirty-six hours."

Closing the door, she bit back the sharp protest and went to him. Sliding her arms around his waist, she leaned her face against his back and kissed the smooth, supple skin while he listened. How she'd missed him, she thought. He had been gone for almost two weeks, and the phone was a poor substitute.

His deep voice rumbled in his chest when he spoke again. "No, that can wait. I'll call you back tomorrow morning."

Robert hung up the phone before he turned around. "I didn't mean to put an end to your party," he said abruptly, stepping back. He spoke in that odd, flat tone he used when he was annoyed with her.

Marianne's eyes narrowed. "We were studying for the math final. We didn't meet at the library because Bobby has a cold and I didn't want to leave him with the babysitter." Her voice was still level but temper was welling up in her. "If you'd have let me know you were coming, they would have been gone."

He looked at her with expressionless green eyes. "This is your home," he said, walked to the closet and shrugged into the dark green velour robe she had given him for Christmas.

"It's *our* home," Marianne corrected him. He acted as if he couldn't bear to be near her, she thought. She sat down on the green satin comforter and asked abruptly, "What's wrong?"

Robert tied the robe, then raised his head. "I'm tired. Did you take Bobby to the doctor?"

He so rarely admitted to not feeling well, her anger vanished at his words. "It's just a cold, and his temperature was back to normal tonight." Then she added softly, "I'm glad you're home."

He looked at her as if he didn't quite believe her. "Did you finish studying? Don't let me keep you if you still have work to do."

He was pushing her away. For a moment Marianne wanted to tear down the invisible wall between them, itching for a fight. But they had only thirty-six hours together, and she didn't want to spend them fighting. "Fine," she snapped, surging to her feet. "I won't keep you from your sleep."

She brushed past him with tears shimmering in her eyes. He had been gone for two whole weeks, and she had missed him terribly. Yet, now that he was here, they were behaving like strangers who had nothing in common. If they had been married, truly married like her parents were, they would have been able to talk about their problems.

She stalked back down the hall, switched on the lights, grabbed the paper bags and took them down the hall to the incinerator. When she returned to the foyer, she collided with Robert. Angrily she tried to storm past him, but his arms shot out.

"I'm sorry." He ran a hand over his face as if he was trying to achieve calm, clear thinking.

She stopped pushing him away, but she wasn't ready to forgive him yet. There had been too many other fights lately, and she was still raw. She rested her hands against his chest to keep some distance between them.

"Robert, what is happening to us? Every time you come home, we seem to fight." She swallowed, then asked the question that had been tormenting her for months. "Is there someone else? Is that what it is?"

"Good God, no." The tenderness in his voice made her sway toward him. With a sigh of relief she leaned her head against his chest, feeling the curls tickling her nose. "Would you believe I'm jealous?" His voice was muffled as his lips brushed her hair, but she still heard the mixture of humor and disgust in it.

She tilted her head back. "Jealous?" she asked, feeling like laughing and crying at the same time. If he was jealous, did that mean he loved her, just a little bit? "Jealous of whom? Cal, Dan or Ben? They're friends, that's all." Didn't he know that there never had and never would be anyone else but him?

"They seem to be here every time I come home."

Marianne listened to the possessive sound in his voice and the hope died a little. "You are not being quite fair, Robert," she said quietly, hoping the pain in her throat did not roughen her voice. "I'm lonely," she said quietly. "You resent the friends I've made here. But you don't want me to move to Washington."

"I don't know how to talk to college kids," he said, brushing his lips across her face.

Easing away, she stared at him with troubled eyes and wrapped her arms around herself. There was no more anger. It had been smothered by despair. "*I'm* a college kid," she said wearily.

His face tightened and his eyes were as dull as the sea on a cloudy winter day. "You're my wife," he said, reaching for her again.

She couldn't deny him. She loved him too much. But her voice was heavy with tears when she whispered against his lips, "I am the mother of your son and your lover. I am not your wife. I am your legal mistress . . ."

I was a well-kept mistress, Marianne thought, looking at her watch. Only three minutes had crept by while she had been reliving the past. The Bedouin was sitting across the aisle with Rafe's book in his hand, and there was still no sign of Robert.

She'd never had to scrimp and save like her friends. The Manhattan apartment she'd shared with Robert had been twice the size of his Washington, D.C., studio. She also had a substantial bank account and a late-model car. She would have gladly exchanged them all for a shack, a cookie jar and a bicycle for the chance to live with Robert as husband and wife.

Now she knew why he had not wanted her to move to Washington. Not because he'd traveled a lot and had wanted her to live close to her family. But because if they had lived together as husband and wife, he couldn't have hidden that side of his life.

Now that she knew, so many things made sense. The reason why he had missed his son's birth, her graduation and all their anniversaries suddenly became clear. She remembered each incident, the pain, the ever-growing feeling of rejection. Damn you, Robert.

And then she remembered his words, *"When I was with you, I could relax."*

Suddenly those words took on a deeper meaning. Did a man feel comfortable enough with a mistress to fall asleep? Only husbands napped on a boat or in front of the TV. She had been his solid base, someone to come home to and feel safe with. But the insight had come too late. Four years too late, she thought, as a single tear ran down her face.

Why couldn't she have fallen in love with an uncomplicated man like her father or her brother? Her father had channeled his energies into building the small family boat yard into a thriving business. Colin's obsession was to race in the America's Cup. Perhaps, because her life had always been easy, she'd looked for the risks and the hard-to-get. Falling in love with Robert had been a kind of madness, like sailing before a storm, exciting and challenging. She had paid dearly for her recklessness.

And now she was falling in love with Robert all over again. She was a sucker for punishment, she thought, taking another look down the aisle.

Finally she heard footsteps and expelled a sigh of relief. But it wasn't Robert she saw emerge from the business class. It was Hamid.

She clutched at Rafe's sleeve. "What have they done to him?"

"Easy does it," Rafe warned grimly, pulling the back of his seat upright to shield her as best he could.

In bright daylight, with a day's growth covering his chin, Hamid looked cruel.

"Where's my husband?" she demanded the moment he came within hearing distance.

Ignoring her, Hamid stopped for a word with the other terrorists, raking his fingers through his hair while his hand beat a tattoo on the butt of the rifle slung over his shoulder. Suddenly he lifted his head and looked straight at her. "You come here."

Marianne caught her breath. For a moment she wanted to refuse, to crawl beneath the seat, to yell at him to go to hell. Rafe was sitting there with his body coiled, as if he was considering jumping the man. Behind them a real estate mogul from New York muttered, "Leave her alone." The blond giant who had sat across the aisle from her in the first-class cabin, snapped, "Pick on someone more your size."

Because the passengers had not been allowed to talk across the backs of the seats, she had spoken less than ten words with each of them. Their sudden defense brought a lump to her throat.

It also made Hamid feel threatened enough to reach for his gun. "You come here."

Marianne took a deep breath, gritted her teeth and slowly stood up. If she resisted or struggled, someone else would get hurt. She buttoned her blazer and inched past Robert's empty seat.

When Rafe got to his feet to block her way, she shook her head and said with quiet determination, "Let me pass. He's only going to take me to Robert." Oh God, what if they'd killed him? She squeezed past Rafe, almost shoving him into his seat. She had to get to Robert. She hadn't told him that she loved him. She had told him to go to hell, when all she wanted was—another chance.

She stumbled over Rafe's feet, then almost fell into Hamid. She caught herself, brushed past him and ran down the aisle.

"Stop," Hamid shouted and raised the automatic threateningly.

Rafe was already on his feet, arm raised to knock it out of his hands.

But the Bedouin was closer. "You're going to blow us up," he shouted in Arabic, wrestling the weapon from Hamid.

At their shouts, Hamid's friend ran from the business section where he'd rifled through briefcases and purses. His hands were full of bills. Stuffing them into his pockets, he blocked her way. Marianne turned sharply, slipping past him before his hands were free. She could hear the shouts to stop, but she paid no attention to them. Robert. She had to get to Robert.

At that moment she felt someone grab her blazer and jerk her back. The last button popped off the jacket as she was spun around. She struggled, kicked with her bare toes, twisting, scratching.

"Stupid bitch," Hamid growled, grabbing her hair and slapping her across the face.

Off balance, she reeled, falling backward into a seat. She hardly felt the pain when her hip hit the armrest. He was going to kill her now, she thought above the roaring in her ears. Dying was better than feeling his hands on her, but she wouldn't make it easy for him. She wasn't going to cower in a chair, she thought, her head snapping back, preparing herself to meet another assault. None came.

The Bedouin was shouting at Hamid with his eyes flashing and his hands slashing the air. Hamid and his friend were shouting back. Dazed, Marianne tried to interpret the meaning of their gestures. And then she saw Robert, towering above their heads, struggling against the hold of the two terrorists who had taken him away a lifetime ago. His eyes were blazing like emeralds in his furious face. He was alive and well. She slumped back into her seat.

Robert saw the red imprint on her face that was already beginning to swell. He made an enormous effort to control the rage pulsing through him, and lost. He turned with such deadly fury on the two men holding him that their grips on his arms eased. He twisted free.

He still had enough control left not to slam his fist into Hamid's face. He lashed out with words, calling them cowards and thieves. His fluency in Arabic momentarily stunned the three men.

Marianne sat frozen with fear. She wanted to shout at Robert to stop his verbal abuse. At any moment the terrorists would retaliate with physical abuse.

Hamid was yelling back at Robert, his hands moving feverishly, but he did not attack him. He had no gun. His friend also had no weapon—his pockets were overflowing with money that he had tried to stuff out of sight. The Bedouin's reaction was strange. At first he glowered. Then he grinned. But the grin on his face was replaced moments later by a look of angry disgust. Suddenly he took a few steps toward Hamid's friend, dug his hands into the pockets of the army surplus jacket and tossed bills into the air. Hamid's friend grabbed the Bedouin's loose shirt in retaliation and shook the younger man. With angry shouts, Robert's escorts threw themselves between the two struggling men, pulling them apart.

Marianne's gaze flew to Robert's face. The grim look of satisfaction startled her. He had planned it, she thought, as understanding dawned. He had deliberately set the men against each other, moving them like pieces in a deadly game of chess. With a mixture of relief and admiration she slumped back into the chair. For now the danger was over.

Robert slid past the men and knelt in front of Marianne. Her eyes were dark and wide with shock and her lips pale. "Are you all right?" he asked, raising his hand to her cheek. Nothing had ever scared him as much as the scene he had just witnessed. His heart was still beating in his throat and his breathing had yet to return to normal.

When he gently soothed the bright red swelling, she flinched. "Yes," she said, feeling foolish and stupid. She had behaved like a child, blindly charging into danger.

"Can you tell me what happened?" he asked, suppressing his need to draw her close, to hold her and whisper soothing nonsense into her ear.

She hesitated, running her fingertips over her stinging face. She wanted Robert to be proud of her, to admire her. Not soothe her with gentle concern as if she were his child. "I panicked."

Her hands were trembling, he noticed. So were his own. He had never hated before, not with such intensity, not with every muscle fiber shaking, not with this driving need for revenge. It was clouding his thinking. Slowly he willed his mind to go blank. "We're both fine. Look at me, Marianne."

She did. Her eyes strayed from the dark hair falling onto his forehead to his tautly stretched skin. The blank look in his eyes frightened her. She could almost feel the violence, the rage he tried to control. "I am all right," she said softly, insistently. "What happened was my fault." She covered his hands, talking to him in the same way that she soothed Bobby after a nightmare, but at that moment it did not seem strange. "Rafe tried to hold me back, but I slipped through his hands."

There was more to this than she was telling him, Robert thought grimly, drawing her to her feet, but the explanations could wait.

He threw a look over her shoulder at the five terrorists. The incident had caused a rift between them, pitching fanatical idealism against greed. Things were looking up,

Robert thought, as the Bedouin returned to his post and his own escort left.

Hamid glared at him with clenched hands and gritted teeth. "You go back to your seat," he snapped. "The woman goes to the galley to make coffee and food."

"I'm not letting her out of my sight again," Robert said in a dangerous voice.

"You return to your seat. Now." Hamid's dark eyes glittered as if he would enjoy enforcing his order.

Marianne gave Robert's hand a reassuring squeeze. "I'll be all right," she said. "I could do with a cup of coffee and a bite to eat."

Robert doubted that Hamid would risk another incident so soon. Reaching into his pocket, he handed Marianne the bottle of Perrier. "Use it if he gets too close," he advised her softly, then reluctantly let her go.

The layout of the galley was almost identical to the one in the upper lounge, except that there was an exit on either side. Marianne set the dials to heat the oven and searched for packages of coffee in the cupboards overhead. It felt good to work, to concentrate on mundane tasks and forget about the violence, the hate and fear.

When the coffee was brewing, she pulled out a section below the counter, checking for food. The plane's supplies had been restocked when they'd landed in Paris. One cart was filled with stacked trays that contained everything from rolls to plastic cutlery. She took a sidelong look at Hamid, then snitched a roll while he lit another cigarette. None of the hostages had eaten since before the hijacking, while the terrorists had snacked constantly between their cigarettes. Putting the roll into her pocket, she tore a piece off with one hand while checking the next cart. The bread was stale, but Marianne was too hungry to care.

The main courses, in foil-covered dishes on heating trays that would slide into the oven, were stacked on another cart.

Hungrily she studied the contents labels stuck to the front. There were two choices: fresh ham in burgundy sauce, new potatoes, carrots and peas; and chicken cutlets, princess potatoes and broccoli.

Marianne wondered grimly if this was a joke. Muslims did not touch pork; they believed it made them unclean. Someone had deliberately sent dishes the terrorists wouldn't eat. Then she realized that the ham must have been meant for the hostages.

She threw a cautious look over her shoulder at Hamid, but he was keeping his distance, leaning against the outside wall. Reassured, she transferred the rack of chicken cutlets into the oven, then reached for the ham. "How many trays do you need?" she asked, closing the door.

"Eight."

That meant that there must be a total of eight terrorists on board. Marianne hid a small grin of satisfaction and pulled out eight trays. "Do I take the trays to the major and the other men? Or is it your job to serve the food?"

"That's women's work," Hamid snapped.

It was exactly the response she'd wanted to hear. She only hoped that the rest of the terrorists had the same low opinion of her sex as Hamid and would ignore her presence as she served their meals.

Twenty minutes later, watching Hamid stab at the elevator button, Marianne sighed in defeat. She'd learned absolutely nothing. The major had intercepted her in the business class, telling her to leave the cart. Now she fully expected to be told to leave these trays outside the flight deck. The elevator door opened and she pulled out the cart.

She must be mad believing they might escape. There were eight heavily armed men against no more than twenty helpless hostages.

As she pushed the cart toward the door, her stomach growled. She was starving. She was tired. She was miserable. Giving the cart a strong shove that sent it shooting down the hall made her feel a little better.

Hamid ordered her to stop in front of the cockpit door, then knocked and called out. After a few words with the terrorist guarding the crew, the man stepped down to make room for Marianne.

The three men inside the cockpit sat in their shirtsleeves. Their faces were haggard and grim, and their eyes red-rimmed with lack of sleep.

"Coffee, anyone?" Marianne picked up the pitcher and poured the hot brew into Styrofoam cups without waiting for an answer.

"What are you doing here?" The gray-haired captain stared at her with bloodshot eyes. "I thought all the women were gone."

"All except me and twelve other hostages." Marianne handed him a cup and a plastic package containing sugar and powdered cream. His face was deeply lined, and exhaustion seemed to add at least ten years to his age. "I hope you are on autopilot," she joked. She was rewarded with a weak smile.

His gaze slid from her face to the torn sleeve of her blazer. "That's a nasty bruise you have on your cheek," he said quietly, anger flushing his gray face.

"I'm all right," Marianne assured him, handing the second cup to a younger man with blond hair and eyes as blue as the sky on the horizon. The captain had enough worries without adding her well-being to his list. "I hope you're hungry. I brought you ham in burgundy sauce."

"An angel of mercy," the first officer quipped. "How are things downstairs?"

"No talking," Hamid snarled.

"Everyone is fine," Marianne said, ignoring him and handing the third cup to a slender man in his mid-thirties.

While she pulled out a tray and added the hot meat dish, she listened to the disembodied voice of some air traffic controller. "Flight 409, do you read me?"

"Answer it," the terrorist ordered tersely. Then he told Marianne to hurry up.

As the captain acknowledged the voice, Marianne handed the tray to the first officer, then listened as a new voice sounded. "This is Beirut airport. Our decision stands firm. We will not allow you to land. I repeat, we will not allow you to land. If you attempt setting down anyway, we will shoot."

"Damn it," the captain swore. "Where can we land?"

Chapter 7

Someone's got to let us land," Rafe said two hours later. He sat on the armrest across the aisle swinging his booted foot. "First Beirut, then Amman and now Cairo have refused."

"The question is, who is going to?" Jimmy Dobson, a cattle auctioneer from Texas, left his seat in the last row, stretched his arms and hitched the pants over his thickening waist.

"Sit," the Bedouin ordered, but made no threatening move when Dobson merely leaned against the seat. Since Beirut, their guards had changed twice. Upon their return to the cabin an hour ago, the Bedouin and his companion had somewhat relaxed their rules, allowing them to step into the aisle and stretch their legs.

Marianne guessed that they were too tired to enforce silence and also somewhat afraid. They hadn't expected to be trapped in the sky. They certainly hadn't envisioned being shunned as criminals by one Islamic country after another instead of being welcomed as heroes.

"Sullivan, what do you think? You're familiar with this part of the world." The blond giant, whose name was Sven Hammond, wiped his brow with the back of his arm.

Marianne watched Robert lean on his forearms atop Rafe's seat. "Kuwait might let us land," he said, his deep voice raspy from lack of water. "One of their planes was once in a similar situation. But that's a long shot."

"What happens if no on will allow us to land?" A red-haired man with freckles that stood out sharply against his pale skin asked the question that had been at the back of everyone's mind.

Robert's tired face creased into a grin. "There's always the sea," he joked, trying to ease everyone's fear. "Our navy is in the Persian Gulf. Someone should pick us up sooner or later."

"Very funny," Jimmy Dobson growled. "I can't swim."

"Are there sharks in the Persian Gulf?"

"How about jellyfish? I'm allergic to those suckers."

"Perhaps there's antihistamine in the life rafts."

"I haven't seen no life raft," the auctioneer from Dallas drawled. "You don't happen to know where they hide them, Sullivan?"

"They're stored in the overhead ceiling compartments or in the front closets," Robert explained, rolling up his sleeves. It was hot in the cabin, a result of the captain's attempt to conserve as much fuel as possible. How much longer would it last? he wondered uneasily. Another hour? Two? Would it be enough to make Omari?

Thoughtfully he massaged the back of his neck. He knew he could count on Jamal to get them a landing permit. But how could he convince the major to head for Omari? Old Yussuf was known for his swift, hard justice. The major must know that he and his men could expect no mercy from him. So the problem was how to convince Yussuf to extradite the terrorists to the U.S. where they could expect lifelong imprisonment instead of the death penalty.

Marianne leaned back against the wall and drew her knees up to her chest. Her gaze was glued to Robert's face. She had never seen him so open with strangers. There had always been a certain reserve that had set him apart from other men. She guessed that like everyone else he was afraid, although looking at the laugh lines slashing his cheeks it was difficult to tell. Only because she was watching him closely did she notice that he glanced over his shoulder too frequently and that the fine tension tightening his jaw never completely relaxed.

He was worried. They all were. But Robert had more information. He had talked with the major three times now. Some of the knowledge he had shared with the rest of the men, but she could tell there had to be much more that he was keeping to himself.

She sighed and closed her scratchy eyes. She wished he would talk to her, share some of his fears and sound out his ideas. She wasn't a stranger like the rest of the men, but someone he could trust. But he hadn't shown any need to confide in her. And she hadn't asked, because she was afraid that he would stare at her in that silent way of his, then smile and talk about something else.

And then she wondered why it should be so important to her. It was only desire that made her want to run her fingers through his tousled hair, slide beneath the unbuttoned collar, push back the unruly hair falling rakishly onto his forehead. Wasn't it? It was fear for his life and her own need for reassurance that made her want him. Once they were free, she hoped these feelings would pass.

Why then did she so desperately want him to need her? And why was the thought they might go their separate ways again when this was over so painful?

He had stayed away from her long enough, Robert thought, but his impatience faded when he turned to her. She looked so damn fragile, so drained. The swelling on her cheek had faded into a faint bruise. Her skin was almost as white as her blouse and there was a droop to her lips that he had never seen before.

Yet not once had she turned to him for support, he thought, his fingers curling over the top of the seat. It was as if she were afraid to lean on him and let down her guard.

He had promised her no complications. But after their many near brushes with disaster, it was getting more difficult to keep his distance.

He wasn't joking when he'd said that they might land in the sea. The possibility was growing with every minute. If Kuwait refused, there were only two choices left: Omari or the Persian Gulf. Yussuf's justice or almost certain death. If they had only two hours left to live, he wanted them to be happy ones. For both of them.

"You're very quiet." He watched her eyes slowly open again.

"I enjoy watching and listening."

Robert slid into the seat next to her, running his hand over his jaw. He grimaced. "I need a shave. Unfortunately my razor is in my briefcase."

"You look like a pirate." She suppressed the desire to run her hand over the bristles, to stroke the tired lines from his face. "Did you have anything important in your case?"

"Some business papers I wanted to discuss with Jamal. Nothing that can't be replaced," Robert shrugged. "I hope you have another photo of Bobby at home."

Resting her chin on her knees, she shook her head. "You can have mine." She hesitated briefly, then added, "I didn't know he'd signed the photo for me. It must be rather awkward for you when you show it to your—friends." She had no right to ask about the women in his life. But that didn't stop her from feeling a hot stab of jealousy. She hoped he hadn't noticed the slight hesitation and the slight coolness of her voice.

But Robert had noticed and her reaction pleased him. Masking the gleam in his eyes, he said quietly, "And I'd hoped he'd done it with your approval. He's been doing it for years. He's also invited me to visit him in New York." He paused, giving her the chance to respond. When she didn't, he pressed on, "I thought I'd take him up on it, once we get back."

He had the most gorgeous, thick, curling lashes she had ever seen, Marianne thought. "I don't see why not," she said cautiously, hiding the swift pleasure she felt at his words. Two could play at the same game. But her heart skipped a beat at the thought of Robert spending his weekends in New York.

She wasn't exactly eager to invite him into her home, Robert realized with disappointment, but she wasn't rejecting the idea, either. That gave him hope. "Bobby's been wanting to go to the Museum of Natural History to see the dinosaur exhibit. Perhaps you'd come with us, or you could meet us for dinner afterward."

"I'd like that," she whispered and closed her eyes against the sudden flood of emotions. "Bobby would be ecstatic," she added cautiously. "We can plan it all once we're free."

At least it wasn't an outright no. Robert moved closer, lifted her legs over his thighs and let his hands rest lightly on her ankles. They were fine-boned, almost delicate, slender enough to span with his fingers. "And maybe you'd like to come to Washington some weekend. I bought a house in Virginia, so you wouldn't have to stay in a hotel."

"Bobby told me about your house. For weeks he talked about nothing else but the huge skylights through which he can see the stars at night. He can't wait to use the swimming pool. And he says that the garden is big enough for a dog. He wants an Irish setter."

Robert chuckled. "He wants *two*. One, he says, would be lonely when he wasn't there to play with it. Do you like dogs?"

She nodded. "Mother is allergic to animal hair. I used to go to the boat yard and play with Caesar and Rex, the German shepherds guarding the place."

"Are you talking about those two big brutes that licked everyone's hands?" Robert teased.

She smiled ruefully. "Dad always says I ruined them." She swallowed, wondering if she would ever see them again. "Bobby was so excited when you allowed him to choose his own bedroom furniture. And you really made his Christmas when you gave him that big computer. At home he has to share our computer with me, and at tax time he rarely gets a chance to use it." It was petty to resent the fact that Robert was able to give their son so much more than she could. But sometimes she wished she could afford the down payment on a house with room enough to buy that extra computer and the dog Bobby asked for constantly.

"It wasn't a real Christmas gift," Robert said roughly. "When he opened it in January, there was no tree, no Christmas music in the background and no one else to show it off to." He cupped her chin and tilted her head back. "Perhaps we could celebrate next Christmas together?"

"How about Easter?" Her eyes were shimmering with tears at the loneliness his words showed. "Memorial Day comes next and then the Fourth of July. You're welcome to join us, if you have the time."

He grimaced. "I'm afraid I'll miss Easter this year. But Independence Day in Washington is something special." He flicked her chin lightly before dropping his hand. The need to pull her closer was a hunger growing with each passing moment. "I don't travel nearly as much as I used to, so I'll be home most holidays."

She desperately wanted to believe in the dreams he was spinning for her. She could almost picture them sitting on a couch in front of the fireplace in his den, touching, smiling, making love. But she couldn't see them talking, discussing more than their plans for the weekend, or Bobby's school. She needed more from Robert, so much more. "Perhaps it would be better if you'd come to Stony Brook instead," she said. It would be easier to fight her desire for him with her family around.

She wasn't going to reject him outright, but he could feel her reluctance, the doubts. For a moment, Robert wished that she was nineteen again, that she could come to him as she had on that sunny Labor Day, eager, warm and trusting.

"It wouldn't be like the last time," he said, choosing his words carefully. So much depended on the right phrasing, on making her understand the differences, that his voice was rather clipped. "When we met, we weren't ready for marriage."

Marianne searched Robert's taut face and tried to see past the fatigue etched into it. She almost despised herself that the mere touch of his hands could make her want to forget the past. But they had to deal with their scars if they were to be friends in the future. "I told you a long time ago that I was nineteen, not nine years old. When my mother was that age she married my father and followed him to a foreign country thousands of miles away from her home."

He had known that this wouldn't be easy, Robert thought grimly. This time she wasn't going to come to him with blind trust and without doubts. But he thrived on challenges. He had learned a long time ago that the things he cherished the most were often the hardest to get. "Your father worked in the family business three miles away from your house. I was working in a job that would have put a strain on any marriage. My position as a liaison officer between the Pentagon and the State Department was a cover for my work with the anti-terrorist division.''

So her suspicions had been true. Even now, three years after he had shifted careers, she could sense a certain wistfulness when he mentioned those days. And suddenly she was glad that she had not forced him into switching careers, but that he had done so of his own free will.

Looking down at her clenched hands, she tried to restrain the bitterness. ''Another secret you didn't trust me with.'' But she had been old enough to raise their son virtually alone.

His eyes mirrored his regret. ''I didn't want to add fear to all the other burdens you were too young to carry.''

''Or was it because you thought I would blurt it out?'' Marianne challenged him. ''I know my parents always teased me that I couldn't keep a secret. But I would have bitten my tongue off rather than harm you in any way.'' Looking at him, she added, ''You loved the challenge, the gamble, the life without roots. How you must have resented it when I became pregnant and tied you down.''

His eyes narrowed at her flat tone. ''I thought we'd settled that a long while ago,'' he said levelly, but his fingers tightened around her ankles. ''Yes, I felt tied down, but not by you. The Iran crisis exploded into our faces right after we were married—first the revolution and then the hostage situation. I spent more time overseas than at my office during those moments. It seemed that every time I was on my way to take the shuttle to New York, some new emergency arose, calling me back. Oh, I wanted you there where I could see you, if only for an hour. But it would have been selfish to ask you to move to Washington under those conditions. You needed to be with your family.''

"I needed to be with you." This time she did not hide the bitterness, the loneliness, the desperation. "I wanted to share your life, but you shut me out. You never gave me a choice. You set me up in an apartment in Manhattan. It was convenient to have a wife who didn't know what was going on, who didn't ask any questions and demanded no explanations."

Robert's eyes narrowed. "It was damned *in*convenient," he said, his voice low and taut. "Sometimes I was so dead on my feet I wanted to sleep around the clock. But I needed you more."

She swallowed to ease the lump in her throat, and her nails bit into the palms of her hands. "Damn it, why did you never tell me?"

His lips twisted, then he said simply, "I thought I did. Every time I kissed you. Every time I made love to you."

She closed her eyes against the pressure of tears, remembering how he would throw open the door, drop his garment bag and call her name. There had been such hunger in his eyes, such need, that she would forget all the questions she had wanted to ask. But later, when she was alone again, she would call herself all kinds of fool. And as the years passed, her resentment had grown.

"That hasn't changed," Robert said huskily, searching her face for the emotions that had once blazed so openly but were now hidden. He lifted his hand and touched her cheek with the back of his hand. "You're still very special to me."

If he'd said that he loved her, Marianne would have kissed him. Here. In clear sight of everyone. She remembered the blind panic she had felt only hours ago, the fear and the utter relief when she had seen him standing there, alive and safe. A part of her would have died if anything had happened to him.

But was this need, this hunger, real, or was it an illusion created by danger? And, if it was real, was it strong enough for her to take the risk and begin again?

He had talked to her more freely in the last five minutes than he had in four years of marriage. It was a start, wasn't it?

But there was Bobby, their son who loved them both. He had coped with their divorce once, but he had never completely accepted it. She knew that now. They could not raise his hopes, unless they were certain that it would work this time around.

"You're very special to me, too," she whispered, running her finger over the scratch on his jaw. She knew he was asking for more, but it was the only answer she could give him. For now.

At that moment, Rafe slid back into his seat. The talk and laughter died abruptly. Their two guards sat up straighter, with their weapons once again firmly in hand, and looked down the aisle as the major came into view. Accompanying him were Hamid and the two terrorists who had previously escorted Robert.

Swinging her legs to the floor, Marianne noticed that the major looked as tired as she felt. His forehead was lined, and a bluish stubble covered his jaw. But he still wore his suit jacket, his tie was still straight, and his steps were impatient rather than lagging. He wasn't beaten yet, she thought as he stopped in front of them.

"Sullivan, I want to talk to you."

Robert slowly crossed his arms over his chest and said calmly, "I'm listening."

"Kuwait has just refused to allow us to land. I want you to talk to them and convince them that our situation is desperate."

Robert tilted his head. "What's in it for us?" He seriously doubted that he would be able to accomplish anything, but he was curious to know how far the major was willing to bend. "Will you set us free?"

"Perhaps." The major put his hands in his pockets and rocked on his heels. "Except you."

"Perhaps isn't good enough, Major," Robert responded, his tone implacable.

"We'll see." The major's dark, expressionless eyes slid to Marianne. "Mrs. Sullivan, I want more coffee," he snapped, "and find us something to eat."

"She's staying here," Robert refused curtly.

Marianne could feel Robert's body coil with anger as she hastily rose to her feet. "I don't mind making coffee," she told him, laying a soothing hand on his tense shoulder. As tired as they all were, tempers would flare easily. Above all, she did not want to see Robert's pride beaten into submission. She loved him too much for that. "I'd rather move around a bit," she added softly. "It helps pass the time."

She slid a look at Hamid and found his slightly unfocused eyes fixed on her chest. Marianne had removed the credit card and traveler's checks from their hiding place a long time ago, so the blouse fell loosely over her curves. But her skin was damp, and the thin silk tended to stick. Reluctantly she reached for her wool blazer and shrugged into it, wishing she hadn't drunk the Perrier Robert had given her earlier and thrown the bottle away. Her fingers curled around the stickpin Bobby had given her. She'd hate to damage it, but in an emergency it was a weapon.

"Please let me pass," she demanded softly when Robert refused to move his legs.

She was doing it for his sake, Robert realized grimly. That was a bitter pill for him to swallow. Not that he had much choice in the matter. Still, he preferred to be forced instead of obeying with only a token defiance. But he couldn't resist the pleading look in her eyes. Reluctantly he rose and made room for her. "Keep a close eye on that bastard," he muttered as she slid past him.

"I will."

"Very sensible, Mrs. Sullivan," the major commented with a sneer.

Marianne shot him a look of such intense hate that his eyes narrowed. "You're a coward," she threw at him. It felt good to release some of her hate. "Make sure that Hamid keeps out of my way, or I'll—I'll pour hot coffee into his face."

"If you were a man I would let him kill you for that," the major said between clenched teeth. "Hamid, take her to the galley. Have her bring the coffee to the cockpit." He turned sharply and walked down the aisle with the two terrorists in tow.

Marianne followed Hamid with her head held high, feeling better than she had in hours. She had lived with fear so long, she refused to be cowed anymore. Behind her she could hear the men chuckle appreciatively.

"I'm going to wring her neck," Robert muttered. He turned to Rafe whose lips were twitching. "Let me have your seat. I don't trust him."

When Hamid entered the galley instead of keeping his distance, Marianne faced him determinedly. "Stay out of here," she warned, "or your major won't get his coffee."

Hamid's eyes glittered furiously, but he moved to the end of the galley. By now Marianne was quite familiar with the place. Within minutes the coffee was brewing and the oven heating. There were a few meat dishes left and she decided to heat them all. Reaching for the remaining unused trays, she wondered what would happen if they would not be allowed to land in Kuwait. How much fuel was left in the tanks? How much longer could they stay in the air? Were they going to die? Was that why Robert had brought up the past?

She slammed the last tray on the counter and kicked the cart, wincing when she hurt her toe. Robert would come up with a solution, she thought. He had dealt with terrorism for years. She didn't doubt that he still had a few tricks up his sleeve.

She glanced over her shoulder at Hamid. He hadn't moved from his position in the entranceway, but his eyes followed her everywhere and his hands moved restlessly inside his pockets, banging the automatic slung over his shoulder against the doorjamb. He was cracking under the strain, she thought. She would have to keep her eyes on him constantly.

When she checked the coffeepot, she frowned. It had stopped dripping, and only an inch of dark liquid covered the bottom of the carafe. The last time, she had simply pressed the button and the water had run freely. Perhaps, like at home, there was a tank that needed refilling. She turned the machine off and took out the filter, but behind it was a stainless steel wall. The water, dripping through a narrow spout, must come from a central supply, she guessed. Crossing the aisle to the small sink, she pressed down the faucet handle. It sputtered, dripped and sputtered again. She drew a sharp breath. They were running out of fuel. They had no water. What would come next?

"We're out of water," she told Hamid. "I can't make any coffee."

"Fix the food," he snapped. The rapid tattoo on the doorjamb became louder, more irregular, grinding on her nerves.

When she opened the oven door to check on the dishes, the noise stopped.

Before she could escape through the other galley exit, she felt his hand on her shoulder, spinning her around. Off balance, she fell against the counter, jerking her head away from the hot oven door.

Then he was kissing her, grinding her lips against her teeth. Marianne gagged with revulsion, twisting her head away, but he grabbed her hair and pulled her head forward again.

He stank of sweat and unwashed skin. Marianne felt nausea welling up in her. She kicked him. "You filthy pig, let me go," she yelled, before his mouth silenced her once again. She scratched him. But she was no match for his strength. In desperation she grabbed his hair and pulled on it viciously. When he let out a yell and loosened his hold, Marianne jerked up her knee.

But her knee never connected.

"Take your dirty hands off her." Robert hurled himself at Hamid, grabbing him by the scruff of his neck, shaking him so hard that the automatic rifle dropped from his shoulder and clattered to the floor. Hamid tried to reach for it. At that moment Robert pulled back his head and planted his fists into Hamid's face with a satisfying thud.

Hamid slumped forward, seeming insensible. Then Marianne saw him reach into his pocket and cried, "Watch out." But her warning came too late. Pistol in hand, Hamid spun around and pressed it into Robert's stomach. With frozen horror Marianne watched him take up the slack on the trigger, slowly as if enjoying every second of it.

With his back pressed against the counter, Robert stood utterly still, his face frozen, his eyes glittering silvery green. "You'd better kill me with the first shot," he said, his voice cold and hard.

Wildly Marianne looked around for a weapon—a bottle, a spoon. The rifle was beyond her reach. Then her eyes focused on the open oven door. She grabbed the first foil-covered dish—ham in Burgundy sauce. She didn't feel the heat burning her skin. She didn't hear the hijacker with the crooked nose yell a warning at Hamid. All she saw was the blue-black barrel of the gun pressed against Robert's waist. She threw the ham at Hamid the instant Robert knocked the gun upward and out.

Later, when she was asked to describe the scene, she could only remember Hamid's screams. She could remember leaning against the counter with her knees shaking and thinking that the world had finally gone mad, because the terrorist with the crooked nose was hitting Hamid, hijacker fighting hijacker.

Robert stood a foot away, watching the thugs while brushing a slice of carrot from his sleeve. Marianne noticed that the scratch on his jaw had begun to bleed again, and there was a rapidly swelling bruise on his chin. But he was alive and well. It was at that moment that Marianne admitted to herself just how much he still meant to her. If Hamid had shot him, her heart would have died with him. Then their eyes met over the struggling men. "Get out of here," Robert yelled above the noise.

Marianne's knees were shaking so badly she was afraid to let go of the counter. Slowly, still holding on to it, she inched toward the end of the galley, stubbing her toe on a hard object. Bending down, she spotted the pistol Robert had knocked into the air. Picking it up, she slid it beneath her jacket.

Before she could reach the aisle, the major pushed his way past the Bedouin and stepped between his men. His cold hard voice sliced through their fighting heat with the sharp thrust of a rapier. The terrorists following him pulled Hamid and his opponent apart.

"You bloody imbeciles." The major raged, his hands clenched into fists. "You stupid peasants. By Allah, I will throw you out of the plane."

Marianne stared from the major to Hamid. A slice of ham was slowly sliding down his arm, and there were peas and carrots in his hair. A hysterical giggle burst from her lips.

Hearing it, the major turned on her. "Shut up," he snarled, his eyes narrowed on her lip, which was beginning to throb painfully. "Abdul," he swerved to the Bedouin, "take her back to her seat. And keep your hands off her."

The Bedouin's face flushed furiously. With his finger pointed at Hamid, he protested in a spate of Arabic that he was a warrior, not a defiler of helpless women.

"She's a temptress," Hamid defended himself heatedly. "She wanted me to kiss her, she asked for it." His eyes restlessly searched the galley floor. "She did it to get my gun."

The major snapped, "And where is your pistol, Hamid?"

Hamid shifted from foot to foot, once again searching the floor. "I don't know. It must have slipped under one of those carts."

"Imbecile," the major ranted. Then he became still, fixing Marianne with a penetrating look that made her squirm. "Give me the pistol, or I'll have you stripped."

Since the major had spoken in Arabic, Marianne didn't understand his order or his threat. Her eyes flew to Robert.

"He wants the gun." Robert wanted to kiss and strangle her for being such a brave little fool.

With a sigh of defeat, Marianne held out the pistol.

Taking it, the major looked at Abdul and jeered, "Beware of defenseless women, Abdul. Take her back, but watch her carefully."

Back in the cabin the men were standing in their seats, asking anxious questions about Robert. "He's fine," Marianne said wearily.

Rafe tilted her face and gently touched her swollen lip. "Does it hurt?" he asked, his eyes flames of fury.

"It's not bad." The throbbing was tolerable, but the stench and the sensation of those thick wet lips was still with her, making her gag. She wiped her mouth with the back of her hand. Swiftly she scooted to her seat.

Rafe's eyes softened with understanding. "Let her go to the rest room and wash her face," he asked the Bedouin.

Marianne shook her head. "There's no water."

The news shocked the men into silence.

Only Rafe seemed unaffected. "There are emergency rations for the life rafts somewhere around," he said thoughtfully. Turning to the Bedouin, he suggested, "Let's look for the bottled water."

"Later," the hijacker motioned Rafe to sit down. "Later. When my friend comes back." Then he turned to look over his shoulder at the galley, wondering, like everyone else, what was happening. . . .

"I told you not to touch the woman." The major raked Hamid with a cold, scornful look. "And pick up the rifle. You're stepping on it."

"You don't tell me what to do." Hamid shot a hateful glance at Robert before bending to pick up the weapon.

"Now give it to me." The major took the rifle from Hamid. "I wouldn't want you to lose the automatic, too."

The other hijackers snickered. Only Hamid's friend came to his defense. "What's so special about the woman?" he growled. "You treat the infidels better than your own men."

"That man," the major snapped, pointing at Robert, "is important to our mission. Molesters of women and thieves are not. Hamid, clean up, then report to the cockpit. Sullivan, you come with me."

Following the major, Robert briefly mourned the loss of the gun. But the deepening rift between the hijackers was nothing to sneeze at. And he doubted that the major would use Hamid to harass Marianne again.

In the upstairs lounge, the major once again climbed on what seemed to be his personal bar stool, then sent his men away. "I apologize for the incident," he said, reaching for a can of cola. Apparently he'd run out of Perrier. "Go find yourself a brandy," he said, pulling the tab open.

Robert crossed his legs and leaned against the bar. "I only drink with friends," he said, wondering what the major was up to.

The major poured the cola down his throat, then set the can down with a snap. "I don't know how you managed it, but you've stirred up trouble between my men."

"I warned you that you'd regret keeping my wife," Robert smirked, watching the major wipe his hands on a paper napkin, as if he were debating what to do next.

Abruptly the major crumpled the paper in his hands. "I'll make a deal with you, Sullivan. Your wife's freedom for getting permission to land in Omari. I want two army helicopters waiting for us at the end of the runway, fueled and ready to take off. No soldiers. No police. If Yussuf doesn't agree, we're going to blow this plane and everyone on it to the sky."

"I'll see what I can do," Robert said. Things were looking up indeed.

It was almost nighttime, and the cabin lights had come on when Robert returned to the coach section.

Despite the deep lines carved on either side of his mouth, Marianne noticed a new spring in his step, as if the news he carried was hopeful. He stopped at Rafe's seat and said, "We're going to land in Omari."

His words were greeted with an outcry of relief.

When the men's voices died down again, he warned, "That doesn't mean that we are being released. But at least you won't have to worry about sharks and jellyfish."

He didn't mention the helicopters Jamal had promised to have waiting for the terrorists. The major would have to leave the hostages behind when he tried to escape. Would he kill them all as a warning not to follow him? To worry the others unnecessarily would be cruel and pointless. They deserved a few hours of hope.

When Rafe stood up to let him slide into his seat, he muttered for Robert's ears alone, "What's the catch?"

"Two helicopters," Robert muttered, as he stepped past him. Rafe was too experienced a man not to question the major's move. Their eyes met, both remembering another time, a similar escape attempt that had ended with terrorists and hostages being shot out of the sky.

Whatever was going to happen, though, Marianne would be free.

Robert dropped down beside Marianne, his face grim, his expression haunted, when he looked at the swollen bottom lip. "I shouldn't have let you out of my sight," he said harshly, grabbing her shoulders and drawing her into his arms. Tracing the lip gently, he asked, "Are you hurt anywhere else?"

"No." Marianne leaned her head against his shoulder. It felt so good to stop fighting her own feelings, to be cradled in his strong arms. She lifted her hand to his jaw. "That is a nasty bruise."

Her fingers felt cool and tender on his skin. Robert turned his head into her palm, caressing her blisters with his lips. Suddenly he remembered the ham sliding down Hamid's clothes and the sauce and vegetables stuck in his hair. He chuckled. "I wish you could have seen Hamid. There's a burn on the side of his face. He had no water and couldn't wash the stuff out of his hair. I doubt that he's going to molest another woman again soon."

He felt her shoulders shake with silent laughter and added softly, "Our son is going to love that story. Modified, of course."

"Don't you dare tell him." Marianne groaned. "I'll never live that down. One of his aunts already told him how I once dumped a strawberry cream pie on cousin Ronnie's head.

He's been waiting for an opportunity all winter to try out the idea.''

"Jolly, six-foot-four Ronnie with the full beard?" Robert asked dryly, staring down at her smiling face. "I wonder why I never heard that story."

"Because he wasn't jolly then, but a mean brat, and because he'd like to forget how he got his just desserts," Marianne said with a grin.

Robert's chest rumbled with laughter. "And who's been stepping on Bobby's toes?"

She grimaced. "Melissa, Ronnie's thirteen-year-old daughter, wouldn't you know? On Christmas Day she told him to play with the kindergarten crowd."

"I think I'm going to have a man-to-man talk with my son." Robert tried to look stern, but his lips twitched. "Perhaps it is wiser not to mention the ham."

He hesitated for a moment, then added, "Talking of ham reminds me of Easter. If everything goes well, you'll be hiding eggs for Bobby."

For a moment she closed her eyes in utter relief. "Then you've done it," she whispered shakily and turned her face into his neck. They'd be free! They could go home! "I always knew that somehow you'd find a way." She wasn't going to cry, not now. But her voice was hoarse when she whispered, "When will they allow use to leave? Tonight? Or do we have to wait until morning?"

Robert buried his hand in her silky hair, lifting the short strands, then letting them slide through his fingers. "It will be too late when we land in Omari." The major was taking no chances of ambushes in the dark.

She wanted to ask why they would have to wait until dawn. But already her mind leaped ahead, to their son, to her family. She thought of the old village church where her mother had been baptized and married. They would give thanks there, together, as a family. She thought of tulips and daffodils and the cake, shaped like a lamb and sprinkled with coconut flakes, sitting among the flowers as a centerpiece on the big dark oak table in the dining room, and . . .

Abruptly she raised her head. "Why didn't you tell the others?" she asked. She read the answer in his hard face, and the light faded from her eyes. She shook her head, rejecting the message she read there. "I'm going to be the only one?" she whispered.

"The rest of us will follow you in a day or so," he said roughly, laying a finger across her lips to stop questions he didn't have any answers for. "Jamal will take care of everything for you. Before you can leave Omari, there are going to be delays, like the debriefing and a medical checkup," he warned. "The embassy officials will want to fly you to Frankfurt, Germany, for that. Just tell them you want to spend Easter with your family. You can join the rest of us at the army medical center after the holidays."

"I don't want to be pricked and prodded. I don't want someone to take my blood only to tell me what I already know. I'm fine." She hated doctors and hospitals. She hated his cool, calm words even more. Angrily she inched away from him. "I feel like a piece of luggage to be shipped out on the next available fight. I don't want to leave while everyone else is still on the plane."

Robert studied her face and saw the temper flashing in her eyes. He wondered what she hated more, the thought of a medical exam or that he wanted her to leave Omari. "You're going to be better off with your family."

"That's for me to decide," she whispered, wishing she didn't have to keep her voice down.

"And what are you going to do while you wait? In Basjad you can't walk around as freely as you do at home. This is a Muslim country where the women still wear veils. Yussuf's and Muhrad's wives will drive you nuts within hours. And reporters will hound you."

"I'm not a child that needs to be entertained." Her fingers clenched the gray flannel of her skirt, twisting it. "A few hours ago you said that you needed me," she whispered. "But you don't know the meaning of the word."

She was wrong, he thought, so very wrong. The need to touch her, to hold her, was so strong that his hands balled into white-knuckled fists. He was selfish enough to want to ignore his son's needs, to want her to stay and find her waiting for him. But he wasn't such a bastard that he'd want her to be alone if things went wrong. "Bobby needs you more than I do," he said.

She sucked in her breath at his words. She knew he did not love her, but did he have to state it so clearly that he wanted her only for his son's sake? She turned to look out the window at the ever-darkening sky, her back stiff with pain and fear.

"Yes, you're right," she said. "I'll leave Basjad as soon as I can."

Dawn rose over the desert, brushing the sand dunes with orange and pink hues. From the top of the minaret in Basjad's main square, loudspeakers called for the first prayer of the day. But this morning the plaza in front of the mosque remained deserted. The traders, shopkeepers and street urchins of the capital of Omari had camped out on top of the desert hills beyond the airport to watch what was going to happen to the hijacked plane that had landed during the night.

Prince Jamal stepped from the black nomad tent that had been erected at the edge of the runway and breathed in the crisp, clean desert air. It was almost time now. Minutes earlier, the helicopters had landed about fifty yards away from the plane. They now stood side by side at the edge of the runway, as Robert had asked for.

Raising high-powered binoculars to his eyes, Jamal swept the dunes beyond the edge of the tarmac. Among the crowd of traders, bakers and nomads he spotted familiar faces. He smiled tautly, a dangerous grin that revealed strong, brilliantly white teeth. Mingled with the citizens of Basjad and the veiled women now selling food and water to the crowds were the Emir's palace guards, a crack unit he had trained with Robert's help.

He raised the radio to his lips. "Major. We've fulfilled our side of the deal. The helicopters are fueled, with keys in the ignitions. We're rolling the stairs up to the plane now. The men are unarmed. Don't use them for target practice."

Long minutes later the door opened.

Marianne stood at the gaping hole, staring at freedom with burning eyes. Behind her Robert watched the staircase being rolled closer. "If you need money, Jamal will loan it to you."

Marianne nodded mutely. Ever since she had watched the arrival of the helicopters she had been sick with fear. Would the nightmare never end? she wondered.

She turned and threw her arms around Robert's neck. "Don't worry about me. Just take care of yourself." She took the pin Bobby had given her and pinned it to Robert's collar. "A good-luck charm," she whispered. "Bobby gave it to me for Christmas. He would want you to have it."

Then her gaze flew to the major. He was staring outside, watching the metal structure come closer.

Robert looked at her for a long moment, his eyes ablaze. Then he kissed her with a reverence that made tears shimmer in her eyes. She wanted to tell him how much she loved him, but the words wouldn't come. A few seconds later it was too late.

She was gently spun around and pushed through the door the moment the stairs hit the side of the plane. "Give Bobby a hug from me."

Marianne gripped the side of the still slightly moving railing to steady herself. At the edge of the platform, she turned back. But all she saw was the major with the gun in his hand. "Get out of here. Before I change my mind."

Chapter 8

"What do you mean, you're not going to do anything?" Marianne jumped to her feet and, placing her hands on the gleaming desk in the ambassador's office, argued heatedly, "There are fifteen Americans on board that plane, three crew and twelve hostages. They have no water. They are almost out of food. The temperature inside the plane must be hell, and you say you can't do anything but wait. Surely something could be done. At least see to it that they get water."

"Please, Mrs. Sullivan, you are slightly overwrought." His Excellency Ambassador Thomas Rossman spread his pudgy hands helplessly. He was a heavy-set, gray-haired man in his early sixties who was planning to retire before the summer. Emma, his wife, had already left for the States to look for a house near their children. Emma, Rossman thought, would have known how to calm down the young woman and explain to her that U.S. policy would not change. "Perhaps you'd like another glass of iced tea."

"No, thank you." Marianne saw the regret in his tired brown eyes, the helpless sympathy, and her burst of angry frustration faded. She slumped down in the leather chair in front of the desk, leaned her head against its high back and stared at the flag that stood for liberty and freedom. "This waiting and uncertainty is getting to me."

"You've been through quite a lot," Rossman agreed.

Marianne gripped the carved wooden arms of the chair. She was free, but her ordeal wasn't over. She was worried. She was scared. And she felt guilty to be able to take a bath, to eat and drink her fill, to change her clothes. She felt like apologizing to Jamal, to her parents, and especially to her son, for deserting Robert. Even telling herself that Robert was better off without her hadn't eased her guilt. "Is there any news from the airport?"

"The matter has been taken out of our hands. We've been asked, very politely but very firmly, to stay away from the vicinity." Clearing his throat, he went on, "I've known Robert for a number of years. He's a very resourceful young man."

"One of the best men we've ever had." One of the two agents who had questioned her—debriefed her, as Robert had put it—walked into the office with another folder of mug shots in his hands. "I'd like you to look at these," he said, spreading them out in front of her.

Her gaze slid over the mug shots. She had already spent close to two hours staring at faces that all seemed to resemble each other. Closing the folder with a snap, she shook her head. "Why don't you try to get the hostages off the plane? Robert will do a much better job of identifying those men."

"We are trying, Mrs. Sullivan," sighed the man who had introduced himself earlier as Jerry. "Describe the man called Major to me again."

"About five-foot-eight, late thirties, high forehead with thinning black hair. Fine-boned. He was probably educated in England because he speaks English with a slight British accent. And he isn't in any of your files." She pushed back the chair impatiently and picked up her purse. "Gentlemen, if you don't need me anymore, I'd like to go back to the airport."

Thomas Rossman also rose. "You still need a medical checkup."

Her eyes snapped. "There's nothing wrong with me that a few days of rest won't cure."

"We prefer that you stay right here at the embassy until the situation has been resolved."

Marianne's chin tilted upward. "And how long is that going to be?"

"Mrs. Sullivan, we're doing everything possible to free the hostages."

"Yes," she said, wearily pushing back her hair. "I'm not blaming you. I prefer a little bit more action, though."

She whirled out of the room and was halfway down the hall before Jerry caught up with her. "Mrs. Sullivan, we may need you to identify—"

Marianne cut him off. "I'll be back later. Now I'm going to the airport."

"You can't do that."

"Watch me," she said and ran down the stairs. "I am not a member of the diplomatic corps, so my hands aren't tied."

He was right behind her. "We've received permission to use the military airport and fly you out of here."

The thought of getting on another plane made her shudder. She stopped halfway down the sweeping staircase and gripped the wood and wrought-iron railing and asked hoarsely, "You'd said you wanted me to stay until this is resolved. Now you expect me to fly out of here today?"

Jerry's face became human. "We've decided it'll be easier to get you on a plane out of here right away. Your family must be anxious to see you."

"My family understands." Marianne recalled the phone call to France, her mother's sobs, her father's hoarse voice and Bobby asking, "Mom, when are you coming back? Is Dad coming with you?" She hadn't been able to tell him the truth, that his father was still on the plane, that it might be days, weeks or even months before he saw Robert again. She'd simply told him, "We'll be back soon." But it wasn't because she did not want to face Bobby alone that she was staying. She loved Robert too much to leave.

"Robert wouldn't want you to stay here, either," Jerry pointed out.

"Probably," she said with an ironic inflection. "But until he tells me so himself, I'm staying." With a swirl of blue silk she turned and ran down the rest of the steps, past the marines flanking the entrance, past reporters who had dogged her steps ever since she had left the palace, where she had spent the night, down the wide stairs to the street outside.

A wave of intense heat hit her as she descended toward the limousine Jamal had put at her disposal. The driver, Hassir, a brown-robed man with a huge nose and bushy black brows shading black eyes, was leaning against the hood of the car, trying to keep a group of street urchins from marking the gleaming polish. When he saw Marianne, he straightened and pulled open the rear door. "Where to, madam?" he asked in fluent, if heavily accented English.

"I don't know." Sliding into the maroon velvet seat, she realized that Hassir might have orders to keep her away from the airport.

When he slid into the driver's seat, he spoke through the microphone: "My master suggested the shops. We have a number of excellent boutiques in Basjad." His voice was polite, but Marianne sensed a certain dislike and impatience, as if he resented taking a mere woman shopping when he wanted to be at the airport with his master.

Hassir was Jamal's personal servant and bodyguard. He traveled everywhere with the prince. She had met him at her wedding and on a few subsequent occasions. Perhaps because of his heavy, powerful build, she'd always thought of him as a fighter, not as a chauffeur or valet.

Marianne pushed the button, which lowered the window between them. "I guess you're right. I can't borrow clothes from the Lady Rana indefinitely." Upon her arrival at the palace, Lady Rana, Prince Muhrad's second wife, had presented her with several outfits: dresses, suits, shoes, underwear and the most beautiful peignoir Marianne had ever seen.

The clothes were almost a perfect fit. Marianne had never dreamed of wearing a Paris original like this blue silk shirt waist dress with long pleated sleeves and kid-leather collar, cuffs and belt. The matching kid sandals were half a size too small, but that was because her feet were still swollen after sitting for so long. Still, she felt uncomfortable wearing borrowed plumes. She needed makeup, and wanted a pair of sunglasses to shield her eyes from the brilliant sun.

"Lady Rana is generous," Hassir agreed with a gleam in his eyes. "She loves shopping and has more clothes than she could wear in a year. She will not miss a few dresses." He put the key into the ignition. "Do you still want to go to the shops?"

A smile curved Marianne's lips. "You've reassured me, Hassir. Where would you like to go?"

Beneath the checkered cloth covering his head, his swarthy face creased, revealing three gold caps among his white teeth. "My master gave orders to take you anywhere you wished to go."

"You are a devious man, Hassir," Marianne chuckled. "Let's stop at a drugstore first. Then I'd like to go the airport."

"Yes, madam," he said and started the car.

The "drugstore," just down one block on Basjad's main street, carried everything from soaps to velour robes. When Marianne entered the scented store, a dusky-skinned sales-girl ran into the back to call the owner. At first Marianne thought that the royal limousine was the reason for this personal attention from the chic, brunette Frenchwoman. The idea amused her. But her amusement fled moments later when the woman said in French, "You poor dear. That was such a terrible ordeal you went through. You will need everything from moisturizers to sunscreens. You've come to the right place, Mrs. Sullivan. I carry a complete line of cosmetics." She began piling small boxes on the glass-topped counter.

With each box Marianne saw her cache of traveler's checks dwindle and almost turned to run. "I only need a mascara and eye shadow. How do you know my name?"

"Nonsense. With your fine pale skin you need special creams—oh. How do I know you? It's in all the papers." She pointed to a stack of newspapers, two printed in Ara-bic and yesterday's edition of *Paris Press*.

Marianne stared at the picture of Robert and herself on the front page of the French daily and read the caption be-neath. "American diplomat Robert L. Sullivan and his di-vorced wife Marianne Lloyd Sullivan are among the hostages of the hijacked TAA airliner. Mrs. Sullivan, whose mother is French, had planned to spend the Easter holidays with her grandmother near Chamonix. Mrs. Sullivan's par-ents and her eight-year-old son had arrived in France the previous week. They have not been available for com-ment."

Behind her, the door to the store opened, and Hassir filled the doorway, holding a crowd of reporters at bay. Flashes blinked through the display windows. "Just give me the mascara," Marianne told the Frenchwoman hurriedly. She had been cautioned to avoid all interviews. Not that she had needed the warning, Marianne thought grimly. Her fears were private.

"Nonsense, my dear, you want to look your best when that handsome husband of yours gets off the plane." She packed the small white boxes into a shopping bag and slid it across the counter. From a small tray next to the cash register she picked up a little blue, pink and yellow stickpin in the shape of an Easter bunny and pinned it on the bag. "Happy Easter, my dear," she said kindly. "Is there anything else you need?"

Marianne shook her head. She just wanted to get out of there. "How much do I owe you?" Outside, a group of khaki-clothed policemen arrived to disperse the crowd.

"It's a gift. No. Please," she said firmly, when Marianne insisted on paying. "And don't worry too much. God won't let anything happen to those poor men. Not on Easter."

"Thank you." The woman's kindness brought tears to her eyes. "I hope you're right."

Once she was back in the privacy of the limousine, Marianne said to Hassir, "I feel guilty. She refused to let me pay for any of this."

"She is a smart businesswoman," was Hassir's cynical comment as he started the car. "Those photos the reporters took will generate more than enough business to make up the loss."

"Perhaps," Marianne agreed, pinning the Easter bunny to her collar. "But she was also very kind and generous."

On her trip into Basjad, Marianne had been too tired and too drained to pay any attention to her surroundings. Now she looked with interest at the place where Robert had spent so much of his free time. Basjad consisted of deep blue skies, brilliant white buildings and lush vibrant green foliage. High-walled palaces towered over adobe shacks. Camels and mules slowed down the traffic of gleaming limousines and European sports cars. Everywhere Marianne looked, she saw an uneasy balance between the old and the new, tradition versus progress, poverty and wealth.

At the outskirts of Basjad, the desert began. Plumes of fine sand whirled and danced across the sand dunes rolling toward the horizon and across the black band of tarmac cutting straight through the dunes. Robert had once described to her the whirling dervishes of sand out in the desert, and Marianne was fascinated. At noon, the sun had a metallic sheen, almost blinding despite the smoked glass of the car. The limousine's climate-control kept the interior comfortable, but when Marianne touched the roof she could feel the heat. "The inside of the plane must be like an oven," she said. "They're still on it, aren't they?"

"Yes. The dunes beyond the helicopters are crowded with spectators," Hassir explained. "It is difficult to disperse them with all their camels, mules and horses, without the help of soldiers and police."

"You mean the terrorists have been trapped inside the plane because of a few mules?" Marianne frowned worriedly. "The major is not a man to be crossed easily. I hope he hasn't vented his anger on the hostages."

"I can't say. Prince Muhrad has been negotiating with them. He has tried to disperse the crowds with helicopters. Some have left, but others have arrived. Most of the traders from Basjad are returning home now." He pointed at the steady stream of crowded buses, trucks and cars on the opposite side of the road. "They don't want to be caught in the storm. The nomads, though, are used to them. So they stay. And the major won't move until the crowds are gone."

Marianne looked at the sky. It was still deep blue, if a little hazy at the distance, but there were no clouds. Only the whirling plumes.

Five minutes later, they reached a military roadblock.

The soldier standing in the shade of the army truck halfway across the road recognized the banner fluttering from the left fender and, snapping to attention, waved them through.

Hassir slowed down, lowered the window and asked a few questions, which the soldier answered with shrugs.

"Is there any news?" Marianne asked the moment they'd left the roadblock behind. Hassir shook his massive head, pointing at the airport buildings rising out of the desert.

Minutes later they saw the plane, a big silver bird shimmering in the heat. Marianne noticed that several of the plane's doors were cracked open. The staircase she had used stood a few feet away. Her eyes briefly swept the crowded dunes, then settled on the three ambulances and several fire engines that seemed to be the center of activity.

The limousine stopped in front of a black, sprawling nomad tent whose sides had been rolled up for cross ventilation, revealing fold-down tables and chairs and communications equipment.

Jamal stood in front of the tent with his tawny head bare and his arms akimbo. "I told you to take Mrs. Sullivan shopping," he snapped.

Hassir opened the passenger door and said, "No, master, your words were to take her anywhere she wanted to go."

Jamal's bloodshot eyes slid from his servant's expressionless face to Marianne's defiant one. He waited until she stood right in front of him, then asked, "Why aren't you on your way to France?"

She could have lied, saying that she was reluctant to board another plane soon. But Jamal knew her better, so she opted for the simple truth. "I'm not leaving until Robert is free."

Jamal reached for the glass Hassir was handing him, splashing half the water over his head, drinking the rest. Handing the glass back to Hassir, he dismissed her with a hard, cynical glance. "This is no place for you. Go back to the palace if you insist on staying in Omari." His white desert robe billowed in a sudden gust of wind that whirled sand into the air. "You'll get tired of waiting soon enough." He squinted into the sky. "Especially when the *khamsin* reaches us." Then he left her standing in front of the tent, striding toward one of the tables covered with what looked like a chart.

Marianne drew in a sharp breath. The air was so hot it seemed to scorch her lungs. Fine sand settled in her nostrils and scratched her eyes. "There's no need to be rude," she snapped, trying to keep her temper under control. Jamal had a cynical attitude toward all women, and his treatment of her was nothing personal. He had been pursued relentlessly since he was old enough to know the difference between the sexes, and also, Robert was his closest friend. She tried to make allowances, but his words still stung. "Unless you use force, I'm staying."

Jamal looked up from the plan of the 747 spread out on the table and held down at the edges by rocks. "I'm not rude. I'm tired and worried and in no mood to deal with hysterics." He took her shoulder in a hard grip and propelled her to the edge of the shade. "Look over there." He pointed toward one of the ambulances, where the two men were at that moment rolling out a stretcher. "See that body bag? They tossed a man out about thirty minutes ago."

"Who?" Marianne whispered. Jamal would have told her if it was Robert being lifted onto a stretcher now. But she'd spent almost thirty-six hours with those men, sharing dangers, jokes and hopes. She closed her eyes in pain. "Who is it?"

"Jimmy Dobson from Dallas."

"He was allergic to jellyfish." Marianne bit her lips to keep the tears at bay.

"They've threatened to kill a man every thirty minutes until those dunes are clear of people," Jamal continued in his hard voice. "If you feel strong enough to stomach the sight of a man pitched from twenty-three feet up, be my guest." He could have told her that the doctor who had examined Jimmy Dobson thought that he might have died of a heart attack before the fall. But this account was more effective.

Marianne pressed her hand to her stomach and swallowed. "Why don't you describe the fall in more grisly detail," she said with as much dignity as the bile in her mouth allowed. "You can make me nauseous, but you're not going to make me leave."

Her dignity impressed him more than any avowal of love for Robert could have done. "You've changed," he said quietly, rubbing the back of his neck tiredly. "You're not a spoiled little girl anymore." Before she could protest his defamation of her character, he turned to Hassir. "Find her a *mashlash*."

Marianne thought of the stifling heat and wanted to protest that she would smother beneath the heavy folds of the robe. But when Hassir handed it to her, she slipped into it without comment. Already some of the men walking in and out of the tent had been frowning at her immodest display of flesh and curves. The silk dress had been molding itself to her body with each gust of wind.

"You said something about the *khamsin* reaching us. What is that?" she asked Jamal, tying the string at her neck.

"A *khamsin* is a sandstorm." Grimly he pointed at the distant sky where the color seemed to have changed to a hazy bluish gray. "They can last for only an hour, but sometimes they blow for days."

"The hostages can't survive days without water." Marianne swayed and braced herself on a chair.

"I know," Jamal said harshly. "But the terrorists can't use the helicopters and take off to God knows where, either." He brushed back the hair that the wind had blown onto his forehead. "If I were in the major's shoes, I'd use the sandstorm to escape on foot."

"And what about Robert and the others?" Marianne whispered.

"The *khasmin* is their best chance." He pointed at the plan on the table. "Show me exactly where Robert and the others were."

The sandstorm hit the airport a half hour later.

One moment the sky had been clear and blue, the next, it was dark and the air was filled with blowing sand. Fine sand so thick that Marianne couldn't see her hand in front of her eyes. Sand so sharp it pricked the skin of her hands like needle points as she held the hood over her face. It blew beneath the edges of the tent that had been secured and weighted down and settled on the plastic sheeting covering the radio equipment. The two kerosene lamps Hassir had lit cast a reddish light over the interior.

Night fell and the sand still blew. Soldiers in masks and billowing robes entered and left the tent. No one ate much of the food that arrived at regular intervals. It was filled with grit. But everyone drank gallons of water served in paper cups with lids and straws.

The temperature had dropped dramatically. Marianne huddled in one corer of the tent with her hood drawn low and a scarf tied over her nose. Sometimes she dozed, lulled into fitful sleep by the whining storm. At other times she listened to discussions about which of the exits the terrorists would use to try to escape. They all seemed certain that the terrorists would make a break.

Just before dawn Jamal bent over her and pulled her to her feet. He had pushed up the mask he'd been wearing. His face was drawn and his eyes gritty with lack of sleep and chafed with sand. But there was a fresh sound of hope in his raspy voice.

"Marianne, we're leaving the tent. Hassir will take you to one of the ambulances. The storm is dying down. If they make a break, it's going to happen soon. You'll be safer in one of the trucks."

Inside the plane, it was quiet and dark. The whine and blasting of the sandstorm drowned out the occasional hoarse words the hostages whispered among themselves. The captain and his crew had joined the hostages hours ago, the moment it had become certain that Emir Yussuf would not refuel the plane.

With his eyes closed, Robert exercised his hands and feet, straining against the ropes that cut into his skin. They had been tied down for hours, ever since Jimmy Dobson had attacked the terrorist with the crooked nose for the bottle of water the fool had waved in front of his face. The thirst and the heat had gotten to him. Robert still could hear his screams when they had dragged him away. Immediately afterward they had all been tied hand and foot with thick nylon rope. Since then, the major had personally checked their ties every thirty minutes.

At least Marianne had been spared, Robert thought. He moved his chin and touched the bear she had stuck to his collar. A teddy bear! He wondered if she still collected stuffed animals. Their apartment in Manhattan had looked like a Christmas display from F.A.O. Schwartz. Every nook and cranny, chair and bed, had once been littered with cats and dogs, pink elephants and penguins.

When she had walked out on him, she had left him to pack them. He remembered walking from room to room with their glass eyes following him, accusing him, pleading with him to call her back. He remembered, too, how he had sat next to the phone, waiting for her to call, firmly believing that she was coming back. Why else had she left her zoo behind?

A week later, he had stuffed them into boxes and plastic bags, telling himself that he was better off without her, that the pain tearing out his gut was because she had taken away his son. He had been wrong. Two weeks later, he hadn't been able to stand the loneliness anymore. He'd had his finger poised on the phone, when Don and Cecile had arrived to pick up the boxes and his pride had snapped back. He could manage without her, he'd told himself.

He was used to empty spaces in his life. He'd always been a failure when it came to personal relationships. Somehow he had always known that their marriage wouldn't last. So if she wanted a divorce, he'd give it to her. She had never had a chance to find out what she wanted out of life. If she wanted to spread her wings, he would not hold her back.

But he hadn't known that life had lost its meaning without her, that he would never be free of her, that he would even begin to resent the demands of his job. If he had, he would have swallowed his pride and shredded the divorce papers.

He rubbed his cheek once again over the pin. Was it only a good luck charm or was it a promise? He told himself that if she still cared for him, she would be waiting for him in Basjad. Then he told himself that he was unreasonable. He was asking too much too soon.

"Feels like more than half an hour since the last time they checked on us," Rafe whispered. "I think the wind is dying down."

Robert stopped flexing his arms and legs and listened. The sand blasting against the windows seemed to have slowed down. Then, faintly, he thought he heard noises from somewhere beneath their feet. Rafe must have heard the faint sounds also, because he leaned into the aisle to listen more closely.

When the noise came again, Robert said, "They're going to make a break for it." His tongue was so swollen the words were slurred. "Damn, I wish I had a knife to cut through the ropes."

"There are knives in the galley," Rafe whispered, pushing himself to his feet. "Never tried to saw through nylon with plastic before, but it's worth a try."

Robert didn't waste his breath. He rolled over Rafe's seat and fell to his knees in the aisle. From there, he pushed himself up to his feet. Behind him, he heard Sven follow their example. Because they had to keep the noise down, it took them several minutes to inch to the galley. It seemed to take hours to find the knives in the darkness. The plastic edges of the knives dulled swiftly on the nylon ropes, and the thin handles slipped through their swollen and numb fingers.

Suddenly they heard shots, machine gun fire, yells and screams.

The three men in the galley held their breath. Then they began sawing again. They knew that if the terrorists hadn't been able to make a break, they'd come for them. If one of them had been injured, there would be hell to pay.

Dawn was seeping through the windows when they heard running steps. Robert attacked Rafe's rope with a last spurt of desperation. The rope broke. It was only a matter of seconds before Robert and Sven were free. They were flexing their hands and shaking their legs when a flashlight flooded the galley.

Rafe twisted around and tried to escape through the other exit. Sven tried to follow him. Only Robert sat back and leaned against the cart. At the edge of the blinding light he had caught a glimpse of desert robes.

"Turn that damn light off," he grumbled, shielding his eyes.

Jamal pointed the light at the ceiling, then looked at Robert again. "You look like you've just returned from hell," he said. "But I don't think I've ever seen a more beautiful sight."

The storm had ended as suddenly as it had started, but dust still swirled through the air, dancing in the beams of the floodlights. The ambulances and army trucks were buried up to their wheels in sand drifts. Climbing from the ambulance, Marianne sank knee-deep into the sand. Gaining her balance, she stood and watched soldiers drag three of the terrorists away. With satisfaction, she noticed that Hamid was in custody. But five had escaped into the desert—the major among them.

Jamal and a few of his men had entered the plane minutes before, the same way the terrorists had escaped, through the baggage hatch. Marianne watched and waited with her heart in her throat. What was going on inside? Why was no one coming out?

Dawn crept over the sand dunes as the first man appeared. He had to be lifted down and carried to one of the ambulances. Another followed and a third. Nine familiar faces. Then came the crew. Sven needed no help. And Rafe almost danced as his feet touched the ground, and he spread his arms wide as if embracing dawn.

When another pair of legs appeared, Marianne began to run. The robe billowed behind her, slowing her down. She almost tore off the ties, then dropped it in the sand. She lost her sandals and ran on, barefoot.

Robert simply opened his arms and braced himself as she flew into them. His arms closed around her as if he would never let her go. Their kiss tasted of sand. They didn't notice it. They stood right in the spotlight with hundreds of eyes watching them. They were oblivious to the crowd. For those timeless moments they saw only each other. Robert kissed her with endless hunger, with endless thirst, feeling her melt into his arms, as she had on that summer day in the marsh.

"I told you to leave," Robert finally whispered, running his dry lips over her dusty skin.

"I promised Bobby I'd bring you back with me."

He raised his head and stared into eyes that shone like silver stars. "Is that the only reason you waited for me?"

She shook her head, and her arms tightened around his neck. She wanted to tell him how much she loved him, that she had never stopped loving him, but she could not. And did words really matter that much? Was it really so important that Robert could not say what she wanted to hear? She knew that he was ruthless, disciplined, harsh and dangerous. He'd had to be to get to the top. But he was also passionate and gentle, and he had risked his life to protect her. He wanted her as she had never been wanted before and since their divorce. And she wanted him in the same elemental way. That hadn't changed.

Perhaps in time, when the dust had settled, when the hurt and bitterness had faded, he would find the words. And if he never did, she would learn to live without them.

Chapter 9

Marianne stood on the terrace of the penthouse suite in the Palace Tower, Basjad's most luxurious hotel, her face raised into the warm breeze that whispered among the potted palms, roses and lilies on the rooftop garden. Below her, a million lights seemed to blink and twinkle in the darkness. From the white mosque's minaret a *muezzin* called for the last prayer of the day. To her right the Emir's palace, with its columns and arches, gardens and fountains, looked like a vision from the Arabian nights. In the distance, the sea shimmered like dark blue velvet and the lights of the fishing boats sparkled like stars. The foreign cadences of wailing music were hauntingly beautiful.

"Is this where you usually stay?" Marianne was partly stunned and partly amused by the opulence of their surroundings. The penthouse suite was large enough to accommodate half of her father's entire family. On the floor below were a formal salon and dining room, two conference rooms and three of the suite's eight bedrooms. The upstairs lounge and dining areas were less formal and, she suspected, the women's domain. The furniture was a mixture of priceless European antiques, silk cushions and gauzy veils.

"No. On private visits I stay at Jamal's apartments." Robert poured the champagne into the crystal goblets, placed the bottle in the silver cooler and looked at Marianne quizzically. Dressed in a shimmering sea-green sheath that fell loosely to her feet, she looked cool, exotic and breathtakingly beautiful. He liked the way she had brushed her hair back, revealing the pure oval of her face and the graceful line of her neck.

Although their luggage had been returned to them, she wore no jewelry. He wondered if she still had her wedding rings or any of the other pieces he had given her. She didn't like to wear rings and necklaces, he remembered. He'd rarely seen her wear either the diamond studs or the gold watch, or the two-carat diamond pendant. "Can you see me sleeping on scented satin pillows?"

"I don't know." She felt like a fish out of water. Tonight, at the reception and the celebration dinner at the palace, she'd been awed by the ease with which Robert moved among princes and foreign dignitaries. She herself had been tied in knots. She'd been afraid to say the wrong words, to pick up the wrong spoon—there had been fifteen different shapes of silverware—and the roast quail had almost jumped into her lap.

"You're a different man here, among your friends." There had been no room for her in Robert's life four years ago. And since then, the chasm seemed to have widened. What if she didn't fit into this world of international politics?

Robert shot her a sharp, questioning look. All evening she had been unusually quiet, but he had attributed it to fatigue. From the time they had called their son at dawn he had seen her only briefly and never alone. Was she already regetting this step they were about to take? Did she have second thoughts? Or was she simply overwhelmed by their lavish surroundings?

"This penthouse suite is reserved for the Emir's relatives and friends. Jamal's taste is austere by comparison. And I still prefer a solid mattress and cotton sheets. That hasn't changed," he said, taking off his white tuxedo jacket and bow tie. Rolling up the sleeves of his shirt, he added softly, "Any more than has my need for a golden-haired nymph smelling of the sun and sea."

She laughed shakily, uncertainly, her fingers touching the turquoise gown she had bought, charged at the boutique in the hotel lobby. "This isn't me," she said. "I don't know if I'd ever feel comfortable in silks and brocades." Her eyes slid to the narrow white bandages covering his rope burns. "Do your wrists and ankles still hurt?"

"No." For a moment his face hardened as his thoughts went to Hamid. It had taken little persuasion to get the few facts Hamid knew out of him. As Robert had suspected, he'd been taken on at the last moment on the recommendation of his friend. Most of the information he had given them was useless. His friend, Mahmad, and the terrorist with the crooked nose, Yasser, were tougher to break. So far they had managed to resist even Muhrad's less-than-gentle type of persuasion. He grimaced. Interrogation had always been the one part of his work he'd hated.

In a way he was glad that tomorrow they would leave Omari for a few days. At first, Yussuf had swayed between putting the three terrorists on trial in Omari and extraditing them to the U.S. But because Muhrad had flatly opposed the move he had finally sided with his son and heir. Robert had no stomach for watching public executions, especially not in a market square.

Picking up the glasses, he dismissed the unpleasant thoughts. Tomorrow they would fly to Frankfurt, where their son would meet them. After their checkup they would have little time together, and he wasn't going to waste another moment.

Slowly he crossed the brilliant old Kashan carpet. "You were the most beautiful woman at the reception tonight. Old Yussuf said you reminded him of Jamal's mother as a young woman. 'A golden, graceful gazelle with eyes as clear as moonstones,' were his exact words. He couldn't keep his eyes off you." Stopping in front of her, he handed her a goblet. "And neither could I." Touching his glass to hers, he added whimsically, "I was afraid that the buttons would pop off my shirt if my chest swelled any more with pride."

"I was one of the few women who wasn't veiled," she pointed out dryly. But some of her dejection fled. She was tired, exhausted, running on adrenaline and making mountains out of molehills. She gave him a half smile. "I rather liked Emir Yussuf. He's a crafty old man."

"A sly desert fox," Robert agreed with a hint of a smile. Laying an arm across her shoulders, he drew her with him to the stone balustrade. He could feel her stiffen at his touch, then try to relax against him. His fingers tightened impatiently around the stem of the glass. He wanted to turn her into his arms and kiss all the doubts from her mind. Instead, he forced himself to relax and add casually, "I never thought I'd see you intimidated by gold, crystal and diamonds."

Her head snapped back in pride, as he'd known it would. "It takes more than a few sparklers to intimidate me."

His voice cooled. "Then what are you frightened of? Me?" He placed the glass on a table half hidden by a gently swaying palm, then cupped her chin. In the dim light her skin looked like alabaster, but her eyes were dark shadows. "If you don't want to sleep with me, say so," he said bluntly, his head tilted arrogantly. "There must be at least six bedrooms in this place."

For an instant she longed to run and hide in the bedroom she had picked out earlier. They were rushing things. Why couldn't they take it slowly, wait until they were back in the States? Robert didn't seem to mind one way or the other. She was afraid to get hurt again. She needed time. But tonight she needed Robert more.

She didn't want to sleep alone in that huge bed with pink satin sheets.

When she relaxed, she felt the tension in his arm, which was still draped lightly across her shoulders. So he wasn't as cool as he pretended to be. A small smile tugged at her lips. "Eight. There are eight bedrooms," she said huskily, raising a finger to trace the tired lines on his face. All day she had alternately dreaded and longed for this moment. Now that it was here, she was behaving like an idiot. "And I took the only one with a hard mattress. The sheets are pink satin, though."

He felt almost weak with relief. His arm tightened on her shoulder and slowly turned her into him. Covering her hand, he kissed her palm and felt the scabs where the blisters had begun to heal, the blisters she had received when she'd tried to save his life.

Would he have to let her sleep alone? he wondered. Should he lower his pride and ask her to stay with him? Asking had never come easy to him. He had always taken what he wanted. Even their marriage had been on his terms, with him calling all the shots. And then she had walked away from him, leaving him with his precious pride a little dented, but mostly intact.

Only a fool would prefer cold pride to the vibrant warmth filling his arms. If he didn't want to lose her a second time, the rules would have to change.

They already had.

"Would you share the hard mattress?" he asked huskily. "Or do I have to sleep on the floor?"

She wanted to cry and laugh at the same time. He was leaving the decision and the pace up to her. She wasn't going to change her mind, but she couldn't help teasing him a bit. "Oh, definitely the carpet." And then she spoiled it by laughing. "The carpet is a fluffy salmon pink, with purple, turquoise and bright red tasseled cushions."

Tilting her head up, he kissed her deeply until the laughter stilled and her body began to tremble. Then he turned the tables neatly. "Only if you join me."

"I'll have to think about it," she said, her voice slightly unsteady.

"Then let me persuade you." He wanted to crush her to him and silence her teasing lips. He wanted to slide the silk off her skin and make love to her right here. But he wanted tonight to be different, sweet, with pleasure expanding slowly as if this were their first time. He raised her hand to his lips and kissed her open palm.

"That wasn't one of the options," she protested weakly.

"I changed my mind." His eyes smouldered; his lips were soft and warm against her skin. Heat radiated up her arm. She took a sip of champagne to cool herself down. Then his moist tongue began to trace ever-widening circles, until he reached the sensitive area of her wrist. The bubbles of warmth exploded one by one.

She moaned softly, staring at the white bandages contrasting with the darkness of his tan. She wanted to touch him. But there was no place to put down the precious crystal. She had to watch and feel his gentle assault on her senses while her hunger grew inside her. She hadn't known that the spot inside her elbow could be so ultra-sensitive.

"Robert, you're torturing me." Marianne groaned, trying to snatch her arm away. There was a fire burning in her body, an aching pleasure that grew until her knees began to tremble and she swayed against him. "I want to touch you, too. Only I don't know what to do with this glass."

"Have you changed your mind?" It was torture to take it slowly, but there was pleasure, too, pleasure that sharpened with each taste of her skin. He wanted to explore, to savor before passion burned out of control.

"No. Yes. No."

Laughing softly, he raised his head. "What is it? Yes or no?" But he couldn't resist the pleading look in her eyes and took the champagne from her, placing the goblet on the wide stone shelf. "I want tonight to be special for you. That's why I accepted when Yussuf offered us the penthouse. Once, a long time ago, I promised you romance. I never got around to it."

She spread her hands across his chest, sliding her fingertips over the silky fabric. Beneath, she could feel the heat of his skin, the strong beat of his heart. "Of course you did," she protested huskily, opening one button of his shirt and then another one. "You were my Prince Charming, Lancelot and Heathcliff all rolled into one."

Her words shook him, sobered him. He stepped back, picked up the glass and downed the champagne, wishing for the bite of a brandy. He hadn't known that she had put him on a white charger. No wonder he had fallen short of her expectations. "There's nothing romantic about me," he said harshly.

He needed to lay his cards on the table to dispel any romantic images she might still harbor about him. Now, when she still could walk away. He wanted her to see him for what he was and not what she wanted him to be.

His hands balled into fists. Would he never be rid of the past? He remembered the nightmares in his senior year at West Point, dreading that someone would find out about his past. One of the reasons he'd been drawn to the ATD had been because there a man's worth was judged by his ability, not by the Ivy League schools he had attended or by his past history.

And now he was facing those nightmares all over again.

"Believe me, there's nothing romantic about foster homes. They've improved a lot since I was in one, but thirty years ago they were hell. At ten, I was working in the pool hall where my foster father gambled. There was a private room at the back. The men playing there had no conscience about fleecing a kid of his hard-earned cash. And when I began to win the odd game, they beat the money out of me again. But I went back and learned until I knew I could beat them at their own tricks.

"One day I won big. I ran off with enough cash to keep me for a couple of years. Or so I thought. Two weeks later, when the police picked me up in Las Vegas, I was broke and starving. They took me back to Chicago, and I landed in another foster home, not much different from the last one."

He looked into her pale face and smiled grimly. "Not very romantic, is it?"

"No. It's sad." He'd been only two years older than Bobby, she thought, fighting the sting of tears. She knew that Robert would reject them as a sign of pity. She wanted to put her arms around him, but he would reject that, too. So she stood and waited. "Why are you telling me this now?"

"I was making sure that this time around you have no illusions about what kind of man I am."

"I never did," Marianne said softly. "I always guessed that there was more to your past then you wanted me to know." She tilted her head to one side and gently asked, "Why did you never tell me before? Did you think I'd have loved you any less for it? That I would be ashamed of your past? Or that I would think that you weren't good enough for me?" The taut look in his eyes told her that she had hit the nail right on the head.

Pain shot through her. No wonder he did not love her, she thought. Her temper flared in a mixture of frustration, anger and hurt. "I must say, you had a fine opinion of me. I'm tired of being treated either like a half-wit, a snob or a pretty butterfly. What difference does it make where you came from? You know what I see when I look at you? A man with great courage and determination. A man I admire and respect. And—" her eyes narrowed as she snapped "—a fool I'd like to strangle."

She had punched him straight in the face. No, he thought, straight in the heart, cracking the hard shell protecting it. "Be my guest," he said hoarsely, reaching for her then.

"No. Don't touch me." She was too angry, too hurt, and she twisted away from him.

Eyes gleaming, he caught her up in his arms, subduing her struggles easily. He wanted to dance with her around the room. But there were better ways of showing her how much he adored her. Smiling crookedly, dimples slashing his lean cheeks, he said, "I only want to make it easier for you to strangle me." He blazed a trail of fire down the slim throat arching away from him.

"I hate you," she whispered and turned her head. She wanted to cry and laugh and love him until the past had stopped hurting. How much more was there that he hadn't told her yet? Would she ever learn the whole story? Would she ever know the whole man? Or would there always be a place with a sign reading No Trespassing on it?

"Yes," Robert said roughly, feeling an aching tenderness for this slip of a woman in his arms. "But you love me a little, too."

"I don't want to," she whispered, clinging to his neck. "Loving means pain, and I don't want to be hurt again."

His arms tightened around her protectively. He wanted to promise her a future filled with laughter, filled with love. But the feelings churning inside him were too new, untested and frightening in their intensity. "It will be different this time." That he could promise easily, he thought as they walked through the sitting room and dining room beyond which two of the bedrooms were located.

He heard her draw a ragged breath, and his stride lengthened with the need to show her just how different it would be. He wanted to feel her skin against his. He wanted to look upon her without barriers. Would she look different with love sharpening his senses? His impatience to find out grew.

He chose the first of a set of three doors and pushed the switch with his elbow, illuminating a room straight out of a movie-set harem: a huge bed draped with hot pink veils, satin pillows spread all over the floor, a low divan covered with white furs. In the back there was even a huge black marble pool with floating lotus blossoms and water gently spouting from a solid gold fountain at one edge of it.

"Good Lord." Robert stood staring, sudden laughter rumbling in his chest.

Marianne turned her head and blinked at the soft lights. "It looks even more decadent at night."

"And you chose a firm mattress and pink satin sheets over this?" he teased her with an incredulous look on his face.

"I did hesitate when I saw the lotus blossoms." Her tone was solemn, but her eyes sparkled wickedly.

Robert's laughter caught in his throat when he imagined Marianne among the satin pillows, creamy furs and pink lotus blossoms. He kicked the door shut and, sliding her down his body, put her on her feet. "I always did have fantasies about making love to you in a harem," he whispered hoarsely, capturing her mouth in a hot, burning kiss.

She'd had her own fantasies when she had looked into this room before. Fantasies of making love to him until the words she wanted to hear above all else were wrenched from him. She could tell herself a hundred times that words torn from him in the heat of passion didn't mean much. That's why she had chosen the other room. But, oh, how she wished he would say them only once.

Then she felt his hand on her zipper, slowly sliding it down her spine, and she forgot about meaningless words. She wasn't a teenager with stars in her eyes anymore, she told herself as he slipped the gown down her arms. The less she expected, the less she would be hurt again. "You're a chauvinist." Her fingers only trembled slightly as they dug into his arms.

I've just discovered that I'm in love with you. His hands were trembling as they aligned themselves with her jaw. He studied her features as if it was the first time: the high forehead, the gently curving brows, the pert nose that wrinkled when she laughed, the generous mouth. Her eyes were closed. Tenderly he brushed his lips over the thick lashes, willing them to open. But though they flickered at his touch, she didn't look at him.

She let him draw her against his hard body and blindly raised her face to the hungry kisses he rained on her skin. Had she changed? she wondered. She was older now and much less active than she used to be. Had the firm young body he had known softened too much from sitting all day in an office? She couldn't bear it if she came short of his fantasies. When he raised his head, she drew his mouth back to hers desperately, wanting to prolong the sweet passion.

With their lips fused, he lifted her once again, carefully threading his way to the divan. He stumbled over a huge deep purple pillow with long silky fringes. At the last moment he twisted and landed on the soft furs, still clutching Marianne in his arms.

For a moment they lay stunned, side by side, their faces almost touching. Then giggles burst from Marianne's throat. Raising herself up on her elbows, she teased, "So much for your fantasies. You almost broke your neck."

His mouth curved ruefully. "I must be getting old."

It was so unlike him to admit to weakness, that the words sent a shaft of fear through her. "Are you hurt?" she asked, scrambling to her feet.

Mutely he shook his head. She took his breath away. He stared at her mature beauty barely hidden by scraps of green lace—the firm full breasts, the tiny waist, gently curving hips and her long legs. "You're much more beautiful than my fantasies." His voice was hoarse with desire and his eyes blazed with need.

She fell to her knees beside the divan and slid her hand beneath the shirt. With the knowledge that he still found her beautiful her confidence had returned, and she caressed and teased until he groaned beneath her hands.

He had promised himself to be patient, to go slowly, to give her time. But he hadn't promised to let her torture him. He captured those teasing, stroking hands and brought them to his lips. Then he rolled over, trapping her beneath him. "Now it's my turn," he groaned, kissing her with gentle violence.

Had her skin always been this soft, had it alwasy tasted so sweet, he wondered as he blazed a trail of fire down her throat. Had her breasts always been so beautiful, fitting perfectly into his hands? He couldn't remember the past. As her body shuddered beneath him and strained to meet each new caress, he felt as if this was their first time together.

Her nipples rose proudly, beckoning for his touch. When he circled them with his tongue, she moaned with pleasure. Her hands tugged at his shirt, slid it off his shoulders and down his arms. The rest of his clothes followed swiftly. Then he rolled the scraps of lace from her hips and began a gentle assault on her defenses.

It was torture not to cry out her love for him, Marianne thought, feeling fire burning up her legs. She stared at him with love-filled eyes as he trailed kisses everywhere. He had the most beautiful body she had ever seen in a man—lean, long-limbed, powerful—and he moved with a grace that delighted her. And then she thought of how stiffly he had moved after getting off the plane. He had been too weak to run; he still wasn't his normal self. The graceful Robert might have stumbled over the pillows, but he would never have lost his balance. Oh God, she had come so close to losing him! Her hands reached for him with fierce urgency. "Please hold me," she whispered.

He saw the darkness in her eyes, the memories, the fear. "Hush," he said, sliding his lips soothingly over her eyes. "Don't think about it." And then he set out to make her forget. Touching, stroking, stirring. There wasn't a place he didn't taste. There wasn't a nerve ending he didn't excite. And her responses were so sweet that he almost forgot about protecting her. But this time he didn't want her to come to him because she was pregnant. Because he loved her, he wouldn't settle for anything less than that she come to him of her own free choice.

When he slowly filled her, her eyes began to glow. When he took her to the first peak the shadows faded. And when he finally joined her completely she cried out with pleasure, reaching for him, urging him on. It was the first time he had given of himself unselfishly.

He had, he thought as he gathered her against his heaving chest, never experienced a greater joy.

With aching tenderness, he stroked her damp hair from her face. Once Marianne had tried to teach him about love and trust; how a simple gesture could convey warmth and support; that touch was more than just a tool to arouse passion.

He had been afraid to learn, afraid to wake up some night and find himself alone again. The fear was still there. Fears of a lifetime did not vanish overnight, he thought somberly, pressing her tighter against him. But he wanted to learn to trust. What would it feel like to think of her without wondering how much longer their marriage would last? What would it feel like to come home at night and share successes and disappointments alike? It was exhilarating.

And it was scary as hell.

He had few illusions about himself. He was a man without roots, who came and went as he pleased. He had plans and ambitions. He had always aimed high. Some day he would be at the very top and have Howard Barton's job. He let out a long, unsteady breath. He'd never had to account for his successes or his failures before. Would Marianne think less of him if he made mistakes?

Love scared him, he thought, his arm tightening around her slender form. He knew nothing about it. He loved his son, but a child accepted things without questions, without making a person feel vulnerable. With Marianne it was different.

Once he had believed that his main responsibility as a husband had been to keep his wife comfortable and safe. He was a rich man, but wealth had never overly impressed Marianne. She wanted a husband who gave of himself. He was almost thirty-seven years old. Was he too old to change?

"Are you all right?" he asked, looking at her face. She had her eyes closed, but there was a smile on her lips and her head was turned into him, her breath flowing over his skin.

"Hmm." She stretched, moving away a little, then curled into his side with all the sweet trust of a kitten.

He raised his head and blew a few strands of hair from her face. "Are you awake enough to listen?"

"Hmm." Her lids felt so heavy they refused to open. And she didn't want to talk. He had never made love to her so...so completely. There had always been passion and hunger and need. But never before had she felt such sweetness, such tenderness—such giving. It was as if he loved her. She wanted to go to sleep with that thought.

With a mixture of tenderness and impatience, Robert watched her breathing deepen into sleep. He wanted to tell her that he loved her and that he was going to make her happy.

For a moment he considered waking her. Then he told himself that she needed sleep more than a few words whispered in a fantasy setting. She might not believe them anyway. He would wait until daylight.

Then he remembered that she had not spoken a single word about love, either. Suddenly he felt very cold.

Shifting her slightly, he reached for the quilted silk blanket that had been draped over the foot of the divan. He pulled it up over them. So she didn't love him, he thought, settling her on his shoulder once again. She was afraid to let herself feel again. He could understand her doubts and fears. In a way, it was easier to deal with them than with love. He didn't believe in miracles. They made him suspicious, and he always looked for a catch. But she still wanted him.

His eyes gleamed with the challenge of making her fall in love all over again. On comfortable ground again, he began to map out his strategies.

He fell asleep before his plans had fully developed in his head.

Marianne woke up with fur tickling her nose. She blinked, sneezed and felt for Robert, afraid that she had dreamed last night. Her fingers closed over a slip of paper. She rubbed her eyes, then read, "Gone jogging."

It was ridiculous to feel such pleasure at two little words, but it was the first time Robert had left her a note telling her where he had gone. She pressed the paper against her cheek and laughed out loud. Things were going to be different this time around. Then she stretched and jumped off the furs.

Perhaps she could catch a glimpse of him from the window. Robert had picked up her clothes and draped them over a velvet-covered stool. Her shoes were placed neatly beneath it. Looking around, she noticed that his own clothes were gone.

They were probably already in his garment bag. Robert was well-organized and efficient, something, Marianne thought with a rueful grin, that hardly described herself. Her desk was the only place in her apartment that was meticulously neat, because she often brought work home. But her closets and her drawers were a mess. She never seemed to find the time to sort through her clothes and give the old ones to charity. But now she would have to roll up her sleeves and dive into them and make room for Robert's things. That thought brought another smile to her face.

She reached for her dress and held it in front of her as she hopped over the pillows scattered on the floor. But all she saw from the window were treetops and tennis courts and gardeners watering flower beds. Disappointed, she turned back to the room.

Should she order breakfast, she wondered, or take a shower first? Her eyes settled on a turquoise clock with gold hands. Six o'clock was too early to eat.

Robert's feet pounded the dirt as he jogged through the gardens of the Palace Tower. Adrenaline pumped through him, sweat poured down his body and his breath came out in gasps. He had done only three miles, but it felt like nine. His joints still felt stiff, especially his ankles, where the bandages rubbed with each step.

A second set of steps followed close behind him. "Slow down, Master Robert," gasped the bodyguard Jamal had insisted upon.

Robert slowed down and gave the man a chance to catch up with him again. "When did Prince Jamal leave for the desert?" he asked in Arabic, as the man drew alongside.

The guard wiped his beet-red face with the back of his arm. "About two hours ago," he gasped. "He wanted to try out Sultan, the new stallion, a present from Prince Muhrad."

Robert's eyes narrowed thoughtfully. He had told Jamal about the father of Abdul, the Bedouin. The sheik who raised Arabians in the high desert was the only lead they had. Frowning, he wished Jamal had told him about his plans to pay the man a visit. He wished he could have ridden with him.

Robert knew it could take days or even weeks to track down a nomad who didn't want to be found, but he and Marianne would have to leave in a matter of hours. And, now that Jamal was gone, there was no one who would keep him informed. Muhrad had refused all foreigners access to the terrorists' files.

What bothered Robert was that five men could have disappeared so easily without a trace. No fisherman had seen the major or his men. None of the caravans had reported strangers in the desert.

It was early yet, Robert thought, striding past a bed of roses in full bloom. The terrorists could have been hiding in one of the half-finished buildings that were shooting up everywhere. All buses and boats leaving Basjad were being searched. But Robert knew that if the men had split up they would be almost impossible to find.

He speared his fingers through his damp hair. Usually there were at least some trails, like reported thefts of food, clothing or cars. Damn, the men would have needed local currency to pay for those. Yet despite the ten-thousand *dirham* reward Emir Yussuf had posted, no one had come forward to claim it. It was as if the sandstorm had buried the terrorists.

Or as if someone had helped them to escape.

Thoughtfully Robert stopped at the end of the rose bed, idly touching a half-closed white bud. The major had supporters in Omari; he had hinted as much in one of their talks. Not everyone in Omari welcomed Yussuf's shift to the West. Last night, Jamal had mentioned several wealthy businessmen who would stand to lose a good deal of trade if the treaty were signed.

But only one man had had access to information about Robert's trip: Muhrad.

Robert stopped, untied the towel from around his waist and dried off his face, neck and arms. Apparently Jamal also suspected his half brother; that's why he had left during the night. If he found proof of Muhrad's involvement, old Yussuf would be furious. And how would an internal power struggle between the Emir and his heir affect the treaty? Robert flung the towel around his neck. For the moment they had nothing to go on but hunches and suspicions.

"Are you making another round?" the bodyguard asked.

"No. I'm going back upstairs." He wondered if Marianne was awake yet? She had looked so beautiful when he had left her, all rosy and flushed with sleep. He snapped off the rosebud and broke into a run again. They had at least an hour or two to themselves.

She wasn't in the room where he'd left her. He found her two doors down, packing her suitcase or messing it up, he couldn't decide which. She stuffed socks into corners and squeezed a pink sweater into the side, which bunched up the rest of the clothes into a mountain over which the lid then refused to close.

Grinning, Robert rested against the door frame and watched her lean on the lid. The gray satin robe she wore molded itself over her back as she tried to pull the zipper forward. He eyed the view with male appreciation. For a moment he was content to watch; he liked coming back and finding her here. "Want me to sit on it?" he finally asked when the zipper refused to round the corner.

Startled, she looked over her shoulder. Her frustration fled at the sight of him. His eyes were bright green with laughter. He was sweaty, and his T-shirt and shorts clung to his damp skin. His muscles still quivered from exertion. Only the bandages reminded her of the stiff and tired man who had escaped from the plane yesterday.

She wanted to run to him, but sudden shyness made her turn back to the suitcase. "I didn't hear you come back."

"I wonder why?" Chuckling, he came into the room.

"The presents take up too much space. Once they are gone I'll have plenty of room." With a hiss she gave up the struggle and turned back to him. "You wouldn't have room in your suitcase, would you?" she asked hopefully.

"Depends." Robert looked down at her teasingly. "What do I get for letting you make a mess of my bags?"

She lowered her lids and said lightly, "A nice thank you."

"How nice?"

She went on her toes and pecked his cheek. "Will this do?"

"I'm sure you can do better than that." Throwing the rose on the bed, he placed his hands around her waist, lifted her until her mouth was on level with his and kissed her hungrily. She tasted of mint and smelled of fresh pines. He realized that she had just taken a shower, but since she didn't seem to object that he was sweaty, he pressed her closer.

Her response was so satisfyingly eager that his body tightened with need. "Did you sleep well?" he asked as he bestowed small, teasing kisses on her throat.

"Yes." It was ridiculous to feel shy, Marianne told herself, but that was how she felt when he studied her. Shy, tongue-tied and not quite ready yet to let him see the love she felt must be blazing in her eyes. "Last night—I vaguely remember that you wanted to tell me something."

Robert put her back down on her feet and looked at her bent head. Last night . . . Hell, last night he'd been too tired to think logically. Last night had been emotional, and he felt uncomfortable with emotions. Now, in the clear light of morning, logic warned him that only a fool laid all of his cards on the table before the game was won. So he shrugged and said lightly, "Nothing important."

It had been important enough for him to make certain that she was awake enough to listen, Marianne thought, raising her head. What had happened since to make him change his mind? His face gave her no clues. Talk to me, she willed him, watching him pick up the rose.

But all he said was, "Happy Easter," as he handed it to her.

Easter was the beginning of spring, full of the promise of new life and a new beginning. Be patient, she told herself, inhaling the heady scent of the rose. And then she put her arms around his neck, drew his head down and kissed him. "Happy Easter."

It was the first kiss she had given him without being prompted, Robert thought, tightening his arms around her. He didn't count the moments right after his release, because she had been caught off balance. His tongue plunged into her mouth and prolonged the kiss. Breathless moments later he raised his head. "I need a shower," he said, reluctant to leave her for even five minutes. Then he scooped her up in his arms. "We're going to take a shower together."

"I already took mine," Marianne protested but threw one arm around his neck anyway.

"Not in the lotus pool." He kissed the protest from her mouth and carried her back down the hall. "We never got a chance to try it out."

Marianne felt a flutter of excitement building deep inside her. So he didn't regret last night after all. "Your bandages will get wet," she whispered, kissing him as they went.

"They're already soaked," Robert said, opening the door. This time he didn't stumble but made straight for the pool. He placed her on the wide ledge of the octagonal marble tub. While he'd carried her, her robe had opened at the neck, giving him a glimpse of swelling breasts. He brushed the fabric aside.

In the short time they had been apart, Marianne's thoughts had swayed between dreaming and dread. Now, as his hands smoothed over her skin and stopped to explore each curve and each hollow as if he'd never touched them before, she forgot everything. In a second, his T-shirt was on the floor and his shorts soon followed, along with her robe. Joining her on the ledge, he kicked off his shoes.

"What about your socks?" Marianne idly watched a creamy pink lotus blossom float past.

"What socks?" Robert asked her.

"The ones you're wearing," she said and waited until he bent down to roll them off. Then she scooped up the flower and placed it on his dark hair.

He punished her with a kiss. "You want to play games?" he asked, tilting her backward then shaking his head like a dog until the flower dropped between her breasts.

"No," she gasped, then wiggled to dislodge the wet blossom. She didn't dare take her hands off Robert's shoulder. "You're not playing fair."

"Want me to stop?"

"Yes," she laughed, eyeing her chances of escaping from him. If he loosened his hold just a little bit, she might be able to get her legs over the top.

"All right." The wicked gleam in his eyes should have warned her. He took his hands off her, and she nearly dropped into the scented water. But, with a swiftness that took him by surprise, she wedged her feet against the side and, pushing with her legs, unbalanced him.

He toppled over. But as he hit the water, his arm dragged her close. Beneath the surface their lips met and clung. They surfaced, their laughter stilled, passion and need flaring so strongly even the water could not douse their flames.

Marianne's arms tightened around Robert's neck as a stab of pleasure ran through her. Her hands slid down his shoulders to his sides. He was still sensitive there, she thought, feeling his convulsive response. There were other spots. Lightly she raked her nails through the hairs on his chest, then circled the nipples until they grew hard. She traced the thin line of hair down to his navel and tasted it with her tongue.

"Enough," Robert groaned, dropping to his knees. His flesh burned with her caresses, but he felt a vague uneasiness. Never before had she excited him so completely, giving him pleasure almost beyond bearing. But there was something missing, some indefinable essence he couldn't put into words.

He drew her against him, and, placing her head on one of the pillows, he drew her legs around his waist. He entered her smoothly, powerfully, watching her face as he filled her. She shook her head in wild abandon. Her hands reached for him and drew his head closer to her. Robert surged deeper, wanting to possess all of her and touch every part of her.

Gasping, she moved with him, pleasure expanding with every movement of his body. Robert filled her, covered her totally. She cried his name at the last moment and then she came apart in his arms. With a tight, hard smile Robert found his own release. "I adore you," he whispered, gathering her close.

A while later, the phone rang. Robert reached for the receiver. "Sullivan."

"Hi, Dad. Happy Easter."

At the sound of Bobby's voice, Marianne sat up straight.

"Happy Easter to you," Robert said and pulled Marianne back into his arms. "Relax," he murmured into her ear. "He can't see us." To Bobby he said, "Isn't it a little early for you to be up?"

"If you're still in bed, you're getting lazy," Bobby laughed. "It's not that early, and I've already been out to gather eggs and feed the chickens."

"Easter eggs?" Robert teased.

Bobby's laughter brought a smile to Marianne's lips. "No. Real ones," he scoffed. "I'll tell you a secret. I haven't believed in bunnies and Santa Claus for years."

"I heard that," Marianne spoke into the phone.

"Do I still get to look for eggs?" Bobby asked. There was a pause and then he said, "I just wanted to talk to you and see if you're all right. Are you still coming tonight?"

"We'll be there around six." Robert heard the slight uncertainty in Bobby's voice, so he made his voice sound soothing and firm.

"Good." There was a sound of relief. "I'll see you then. Can I talk to Mom?"

"She's right here."

Marianne almost snatched the phone from Robert in her eagerness and wished him a Happy Easter. "I'm afraid the chocolate eggs I brought with me melted in the heat. I threw them out yesterday."

"That's okay...." There was a pause, then Bobby asked. "Are you sleeping with Dad in the same bed? Is that why you're not up?"

Marianne almost dropped the phone. Her eyes flew to Robert as if seeking an answer. He was grinning at her, the fat, pleased grin of a cat. "Try and get out of that one," he whispered.

Marianne flicked some water at him before she spoke into the phone. "No. We're sitting in the lotus—in the Jacuzzi."

"You mean you're taking a bath with Dad?"

Robert was laughing openly now.

"No." Marianne was trying to keep back a chuckle. "We're relaxing."

"Oh, you're wearing bathing suits."

"Did anyone ever tell you to mind your own business?" Marianne asked her son.

"Sure," Bobby said unrepentantly. "This is my business. See you tonight, Mom and Dad."

When Marianne handed Robert the phone there was a taut look on her face and her hand was trembling. "He has us already married again. We have to be careful not to raise his hopes." When he didn't protest but merely turned to replace the phone, Marianne shivered in the warmly scented tub. She climbed out, reached for one of the fluffy pink towels and wrapped it around her.

And what about my own hopes? Robert wanted to fling at her. Hadn't he shown her in every way he knew that he loved her? "I'll talk to him." Robert rested his head on the edge of the pool and closed his eyes. Not once, even in the heat of passion, had she told him that she loved him in return. That had been the cause of his uneasiness.

Chapter 10

The experts on hostage syndromes had cautioned Marianne that for a while after coming home she would feel strange. They had warned her that she would have nightmares. They had cautioned her that for a time the only persons she would feel comfortable with would be others who had experienced the same kind of trauma.

And Marianne had been skeptical. The cases they had talked about were people who had been kept prisoner for weeks or months, not for a mere twenty-four hours like herself. Those people had been abused and tortured over prolonged periods of time, not merely slapped once like she'd been. She had told herself that once she was home, the feeling of disorientation would fade like an early morning mist with the rising sun. In the familiar security of her own bed the nightmares would cease.

She had been wrong.

She still had nightmares. Every time she closed her eyes, she saw Hamid wrinkling the doily, twisting it, over and over again. She saw Jimmy Dobson. And she saw Robert being hunted by a faceless man.

Sometimes she wondered if she would ever feel safe again.

Impatiently she pulled the blue-and-white striped sweatshirt over her head and drew on a pair of acid-washed jeans. The face reflected in the oval mirror of her bedroom was the same. Perhaps a little paler. Perhaps a little drawn, but that was to be expected. The two-day trip to Chamonix had been emotional, and the flight back to the States exhausting. She was suffering from jet lag, she told herself. Now that she was back in Stony Brook, everything should be fine.

Only it wasn't. Not yet, anyway.

Her family was concerned and loving and protective. They were smothering her. If she stood, her mother told her to sit. If she started to empty the trash, her father took the bag out of her hands. When she'd wanted to take out the sloop yesterday afternoon, Colin had told her that the breeze was too strong. If she put on makeup they looked for signs of poor sleep. If shadows did show under her eyes, they told her to lie down. She felt out of place even here at home. It was as if the "terrible ordeal," as everyone called it, had turned her into a stranger.

Even Bobby was on his best behavior, Marianne thought, pulling a brush through her hair. Although last night he'd almost thrown a tantrum when Robert had sent him to bed. He had become used to being treated with kid gloves and now resented the return to normalcy.

The only person she *did* feel comfortable with was Robert.

He didn't require constant reassurances that she was fine. He didn't wrap her in cotton wool and tell her to rest. He teased her and made her laugh. And sometimes, when she looked at him above Bobby's head, she found him watching her with the same kind of hunger that pulsed through her.

But if the experts were right on all other accounts, how much of her relationship with Robert was real? How much were her feelings caused by the experience of the hijacking? Had the night in Omari been merely a celebration of life after they had been near death? Was her need to be close to Robert another symptom of the hostage syndrome?

She opened the pine dresser and withdrew a pair of white cotton socks. She knew she was going to need time to put her relationship with Robert into perspective. What had happened in Omari had been beautiful. She didn't want to lose the importance of it, but she also didn't want to build it into more than it had been.

Grimacing, she sat down on the quilted spread covering her four-poster bed, pulled on the socks, then bent down to reach for her deck shoes. And how did Robert feel? she wondered, tying the laces. Over the past six days they had been constantly surrounded by family. It had rained the two days they had been in Chamonix and they hadn't even been able to go for a walk, much less talk privately. Since their arrival in Stony Brook yesterday, friends and relatives had come and gone constantly, and reporters had been hounding the house until her parents had finally taken the phone off the hook.

In a few hours there would be a press conference. Later, the family would descend for a combined Easter and homecoming celebration. She glanced out her window. The white muslin curtains framing it were waving in the mild breeze coming off Long Island Sound. The oak and maple trees were budding, and, although it was barely seven o'clock, sail and fishing boats were out on the water. Marianne saw two small birds fly past, pine needles and grass in their beaks. They were building a nesting place behind the black shutters framing her window. Their chirping and squabbling had woken Marianne at dawn.

She was going to escape if only for a little while, she thought, opening the door to the long, dim hall.

Inside the house everything was still quiet. Marianne had heard her father leave for the boat yard about thirty minutes ago. Robert was also up and had followed her father downstairs within minutes. There was a creaky floorboard beneath the thick light green carpet in front of his door. Marianne had also heard it last night when Bobby had sneaked into Robert's room.

Now Marianne stepped over that board carefully as she went to check on her son. Bobby and Robert had shared a room in the farmhouse in France, because there had only been four bedrooms there. But Marianne had hoped that once her son was again in familiar surroundings, he would prefer his own bed. Bending over his curled-up form in the middle of the queen-size bed, she wondered if Robert had felt as frustrated as she had when she'd heard the creaks.

Sneaking down the stairs, she followed the scent of coffee into the sunny, oak-lined kitchen. Mary Lloyd, affectionately called Granny by her large family, was sitting at the butcher-block table beneath the bow window, her hands cradling a white mug that read I Love Granny. She wore the fluffy pink robe and matching slippers Marianne had given her for her seventieth birthday last year. Her gray curls still retained some streaks of gold. Apart from a few laugh lines around her eyes and mouth, her skin stretched smoothly over the high cheekbones Marianne had inherited from her.

"You're up early." Bending down, Marianne kissed her cheek and breathed in the familiar scent of the lavender Granny grew in her garden and which she used in sachets.

"You know I never sleep in." Granny picked up the white-and-blue-flowered thermos, poured coffee into one of

the mugs already on the table and handed it to Marianne.
"But I wasn't the first one down. Don and Robert were up
before me. Robert must have made the coffee," she said,
taking an appreciative sip. "Your father always makes col-
ored water for me. If I'm allowed only two cups of coffee a
day, I want it to be strong."

"You're not supposed to have any coffee at all," Marianne said dryly, sliding into an oak Windsor chair with a
cushion that matched the blue country print of the curtains.

Granny dismissed Marianne's concerns with a slightly
sheepish grin. "Doctors don't know everything." She fixed
Marianne with a sharp, penetrating stare. "I'll bet they filled
your head with a bunch of nonsense when you were in
Frankfurt."

Marianne looked out the window and past the bed of
bright red tulips and yellow daffodils bordering the patio.
They were swaying slightly in the gentle breeze. Two gray
squirrels were chasing each other across the lawn. "I don't
know," she said, wishing she could dismiss the experts' ad-
vice as easily as Granny did her son's. "I'm still trying to
figure it all out."

"What's there to figure out?" Granny asked, looking at
Marianne's pensive profile. "The only thing that's important is how you feel. I *know* that two cups of coffee a day
won't really harm me or I'd never touch the stuff again."

"Oh, Granny, I wish I could believe that how I feel was
all that matters, that it was as simple as that." Marianne
shook her head from side to side. "I'm scared of making the
same mistake all over again."

"If you're talking about your marriage, then you have
good reason to be scared," Granny said bluntly, emptying
her mug. She picked up the thermos for a refill, then reluctantly put it back down. "Personally I always thought that

your divorce was the mistake. You never stopped loving Robert, or you would have found someone else.'' She pushed herself to her feet. "But I never thought it was a good idea to meddle in someone else's business, and I'm not going to start now." Her slippers slid softly over the tile floor as she walked to the sink. She was silent as she rinsed out the mug and placed it into the dishwasher. Then, straightening, she said, "Be honest with yourself, Marianne, and then ask yourself why Robert is still here when he should have returned to Washington almost immediately." She walked to the door, then added, "Or better still, ask Robert himself."

Marianne drank her coffee thoughtfully. She hadn't needed Granny to point out that she had never stopped loving Robert. She had known it for some time. And since that night in Omari she could no longer deceive herself that Robert wanted her only for Bobby's sake. An intensely private man like Robert didn't bare his soul and leave himself vulnerable unless he cared, and cared deeply. A tough and cautious man didn't spill out his emotions even under stress unless he trusted, and trusted deeply. He had opened up to her in ways she had never before thought possible.

Yet, he was holding back.

Wearily she pushed her hair away from her face. She had never been passive, yet for the last few days she had been content to drift with the currents. No wonder her parents had treated her with kid gloves. If Bobby had slunk around the house like a ghost she would have rushed him to the pediatrician. What was wrong with her?

If she wanted Robert, then why was she sitting here, reluctant to go in search of him? Was she going to dwell on the past indefinitely? Was she going to allow her doubts and fears to hold her back and possibly lose the one person she wanted so desperately?

But what if she had misread him? Robert was as human as anyone else. She knew that Jimmy Dobson's death had shaken him badly. What if he already regretted the confidences he had shared? Was that why he had been acting more like a brother than a man who wanted her?

Abruptly Marianne finished her coffee and carried her mug to the dishwasher. If she had wanted guarantees out of life she should have fallen in love with a man with a nine-to-five job, not a man who was as unpredictable and as challenging as the sea. She was caught between common sense and wild emotions, and she would have to make a choice soon. Robert couldn't stay on indefinitely, and before he left they would have to come to some understanding. She went in search of him.

Robert was sitting at the desk in Don Lloyd's oak-lined study. "I'll be in Washington tomorrow," he promised Howard Barton, who was on the other end of the line. Robert's eyes roamed over the collection of racing trophies and design awards lining two of the paneled walls and flanking the fireplace. He'd never felt less eager to return to work.

"I was hoping you would," Howard Barton said crisply. "I need you here. Hamid, Yasser and Mahmad were executed this morning." Robert detected the faint trace of distaste at what must have been a gruesome spectacle. "The ATD finally traced their places of employment to here in the States. Your hunches were right on the button, Robert. Yasser was a sociology major at the graduate center in New York. Hamid and Mahmad worked for one of those small cargo outfits at Kennedy Airport, which explains how they gained access to the plane. And I believe we finally have a lead on that sheik. His name is Selim. We even have some photos of him and his sons that were taken last year when he visited Morocco."

Robert's eyes gleamed at the news. It was a step in the right direction, but there was still no trace of the major yet. *I think I'm going to kill you before this is over.* The major's words still haunted him. Robert didn't know why the terrorist hadn't finished him off before he'd made his escape. Perhaps in the end he'd channeled all his energies into getting away. Whatever his reasons, the major had made a big mistake, because Robert still believed that the world wasn't big enough for both of them. Robert had no intention of spending the rest of his life looking over his shoulder. "I've already made arrangements with the ATD to look through its files."

"Excellent. Dobson's funeral is on Wednesday, and I'd like to have some leads before we leave for Dallas." Barton hesitated briefly, then went on, "Gloria sends her regards. She asked me to tell you that she'd be glad to have Mrs. Sullivan's company, if Mrs. Sullivan feels strong enough to make the trip."

An invitation from Gloria Barton was almost like a royal summons. Robert truly appreciated Gloria's kindness and the offer to take Marianne under her wing, but he doubted that Marianne was ready yet to take such a step. At the moment, she was still dealing with nightmares, and he didn't want to add to her stress. And above all else, he wanted to keep her safe. Still, the temptation to leap at the offer and spend a few hours alone with her was great. Security at the funeral would be so tight even an expert like the major would be foolish to risk anything. "Please give my regards to Gloria," he said evasively, "but I'm not certain yet what Marianne's plans are."

Marianne's moods were unpredictable these days, Robert thought a few minutes later, after hanging up the phone.

One moment she was laughing and teasing and the next she would be silent and withdrawn. Yesterday afternoon, while he had been on the phone, he had watched her and Bobby race on skateboards down the hill. When he had gone looking for her a little while later, she had been sitting quietly at the kitchen table, writing thank-notes for the many letters and flowers they had received.

Their lack of privacy was frustrating.

A week had passed since Easter and their departure from Omari. A whole week of being with Marianne and yet not being with her. During the day they acted like a family, but at night they were still divorced. It was a situation he wanted changed. If he'd had his way, he would have taken Marianne and Bobby to Washington, locked the door and disconnected the phone. Perhaps he would still do just that once the major had been caught.

The press had blown up their reunion into the romance of the month. Robert had hoped that public interest in their private lives would die down, but so far it hadn't. Perhaps after their meeting with reporters this afternoon, they would be allowed some privacy.

Frustration aside, he had enjoyed the last few days with Marianne, Bobby and the family. Marianne's relatives on either side of the Atlantic were down-to-earth people, friendly and warm. Robert had been prepared for some awkwardness, or resentment, or even hostility, but there had been none.

Maybe the time had come for them to talk, Robert thought, getting to his feet and pushing his hands into the pockets of his jeans. Abruptly he crossed the study, determined to make her notice him. There was so little time left, and he had no idea when he would be back once he left for Washington. It could well be a month before he found a couple of days to be with her again. He could handle that, but only if she gave him something to take with him.

Opening the door, he saw her coming down the hall. She had lost weight, he thought. She looked frail, and she walked slowly. But when she saw him, she smiled and her step quickened.

"You're up early," he said, extending his hand. She stepped past his hand and straight into his arms, as if she had missed him the last few days. His arms closed around her, folding her against him.

"I've already had a cup of coffee with Granny." She tilted her head back. He looked tired, she thought. Needing to touch him, she reached up and brushed back his unruly hair. "You work too hard," she said softly. "Come sailing with me? We can pick up fresh croissants and coffee at the deli and have breakfast out on the water."

His arms tightened, drawing her close. "That's the best offer I've had in days," he said, kissing her. He tried not to read too much significance into her having come to him. But when her mouth opened beneath his with the same need that pulsed through him, his hope soared. For a moment he held her pressed against him, wanting to prolong and deepen the kiss. Then he heard doors open and close upstairs and raised his head. "Let's sneak out of here," he muttered, taking her hand and drawing her toward the garage.

"I didn't know how much I'd missed this," Marianne shouted a half hour later. Her hands were on the sailboat's tiller, and her face was raised into the stiff breeze and the sun burned her skin.

It was one of those rare summerlike April mornings that drew Long Islanders out on the water. Motor yachts and fishing boats crisscrossed one another's paths. In the distance, Marianne could see the coastline of Connecticut and the ferry boat on its first run from Port Jefferson to Bridgeport. As she listened to the periodic snap of the sails above her head and to the clean sound of the hull slicing through the choppy water, the nightmares faded.

Robert had let her take the tiller when they'd cast off. Instinctively he had known that she needed to be in control of their destination. He watched her turn slightly away from the wind and adjust the mainsheet to angle it for maximum thrust as she had taught him so long before.

"It's good to be home," she shouted as the sloop gained more speed. She laughed out loud as the sails filled.

"Yes." Robert leaned back and put one arm on the railing, contentment filling him. In the hallway she had looked soft and frail, and he had wanted to protect her. Now she looked warm, desirable and tempting, and he wanted to make love with her.

"I should feel guilty slipping away like this." Marianne laughed as saltwater sprayed her face. She brushed her hair back from her face, only to have the wind toss it right back. "But I'm enjoying this too much." Impulsively she leaned forward and placed a hand on the sleeve of the white sweatshirt he wore. "I am glad you're here."

"Are you?" His eyes narrowed. Over the last few days he had often wished he could read her as easily as he had been able to in the past. Sometimes he had looked into her eyes and seen the same hunger and need that was burning in him. But there had also been times when she had deliberately avoided his gaze.

"Of course. I know you are impatient to get back to Washington," she said lightly, "but your stay with us has helped Bobby tremendously. Did he sleep well last night?"

"Like a rock." As much as he loved his son, Robert didn't want to discuss him now. "I didn't, though," he said, deciding to bring their relationship out into the open.

Nothing could dissipate the constant dull ache her presence brought to him. He hoped that she burned with only a fraction of the frustration and need that disturbed his sleep. Selfishly he prayed that she also didn't sleep well because she missed him.

It was a need that had grown over the years. He realized that now. Repressing that need had only sharpened its edges. There had been years when he'd thought that his desire had eased. There had been months when he had fought that hunger so successfully that he hadn't thought of her for days at a time. But since he had touched her and tasted her again, his passion had become impossible to fight. And when she was close, the ache became a torment.

"I didn't sleep well, either," she admitted, surprising him. And then she rocked him a little further by adding, "I waited for you last night."

He thought of the hours of frustration, the tossing and turning, and smiled ruefully. "And I waited for an invitation," he countered softly.

He had never given her a choice before, he thought soberly, fighting the need to reach for her. This time he was determined to take their relationship one step at a time.

"You never waited for one before." She tore her gaze from his face to watch a sea gull settle on the waves.

"I didn't need one before. We were married. Besides, I'll bet every family member was listening for that floorboard to squeak in front of my door. I prefer a little more privacy."

Marianne bore to the right, luffing the mainsail, and the sloop slowed down. Why had he really stayed away? She doubted it was propriety. If her room had been next to her parents and if the house had been of average size, she would have understood his reluctance. But there were nine bedrooms and five bathrooms separating her from the master suite. Apart from her parents and Bobby, Granny had been the only overnight guest. Colin had moved out of the house years ago and now lived in the apartment over the garage.

Which left the only other possibility, she thought, pain searing through her. He wanted her, but not enough to change his life. He was a man used to coming and going as he pleased. She had accepted that years ago, but she couldn't settle for crumbs again.

When she turned back to him, she had stopped smiling. "I've been wanting to talk to you. But there never seems to be a private moment."

Robert felt a shiver of apprehension and looked at her sharply. "What about?"

"Several things." Marianne watched a sea gull settle on the waves, then turned back to him. "For one, I never thanked you for getting me off the plane."

He watched the wind tousle her hair and wanted to soothe it back. "I believe you did," he said coolly. He wanted to shake her for reducing that night in Omari to gratitude. Damn it, it had been so much more, even if she wasn't ready to admit that yet.

"Did I? I don't remember." Marianne shot him a swift searching look. Robert's face showed no emotion, and she sighed with frustration. "I have been thinking a lot about the past." She raised her voice above the wind. "I always blamed you for the divorce." When he looked at her with guarded eyes, she went on swiftly before she lost her courage. "Oh, I admitted to a few minor mistakes, but it seemed so much easier to find fault with you when our marriage failed. Looking back, I realize that we were both caught up in circumstances beyond our control. You were always the dominant partner, and for a while I was content to let you make all the decisions. But I grew up. Perhaps if we had lived together day by day, the changes would have come naturally, drawing us closer together instead of splitting us apart.''

"That's very generous of you," Robert said quietly, searching her profile and wondering what would come next. "So now we've wiped the slate clean. Where do we go from here?"

She looked at him then. Things weren't working out as she'd planned. Robert wasn't a man to sit back and let someone else take the initiative, and his apparent willingness now made her uneasy. "I want us to be friends," she said uncertainly, wishing he didn't look so remote. "I've managed my own affairs for so long, I don't think I would be content in a relationship in which I did not have equal rights." She bore to the right, toward shore. There was a cove, a small private place not far away, one of the few that so far had escaped Long Island's building boom.

Robert adjusted the sail once again, then turned back to her. He needed so much more from her than friendship. But perhaps she was right and they would have to deal with the past one more time.

"During that last year, I'd thought about handing in my resignation," he said somberly. "But after you left, there seemed no point, even though I'd lost my taste for living on the edge." He hesitated briefly because he still wasn't comfortable baring his soul, then forged ahead. "When I quit the anti-terrorist division, I told myself that I was doing it for Bobby, because I didn't want to become a stranger to my son. But the truth is that even then I wanted you back. Since the first time we went sailing, there's never been anyone else for me." He saw her eyes widen with joyful surprise and he smiled ruefully, wishing he had opened up to her a long time ago. He leaned toward her and brushed his knuckles lightly across her cheek, wanting to drop the anchor and make love to her there. "This is where it all started. We've come full circle now. I realize that the rules will have to change if we decide on a second run.''

"How much longer can you stay?'' Marianne queried as she impatiently watched the shore come closer.

"Trying to get rid of me?'' Robert asked lightly, studying her reaction carefully.

Her eyes widened, and she shook her head. Her artless "Don't be silly'' was, if not amorous, still very satisfying to Robert.

Marianne rubbed one hand on the mahogany rail and chose her next words carefully. "I've enjoyed your company. And Bobby has been happy. But I know you can't stay indefinitely.''

Then come back to Washington with me, Robert wanted to ask. He was planning to draw her into his life slowly, not overwhelm her as he had done before. Patience wasn't easy, especially not when he knew he'd have to leave soon. Only the knowledge that this time there was no room for mistakes made him hold the words back. He was afraid that if he pushed too hard she would retreat, and he couldn't bear to lose her a second time. It was his life he was fighting for, but the frustration was slowly killing him. "I leave early tomorrow morning. I have to be in Washington by ten.''

"So soon.'' The words were out before she could guard against them. She had hoped that he would stay for at least another day. So far they'd barely had a moment to themselves.

So she would miss him. Robert felt like smiling at the thought. "I should have been back Friday,'' he explained, adjusting the canvas. "The negotiations with Omari have been delayed until the week after next. But there are some other things that I need to do.''

From the grim set of his mouth and the hard look in his eyes, Marianne knew his intentions. "You're going to get involved in the search for the major and his men," she said. He would be gone for days, maybe weeks.

"I want him," Robert said, control slipping, his eyes hard with the need for revenge. "He killed a good man." And as long as he's free he's going to be a threat, Robert thought, taking a deep breath of salt air. "There's another reason why we have to find him. He had supporters in Omari. That's why he and his men were able to disappear so easily. I need to know who they are before our government commits itself to spending billions of dollars."

Marianne frowned. Puzzled, she asked, "Are you concerned about the safety of the base? I always thought that protection is the duty of the host country. I know that for instance New York is responsible for safeguarding the UN."

Robert gave her a swift, startled look, struck by the quick leap of her mind. Another few words and she would guess why it was so important to find the major's supporters. "Usually that's true," he agreed cautiously. "But those points still have to be ironed out."

His answer dissatisfied her. There was more behind it than he was telling her. "What about Hamid and the other two men? Surely they must know something."

"They were executed this morning," Robert explained flatly.

Marianne felt a swift surge of relief at the news. It was terrible to be able to breathe easier because men had died. But deep down she'd always feared that somehow Hamid would manage to escape and come looking for them. Now she did not need to fear for Robert's safety nearly as much when he returned to Omari. "Did you find out anything about them?"

Over the last few days Robert had come to trust her as he trusted himself. Without hesitation, he repeated Howard Barton's words. "Without a treaty, old Yussuf won't allow us a look at their files.'' Not that those files would reveal anything to support his suspicions, Robert thought grimly. ''Jimmy Dobson's funeral is on Wednesday,'' he added harshly. ''What am I going to tell his widow? That I don't know who killed her husband? I can't even give her a name.''

Beneath the control she could hear the anger in his voice, the bitterness and frustration. Swiftly she took one hand off the tiller and placed it on his arm. ''Don't blame yourself for his death,'' she said softly. ''You did all you could to get us off the plane.''

He closed his eyes and made a negative movement with his head. ''The major wanted to get rid of you because you were a thorn in his side. I often wonder if he would have released some of the other hostages, if I had pushed a little harder.''

For a moment she saw his control slip and his eyes burn with pain. ''I doubt it,'' she said firmly, coaxing the sloop into the cove. ''If he'd considered freeing anyone else, it would have been the crew. Certainly not one of you.''

Marianne's words were almost a repetition of Howard Barton's reply. But that didn't ease his own conscience or make Jimmy's death easier to bear, he thought grimly. Getting to his feet, he secured the lines and dropped the anchor.

With the sloop riding gently on the waves, Marianne turned to him and asked, ''Do you want me to come with you to the funeral?'' She had struggled with the decision long and hard. To appear with Robert together at the funeral would be almost like a public announcement that they were planning to get married again. His colleagues and friends would especially think so.

Whenever Robert mentioned the future, his words were vague. It could mean everything or nothing at all. But, for the first time ever, she sensed that he needed her. She wanted to be the one to take the weary look from his eyes and make him smile again.

"We leave at 6 a.m.," Robert said offhandedly. Did she know she was killing him with her sweetness and understanding? He put his hands lightly on her shoulders and drew her close. "You'd have to come to Washington the night before."

"If you're busy I can always stay at a hotel," Marianne said, placing her head against his chest. Beneath her cheek she could hear his heart pounding. She hadn't known how much her offer would mean to him or she would have discussed it with him the moment she'd found out that Briggs and Sommers, the accounting firm she worked for, was giving her another week to recuperate.

"I'll give you a key to the house before I leave." His arms tightened, even while making it possible for her to withdraw at the last moment. "There will be six of us. Howard Barton, his wife Gloria, the senator from Texas, Colton, his wife and the congressman. In fact, Gloria already asked if you were coming with us," he added lightly.

"And what did you tell her?" Marianne tilted her head and stared at him curiously..

"That I was going to throw you over my shoulder and carry you onto the plane." Robert's eyes shone bright green when she didn't retreat.

"You didn't. Did you?"

"I was tempted to," Robert teased, brushing her lips. "But, no, I merely said that I had no idea what your plans were. I thought it might be too much for you."

"Don't you start, too. I've had enough coddling from everyone else to last me a lifetime," Marianne protested lightly. Then another thought occurred to her. Perhaps she had misread Robert after all. "If you don't want me there, say so," she said.

"Stop behaving like an idiot," Robert said huskily, capturing her lips. "There will be a certain amount of curiosity, and I wasn't certain if you were ready to face the gossip. And then there's Bobby to consider."

"Mother will keep him," Marianne said. "He'll understand that I want to go to the funeral," she whispered, drawing his mouth back to hers.

He swallowed the words of frustration and the need to force a promise from her now. With powerful urgency he drugged her senses until nothing existed between them but the heat of desire. Lifting her high in his arms, he braced himself against the swell of the boat. There was one way he could show her how much she meant to him. "Make love with me."

The cabin was small with barely enough room between the bunks to stand. But it was private. It had been a week since they had been truly alone, and the desire they had tried to hide from family members now slipped its leash. There was no laughter as there had been that night in Omari. There were no words, no explanations and no hesitation as they touched. There was only hunger and need, sharpened by the knowledge that tomorrow Robert would leave.

Their sweaters were discarded and their jeans followed, and then they were reaching for each other. The kiss was deep, penetrating, hot. Their hands were urgent, moving restlessly over each other. When they broke apart, breathless and shaking with the force of their feelings, what Marianne saw in Robert's eyes made her catch her breath. Perhaps he would never give her beautiful words, but a look from him said so much more. She stepped back into his arms and pressed her lips to the skin above his heart.

He groaned at the moist caress of her tongue and, sitting down, shifted her between his parted legs. Her proud breasts teased him, beckoned him. Someday, he would watch another child of theirs suckle there. And this time nothing would prevent him from being home to watch that child grow up. A daughter would be nice, he thought, cupping her breasts. Tenderly he took Marianne's nipple into his mouth, caressing until she groaned.

His hair felt like strong, resilient silk as she ran her fingers through it. His mouth seemed to cherish her, and his hands were trembling with the need to keep some control. She wanted to slip beneath the restraint that always seemed to stand between them. With firm yet gentle hands she pushed at his shoulders until he fell back onto the narrow bunk. His skin gleamed in the light of the sun shining into the cabin. Bending over him, she trailed her fingernails lightly over his skin. When he groaned, her lips soothed him. When he reached for her, she moved just beyond him. She teased, she laughed, she tortured. His skin grew damp and his breath came out in gasps. In all the years of marriage she had never taken the initiative, not like this, seducing him, stripping him of control, leaving him with raw emotions. Vulnerable. Yet for the first time in his life he didn't fight the feeling.

Finally, on the brink of reason, he reached for her, pulled her until she covered him. With a smooth powerful twist he rolled over and caught her beneath him. Heaving, poised above her, he stared at her with burning eyes. "I adore you," he ground out, crushing her mouth beneath his.

It wasn't enough. Not any more, Marianne thought, raking the ridges of his back lightly with her nails. But it was so much more than he had given her in the past.

Then Robert was taking the initiative. No longer could she think. She only felt desire so hot her skin felt scorched and her lungs burned. He took her, filling her, sending her over the first peak. And before she had time to recover he sent her spiraling higher and higher until she cried out in ecstasy... and in love.

Chapter 11

"Where did you and Dad go this morning?" Bobby asked, bouncing on the edge of Marianne's bed. He was dressed much like his father, in jeans and white cotton-knit sweater.

"We sailed past Wildwood State Park." Studying her son's pouting face in the mirror, Marianne tried to suppress a grin. Bobby was upset because they'd left him behind, but she was too happy to feel any guilt. "I looked in on you before we left. You were sleeping so soundly I didn't want to wake you up." With a few deft strokes, she darkened the tips of her lashes, adding lightly, "You must have been very tired. All this moving around at night is wearing you out. Don't you like your own bed anymore?"

A big yawn split Bobby's face. "It's all right," he grumbled. "But I like to be with Dad, and during the day I hardly see him. He's always on the phone. Did you know that he's leaving tomorrow?"

Replacing the cap, Marianne turned around. "Yes. But he's coming back soon," she said soothingly.

An eager light brightened Bobby's eyes. "To stay? I mean, are you and Dad getting married again?"

Marianne put the mascara down and swiftly crossed the carpet. Sitting down on the bed, she hugged her son. "Isn't it enough that we are friends?" she asked gently, brushing his hair off his forehead.

Shaking his head, Bobby thrust out his rounded jaw. "Friends don't get married," he said stubbornly, gnawing on his lip. "You always say that there's nothing you wouldn't do for me. Well," he half pleaded, half challenged her, "How about marrying Dad again? If you do, I won't ask for a birthday *or* Christmas present this year."

She hugged him tightly, wishing she could answer him with a simple yes. But she could hardly tell her son that he was one of the main reasons why she was determined not to rush things this time. Besides, Robert hadn't asked her yet. "I know you want your Dad to live with us. But at the moment that isn't possible. Dad is going to be very busy in the next few weeks. And I also will have a lot of work waiting for me."

Bobby sighed. "Dad said the same thing," he muttered, tugging on the laces of his high tops. "Is that what you were discussing on the boat?"

"Among other things," Marianne said evasively. Because Bobby's head was turned away from her, he didn't see the faint flush tingeing his mother's face. Dropping a kiss on his wavy hair, Marianne walked back to the mirror and added some blush to her cheeks. Not that she needed it at the moment, she thought ruefully.

"Is that what you're going to tell the reporters? That you're friends?" Bobby slid off the bed and walked to the door.

"I doubt that they're going to ask such personal questions." At least she hoped they wouldn't, Marianne prayed, opening a small box and taking out the diamond studs Robert had given her the first Christmas they'd been married. She hadn't worn them since their divorce. "Isn't Uncle Colin waiting downstairs to take you fishing?" she asked, putting the studs into her ears.

"Yeah." Bobby stuck out his jaw, looking much like Robert when he was determined to have his way. "But I want to say here and watch when you talk to the reporters."

On their way back to the dock, Marianne and Robert had decided that it would be wiser for Bobby to be absent when the reporters arrived. Their son was so eager to see them married he might decide to take matters in his own hands and state his wishes before the cameras. Running a brush through her hair, Marianne said, "I thought you wanted to try out that new fishing pole Uncle Colin bought while you were gone."

"Did he show it to you?" Bobby asked, his determination wavering. When Marianne shook her head, he explained, "It's a real beauty and strong enough to catch a shark with." When Colin called his name, he slid off the bed. "If I catch one, will you cook it?" he asked, the heel of his unlaced high tops dragging over the carpet as he walked to the door.

"Only if you promise to eat it," Marianne called after him. Although Bobby liked to catch fish, he wasn't very fond of eating them.

"How does it taste?" Bobby asked cautiously over his shoulder opening the door.

"A little like fresh tuna."

Bobby wrinkled his nose. "I'll think about it," he said, running toward the stairs.

"Don't trip over those shoelaces," Marianne called after him. Leaning over the banister, she asked her brother, "Colin, can you get him to tie his sneakers?"

"Don't fuss, Mom. Only geeks tie their shoes."

"Bobby, don't talk back to your mother," Colin admonished. "If you don't want to fasten those laces, you'll have to wear rubber boots."

"Oh, okay," Bobby grumbled, thumping after his uncle.

Marianne waited until she heard Colin ask Bobby to carry the tackle box to the car, then returned to her room. She was nervous. For an instant she wanted to sneak out the back door with Bobby and Colin and leave Robert to face the reporters alone. Robert was used to dealings with the press. But if she wanted to fit into Robert's life, she would have to take this first step, she thought, closing the door.

After removing her robe, she took the pink-and-white dress she had ironed earlier from the hanger and slipped it over her head. She had chosen it carefully for color and style. The pink added a little color to her pale skin, and the blouson-type top and loose-fitting slim skirt hid the fact that she had lost a few pounds. She wanted to look cool and confident, not fragile. Inside, though, she was pure jelly.

It wasn't so much the upcoming interview that made her nervous. After everything she had gone through, she could handle a few nosy questions. It was Robert who was keeping her on edge. She wished she could read what went on behind those green eyes. He had given her passion. He had given her answers. He had done everything to show her how much she meant to him. But she needed more, she thought.

Was it only a week ago that she had promised herself that desire would be enough, that she wouldn't ask for anything more if he only returned to her safe and sound? It still was, she told herself, fiercely fastening the wide belt around her waist. But she couldn't suppress a small shiver of apprehension. Without love there was no comfort, no security. Robert wasn't a shallow person, yet she kept wondering whether he would care for her less if she made a blunder. Rationally she could tell herself that she was a fool, but when it came to Robert, she wasn't thinking logically at all.

When she heard his knock on the door, she took a deep breath, then glanced into the mirror to make certain that her smile was firmly fixed in place. "Come in," she called, swiftly smoothing out the wrinkled bedspread.

She looked like a breath of spring air, cool and poised, Robert thought as he came into the room. Only her balled hands told him just how nervous she was. Crossing the carpet toward her, he glanced at the pine furniture, the four-poster bed, covered with a handmade quilt in shades of cream and blue. He smiled at the big bear sitting in a rocking chair near the window like an old friend. The bear was the only familiar object Marianne had moved into the room after their divorce. "Are you ready yet? Or do you want to keep the reporters cooling their heels?"

"Both." He looked devastatingly handsome in his tan suit, white shirt and conservatively striped tie. And, as always when he was close, her heart skipped a beat and she wanted to walk into his arms. But she stayed where she was and said with a small smile, "Reporters scare me. What if I make a fool of myself? What if I embarrass you?" That was her greatest fear.

"And that from the woman who talks about dealing with the IRS without a blink?" He took one of her hands, gently straightened it and brushed his mouth over the back.

"The IRS is a known quantity," Marianne said lightly, her fingers curling around Robert's. "Their questions are always predictable."

"So are the ones the reporters will ask." He tilted her head into the sunshine falling over his shoulder and noticed the diamond studs. Had she put them on to please him, he wondered? Robert brushed her lips lightly. "Except today you can smile, ignore a question, dissemble, even prevaricate. And if they shove too hard, you even can tell them to go to hell."

"Don't put ideas into my head," Marianne groaned. His kiss felt so right, she thought, feeling her pulse quicken. She wanted to lean closer and let his touch cloud her mind, to let him make her forget about hostage syndromes and her doubts, and to listen only to her heart.

Instead, she pushed at his chest. She needed a clear head when she faced the press. "You have lipstick all over you," she said lightly.

"Afraid that will promote the wrong kind of question?" Robert asked, watching her turn toward the dresser.

When she came back to him with a blue tissue in her hand, her defenses were up. "Is there a right kind of question?" she countered, lightly dabbing lip gloss from his mouth. "I'm not used to people prying into my life."

He caught her hand. "If you don't want to go out there, I'll deal with them alone," he said quietly.

Abruptly Marianne shook her head. She thought of the interviews some of the other hostages had given. They had been surrounded by family and friends, some smiling, some crying. Robert had no one. Vaguely she remembered that there was an aunt somewhere out in the Midwest who hadn't cared enough for a six-year-old orphan to give him a home and who hadn't tried to get in touch with him since. Her own family would have gladly given them support, but Robert and Marianne had turned down their offer.

"It's just nerves," she said lightly. Robert had grown up determined not to need anyone, to be independent, to face life alone. It was up to her to undo the lessons of a lifetime and teach him to trust. She had let him down once, but she was determined not to make the same mistakes again. Gently she slid her hand into his.

The moment they stepped onto the front porch, strobe lights flashed and cameras rolled. Marianne counted at least twenty men and women crowded on the circular driveway. They converged like sharks baring their teeth, and Marianne felt a slight stirring of panic. Controlling her urge to flee, she looked away from them toward the azalea bushes flanking the two brick steps leading up to the house. A few bright red blooms were opening up in the warm spring sun, and the branches of the two birch trees standing in the middle of the lawn were covered with budding light green leaves. She felt the breeze on her face and strength pulsing through her veins. The self-confidence she'd seemed to have lost since the hijacking returned. She relaxed her tightly clenched hands.

When Robert took her elbow protectively and steered her to the microphone he noticed the change. The subtle smile in her eyes made him blink and catch his breath. A ripple of desire tightened his muscles, his eyes narrowed and his chest swelled with pride. Slowly his hand slid down her arm, clasping her hand tightly. God, how he loved her, he thought. Facing the press, he promised himself that as soon as they could escape, he would tell her so.

"Over the last few days we have received a great number of letters and flowers. On behalf of the Lloyd family and myself, I want to thank everyone out there for your thoughtfulness and kind wishes. We realize that there are a few questions, and we'd like to answer those. However, I'd appreciate it if you would address your questions only to the hijacking events."

A young woman with cropped black hair took a step forward. "Mr. Sullivan, you have always been in favor of the disputed military base in Omari. Washington has hinted that despite the hijacking the talks with Emir Yussuf will continue. Has the hijacking changed your personal opinion?''

"No. On the contrary. I firmly believe that the base is an absolute necessity to peace in the Middle East.''

"And what is your opinion, Mrs. Sullivan?''

Marianne's thought flew to Jimmy Dobson. Since Omari she had learned a great deal about the Texan from Robert and television reports. He'd had a wife, a son, two daughters and three grandchildren. "If the base will save the life of even one person I am completely in favor of it.''

"Did you feel the same during the hijacking, Mrs. Sullivan?'' a well-known interviewer from one of New York's public stations asked.

Marianne shook her head. "All I thought about was survival. And seeing my son again.''

"When did you realize that your ex-husband was on the plane?'' a bald-headed man from the back asked.

"After the hijackers took over," Marianne said.

"Since then, you have spent a great deal of time together. Are you planning to get married again?''

I hope so, Marianne thought. It wasn't easy to keep her eyes fixed on the crowd when she wanted to look into Robert's face, but she did. "The subject hasn't come up. For now, I can only say we're good friends," she said firmly.

A heavyset man with greasy strands of hair carefully combed over his bald spot smirked as he asked, "The day you left Omari you were seen leaving the penthouse suite of the Palace Tower Hotel in Basjad together. Surely that points to more than just friendship.''

Marianne felt Robert tense angrily. Her voice pitched low, she pleaded softly, "Please, let me deal with him.'' The man who'd asked the question stood off to one side, as if the other reporters didn't want to associate with him. "I've been told the penthouse suite alone contains sixteen rooms. But

I confess I didn't check the accuracy of that count. After what we went through I was too tired to make a grand tour." Her reply caused a ripple of amusement among the rest of the press.

Robert's mouth twitched. She was a natural, he thought, his eyes glued to the man's face, watching as he took out a large wrinkled handkerchief to wipe his sweaty brow.

Stuffing the cloth back into his pocket, the man shot his colleagues a venomous look. "There's a great deal of speculation going on about Mr. Sullivan's dealings with the man called Major," he pressed on. The amusement died down. "Rumors have it that your ex-husband could have saved all the passengers. That instead he chose to make a deal for your release alone." His eyes shifted to Robert. "How did you feel, Sullivan, when they dragged Jimmy Dobson to his death?"

Robert's response was swift, hard and cold, cutting through the uproar. "Those are serious accusations. Perhaps you'd care to reveal the source of your rumors?"

For a moment Marianne was stunned by the vicious attack, else she would have told the reporter to go to hell. Her nails bit into Robert's hand and, instinctively, she moved closer to him until their bodies touched.

"Go back into the house," Robert ordered Marianne sharply, his grip slackening, his jaw hard. But he continued to study the sweating face, the shifting eyes, the strong nose, the thick lips and the big mole on the left side of his forehead. It would be easy to trace the man later on.

Marianne's fingers tightened in response. Did he really believe she would leave him to face this mudslinging alone? He looked grim, aloof. His eyes were blank as he glanced at her.

"Did you know Jimmy Dobson?" Marianne asked the reporter. She raised her voice, wanting to wipe the satisfied smirk off the man's face. "Did you know that he was allergic to jellyfish? Did you know that he couldn't swim? That he was afraid that the plane would crash into the Persian Gulf? That we *all* were? Without Robert we would have all died."

Even as she said those words, she realized that nothing she could say would undo the damage already done. Though the majority of reporters nodded at her words, many faces showed a mask of doubt. Marianne wanted to rage at the injustice of it. Then she felt Robert gently pry her hand loose and step away, and her anger faded, suppressed by rising despair. He was shutting her out, determined to face the slander alone.

"Why did the major allow Mrs. Sullivan to leave?"

The questions seemed to go on forever. As Robert answered, she remained stubbornly at his side.

When it was finally over, they walked back inside. But their hands were no longer touching.

"The man's name is Tobias Splash, and he digs up dirt for the *Western Investigator*." Robert's voice was as devoid of expression as the look in his eyes as he replaced the phone.

"That rag." Don Lloyd crossed the carpet and handed Robert a brandy, his lean, weathered face tight with anger. "I'd sue him for slander if I were you."

"Asking about a rumor isn't slander." Robert rubbed the back of his neck with one hand while reaching for the snifter with the other. He tossed back the drink, welcoming its sharp bite. "Splash was very slick." Slowly he crumpled the piece of paper in front of him. It had taken him exactly seven minutes to find out the man's identity and the paper he worked for and another twenty to discover that at the present time there were at least five lawsuits running against the scandal sheet.

It had taken Splash mere seconds to tarnish his reputation.

"I'm leaving on the next available flight to Washington."

"Make two reservations. I'm coming with you." Marianne pushed herself out of the high-backed chair in her father's study and faced Robert determinedly.

"No." Grimly Robert tossed the paper ball into the waste basket, then reached for the phone again. Pausing a moment, he looked at her. "I want you to stay here with Bobby." It had been a mistake to return with Marianne and Bobby to Stony Brook, Robert thought. He should have gone straight to Washington to clear things up before drawing Marianne into his life. He didn't believe that the rumors Splash had started would take hold, but he was going to protect his family.

Marianne's eyes flew to her father, asking him for help.

"I think it would be better if you both stayed tonight. By the time you get to Washington, Robert, you won't be able to do much anyway," Don suggested in his calm way. Through the French doors children's laughter drifted into the room. Car doors slammed as other family members arrived at what was supposed to have been a celebration. "I realize that you don't feel like joining the family. But we stick together when there's trouble."

Robert met Don's eyes firmly. "I know. That's why I'm leaving Bobby and Marianne here. I appreciate your offer though," he said, lifting the receiver and punching the number for MacArthur Airport.

Don gave his daughter a look that said he'd tried his best, then left them alone.

Marianne held back her anger until the door closed behind him, then stormed to the desk. Leaning over, she pressed down the button to stop the call.

"You're not leaving me anywhere," she snapped. "I'm not yours to leave, remember?"

Carefully Robert replaced the receiver and leaned back in the chair. "That's splitting hairs," he said, studying her. She was furious. Which was a damn sight better than being worried.

His calmness only fanned her anger and frustration. She almost yelled at him. "I thought you had changed," she spat across the desk. "You promised me that this time things would be different. Well, they aren't. You don't need me any more than you needed me before. You don't want a wife, Robert. You want a mistress. Someone you can share the good times with and walk away from when the going gets rough."

He felt his own temper flare, straining at control. He wanted to get up, hold on to her and shout back. Because she couldn't have been more wrong. His need for her was so strong that his fingers whitened around the glass. But he didn't want her to be part of the suspicions, the whispers and sly looks. "I will be able to deal better with Splash if I don't have to worry about you."

"And who asked you to worry about me?" Marianne asked, then drew in a sharp breath when she saw him raise the glass and noticed the tightness of his grip. "I'm not some weak female afraid of a squall," she said, her voice suddenly rough with relief. Oh, he needed her, but he was too damn proud to ask for her help. "Go ahead, Robert, make your call. I can make my own reservations."

Suddenly the door burst open. Bobby stood there, his face flushed, his chest heaving, his sweater streaked with dirt. Clutching a football under his arm, he looked at his father accusingly, "Is it true that you're leaving today?"

Robert replaced the phone and held out his hand. "Yes. I'm sorry, but I have to go sooner than I thought."

Bobby remained stubbornly clinging to the door, biting his quivering bottom lip. "If I promise to sleep in my room tonight, will you stay?"

Robert swiftly rose to his feet. "I'm not leaving because of you," he said firmly. "I promise I'll be back in a few days."

"No, you won't," Bobby shouted, his eyes filling with tears. "You don't like being my father. A real father, not a weekend one. I don't care if you never come back."

Marianne stepped quickly forward, crouching in front of him. "Sweetheart, you don't mean that. And it isn't true. Your Dad loves you."

There were tears running down his face, and he wiped them away with a childish gesture. But the look he gave her was very adult. "Sure. But not enough for every day," he said, his voice shaking. Clutching his ball, he ran down the hall.

Wearily Marianne rose to her feet. "I'm sorry," she said, watching Bobby run upstairs. "This is my fault. I shouldn't have teased him earlier about sneaking into your room at night."

"No. It goes deeper than that." Robert rubbed a hand across his face, wondering how he could explain to his son that there were some things a man had to do alone to protect his family. "Spending this week with you raised his hopes too high. I should've realized that."

And what about my hopes? Marianne wanted to cry out, keeping her back to him. "I have to go after him."

Robert hesitated, staring at her straight back. The need to take her hand and go after their son together was almost more than he could bear. Then his face hardened determinedly. "Go ahead. I'll talk to him before I leave."

He had left her the key to his house.

During the long drive from Stony Brook, Marianne had

tried to see that as a sign that he wanted her to come. Easing her brother's black Corvette down the exit ramp of the interstate, she stopped at a red light then headed north. But the longer she drove through the swiftly falling night, the less certain she became. He had refused her offer to drive him to the airport. With a taxi waiting, he had hugged Bobby and whispered something into his ear to make his son smile. Then he had lightly touched her cheek. "I'll call you," he'd said before turning away.

But later, in the study, she'd found an envelope addressed to her, containing the key, detailed instructions of how to get to the house, and a telephone number where he could be reached during the day to let him know if and when she planned to arrive.

She hadn't called him.

At first she had been too angry and too hurt. The slanderous remarks had made only local headlines, so there had been no need to run after him, she told herself. Especially since the following Monday morning the State Department had firmly and publicly rejected the rumors as unfounded. But with Jimmy Dobson's funeral only a day away, speculations circulated about whether or not Robert planned to pay his last respects; Marianne knew he would go, and she planned to fly to Dallas with him. After the funeral they would sit down and discuss their future openly. She was tired of vague promises. She wanted to know where she stood.

Slowing down at a blinking red light, she leaned forward, trying to read the street sign in the darkness. She had planned to arrive in Washington before the rush hour, but construction on the Long Island Expressway and an accident on the Goethal's Bridge had slowed her down. There was a time when, in her old Camaro, she could have made up the lost time later on, but the ten-year-old car wasn't reliable enough anymore to make such a long trip. Colin's Corvette was too new to drive at high speed, although there had been a small stretch between Baltimore and Philadelphia where she hadn't been able to resist temptation.

The sign read Fox Hollow Road. Marianne sighed in exasperation when she couldn't find the street on the map Robert had drawn. She must have missed the turn at the last fork. Driving into the intersection, she made a U-turn, then sped back downhill. This time she found the Weeping Willow Path. From there it was only another three miles to the turn for Robert's house.

The road was narrow, winding up- and downhill. The houses were set well back, often screened off completely from the road. If it hadn't been for the cherry trees blooming everywhere, she might have been driving down Stony Brook Road.

Five minutes later she drew up in front of Robert's house. Leaving the motor running, she stopped at the curb and wiped her damp palms on her jeans. The sprawling Tudor-style house was hidden by a hedge of rhododendrons already in full bloom. Two fir trees guarded the floodlit driveway. At the sight of Robert's BMW parked in front of the garage, she swallowed hard. She couldn't bear it if he greeted her with a cold expression in his green eyes.

But she had come too far to turn back now, she thought, tilting her chin. Turning into the driveway, she pulled up beside his car. Before she could take the key out of the ignition and unbuckle her seat belt, she saw Robert coming from the house, as if he'd been waiting for her. The brick walkway was lined by landscaping lights whose beams didn't reach his face, but his long smooth stride seemed impatient. Some of her tension eased.

He could have strangled her, Robert thought, pulling the door open, almost lifting her to her feet and drawing her straight into his arms. He had called Stony Brook four hours ago to find out if she was coming, and he had gone through hell since. "You're three hours late," he growled, pressing her head into his shoulder. "Why didn't you fly?"

"You left me the map."

"That was meant for the taxi driver, you idiot."

Marianne smiled into the rough cotton knit of his grey sweater. He was glad to see her, and because he had been worried, he wasn't hiding it. Then her smile faded a little as her thoughts went back to the past, wondering what would have happened if she had shown up at his apartment five years ago. If she had taken the initiative then, would Robert have welcomed her as he did now, with his heart beating unevenly and his arms tightly wrapped around her? She sighed with regret.

"I called home less than an hour ago when I filled up with gas. Dad said he'd let you know."

"He did." Robert slid his finger through her hair, framing her face. Tilting it back, he kissed her lightly and teased, "He also warned me that your lousy sense of direction hasn't improved over the years and that it might be hours before you got here."

"Sometimes I really do wonder why I love my parents so much," Marianne muttered, exasperated. "I've never been lost. Not permanently, anyway," she amended when Robert raised one brow pointedly. "I have a perfect driving record, I'll have you know."

"Of course," Robert said dryly, "All you have to do is smile at a cop and he'll forget about the ticket."

"Is that how you get around lady cops?" Marianne asked. "Your smile is devastating."

"Is it?" he asked, smiling broadly, watching the result. It did make her catch her breath. "I never speed."

"Sure," she scoffed, "I've yet to see a BMW crawl down the road."

"I was worried about you," Robert said softly, laying one arm across her back and turning her toward the house. He knew that she was as good a driver as she was a sailor. But she loved speed. He would have worried less if she had been driving her mother's Bonneville instead of the Corvette.

"I didn't mean to worry you. Traffic on Long Island was awful. It took me almost three hours to get into New Jersey." Sending him an impish look, she added, "But I do like the results."

He pinched her waist lightly in mock punishment, making her squeal in protest. In front of the heavy carved oak door flanked by brass lanterns she suddenly turned serious. "I wasn't certain what my welcome would be."

Over the past twenty-four hours Robert had gone through a whole range of emotions, alternately hoping that she'd come and seconds later telling himself that he didn't want her here. Coming back to Washington had been unsettling. The house had echoed with emptiness. He had gone through the rooms, opening windows, wondering if he had pushed her away too far. Again. Over the last ten days he had become used to looking around and finding her close. He'd missed her more than he wanted to admit. Now that she was here, he felt complete.

"I wasn't going to lock you out." Robert pushed the door open, then stepped aside to let her enter first.

"Perhaps not literally, but mentally you do it all the time," Marianne said quietly, facing him. "I know you don't want me here. I know you don't want my help." When he started to say something, she silenced him by placing her hand across his lips. "I'll only stay until after the funeral. Until the worst is over."

For all her brave words, she was still hovering outside the door, poised for flight. Gently he pushed her into the foyer, then closed the door and leaned against it. The smile slashing his lean cheeks was part arrogance, part tenderness. "If I didn't want you with me so badly, I would send you back tomorrow," he said softly, placing his hands on her shoulders.

Her breath caught in her throat. "You've never said that to me before," she said, blinking to hold back the tears.

"Haven't I?"

"No. Not with words."

He was going to say it to her often, he swore to himself, drawing her against him and kissing her tenderly. There were so many things he wanted to say to her, but they were best kept inside a little while longer. "Let's have something to drink. Then I'll get your luggage."

"Oh, damn, I forgot."

"Forgot what? Your luggage?" he chuckled, his eyes brightening with amusement. There was never a dull moment with Marianne around. "I guess I can loan you a shirt and a toothbrush."

"No. I was going to stop and get us a pizza."

"Will steaks and baked potatoes do?"

"Who's cooking?" she asked him cautiously.

"I'll do the steaks and you cut up the vegetables for the salad."

"Deal. I guess I should call home first. Then I want to see your house," she said, sliding her arm through his. "That is, if you have the time. I know you're very busy and I wouldn't want to keep you from your work."

"If you're not too tired after dinner, you can help me look through some mug shots," he said offhandedly.

Marianne almost groaned at the thought of looking at more beards, strong noses and dark curly hair. But something in his voice, a sound of suppressed excitement, made her hold it back. "You've got a lead?" she guessed.

He shrugged his broad shoulders. "Possibly."

"Show me," she said eagerly.

Smiling, Robert shook his head, his hand curling around her wrist. "I've been staring at the screen for so long that one face looks like another. I deserve a rest. The phone's right over there." He pointed at an antique oak chest, then leaned back against the door and watched her make the call.

He was almost certain he had a lead on the major, but he hadn't told anyone yet. Now that Marianne was here, he wanted her opinion. She wasn't trained to look for certain features that did not change, like the shape of an eye and the slant of a nose. But she had sharp eyes, a quick grasp of the essential, and she knew the major. He had never felt the need before to share his thoughts, but that too had somehow changed over the last ten days.

After she hung up the phone, he asked. "Where do you want to start?"

"In the foyer," she said, her eyes following the curved staircase to the second floor. "I've heard all about the banister that seems to make a perfect slide."

Robert gave her a quick grin. "Want to try it out? The banister, I mean. I'll catch you before you test the floor."

Laughing, she shook her head. "I wasn't certain if Bobby was pulling my leg or if it was true that you'd broken the post at the bottom."

"It was already cracked," he lied, drawing her into the living room.

Judging from the skylights Bobby had described, Marianne had pictured a modern setting with walls of glass and chrome tables. Instead, she saw a comfortable mixture of old and new, velour couches, an antique armoire, wooden floors, oriental rugs. The dining room consisted of dark mahogany and light velvets, and the den was all leather and light oak. It was a big house for one man, especially a man who rarely had time to enjoy it. "It's a beautiful place," she said, looking for familiar objects, but finding none. She wondered if he'd kept any of the furniture, books and paintings they'd bought together, or if, like herself, he had put them in storage or given them away. "What made you decide to buy such a big house?"

"I like space." He had bought the house on a whim, a dream, a half-formed hope. Watching her walk around, running her hand over smooth surfaces and knobby velours, everything clicked into place. He hadn't consciously picked out the house or the furniture with her in mind. But now seeing her in it, he knew that was why he had chosen one couch over another and why he had bought the Flemish armoire. She had fallen in love with it instantly.

Bobby's room was a boy's dream: big, light and airy, with a stereo, a computer and a pinball machine. "How do you ever get him to come downstairs?" Marianne asked, running her finger over the oak headboard.

"Bribes," Robert said dryly. "Rocky road ice cream, popcorn, raspberry fruit slush."

"What ever happened to balanced diets?" Marianne shook her head.

"What's that?" Robert asked, not one bit contrite.

"And you expect me to send him back to you?" Marianne teased.

The light vanished abruptly from Robert's eyes, and he said quietly, "No. I expect you to come with him."

"I don't know." She thought of Bobby's outburst yesterday. Oh, he seemed to have recovered quickly after Robert had talked to him. Still, she couldn't put him through one goodbye after another.

Robert put his hands into his jeans and leaned against the door frame. "Are you trying to pull back, Marianne?"

"I don't think it would be good for Bobby if I came along."

With an impatient oath, Robert pushed himself away from the door. He had promised himself not to touch her, not unless she made the first move. But he could no more leave her alone than he could have sent her back. "Bobby and I came to an understanding before I left," he said, crossing the distance between them. "That leaves you and me." Cupping her chin, he tilted her face back. "Perhaps it's time we, too, come to an understanding."

Dear God, she couldn't agree with him more. She ached to tell him over and over again how much she loved him. When he lowered his head, the emotional distance she had tried to keep between them vanished instantly at the touch of his lips. Her mouth opened and her arms clung to his neck.

He never seemed to get enough of her, Robert thought, lifting her high into his arms. Swiftly he carried her the short distance to his own bedroom and lowered her on the bed. "Words never seem to work with us," he whispered, following her.

At his statement, pride filled her. There had been too few words in the past and too many misunderstandings because of it. And now they seemed to be slipping into the same pattern that had once torn their marriage apart. "I need words, Robert," she snapped, rolling away. "I didn't come to Washington to sleep with you."

He grabbed her shoulders, pinning her body beneath his. "I want you. Damn it, I've told you so often enough."

For a moment she lay perfectly still, staring into those heavily lashed silver-green eyes. The temptation to take what he was offering almost weakened her resolve. Almost. But not quite. "And I've told you I'm not going to be a weekend mistress." She shoved him back, taking him by surprise. Flinging herself to the side, she got her legs off the bed, just before she was pulled backward and pinned down.

"Then how about being a full-time one?" he ground out, his fury leaping at this slur against his honor.

"Wouldn't that be convenient," she sneered.

"Convenient? Hell. You're about as convenient as—as a bag of fleas."

Marianne sucked in her breath sharply, glaring at him. "Now I'm a bag of fleas, am I?" she snapped. She squirmed beneath him, but his solid weight did not shift. "If you don't let me get up, I'll draw blood," she threatened.

Robert felt a grin tug at the corners of his mouth. This was hardly the time to laugh, but it wasn't easy to keep a straight face. It had been years since he'd fought with anyone, had really argued and let go. "Are you threatening me?" he asked gently, nipping at her neck. "Isn't that a little reckless in your position?"

"Perhaps," she started, and then his mouth came down. She struggled, still wanting words, still holding out for promises. But her body was weakening. Because her pride demanded it, she made a token effort to roll away from him when he knelt at her side. But his hands were quick and strong, opening buttons, her zipper, tearing them in his haste. Pinning her body beneath his, he sucked at her tongue, drawing it into his mouth, then circling it with his own. He felt her fists pounding on his back, then change position and push at his shoulders, before sliding beneath his sweater. Her breath was quickening and her resistance began to fade. And with each move, her body sank deeper into the mattress, softening beneath his. He trapped her hands between their bodies and slid his lips down her arched throat.

Her body became a mass of conflicting emotions. She wanted him to stop. She couldn't bear it if he did. Finally her arms locked tightly around him, and she accepted what he could give. At least for now.

They sat on the carpet in Robert's study, with their backs propped against the burgundy leather couch, their plates balanced on their legs and their eyes glued to the screen. Faces flicked by—fat ones, thin ones, smooth, wrinkled, cowed, proud and cold.

"Stop," Marianne said with her mouth full of steak, pointing with her fork at a bearded man with a turban high on his forehead. Placing the plate on the carpet, she crawled over to the screen, trying not to trample the tail of Robert's shirt.

"The high forehead fits," she said, covering the turban with one hand. Placing her other hand over the lower part of the man's face, she stared at the eyes and shivered, even now that she was safe. "It's the beard that bothers me. Somehow I can't imagine the major wearing a long bushy one; short and clipped would be more his style."

"But you still believe it is the major?" Robert asked, folding his arms across his chest.

"Yes," she said with absolute certainty. "I'll never forget those eyes."

"I agree." Leaning forward, Robert reached for her and pulled her down beside him again. "I was almost certain. But the beard threw me off, too. The major always seemed so predictable. He always chose the same bar stool, for instance. Then there was his militarylike carriage and step. He had me fooled."

Placing a kiss on her nose, he got to his feet and took the tape out of the video. "I have to go down to the ATD headquarters. Will you be all right here, alone?"

She nodded. "Please be careful. He could be out there, waiting for you."

Robert placed the cartridge into the plastic box and snapped the lid shut. It was more than likely that the major was somewhere close, waiting for the last round of the game to be played. It wouldn't be tonight and not here in this house. This neighborhood was a beehive of plainclothes police and bodyguards. "My guess is that he's holed up in a rat-infested house somewhere between Beirut and Basjad," he said, giving her a sharp, searching glance.

"No." Marianne got to her feet and wrapped her arms around herself. "I can feel that it isn't over yet."

Chapter 12

The anti-terrorist division headquarters housed some of the world's most sophisticated electronics equipment and arguably the most comprehensive data bank in the world on terrorists and terrorism. Inside the windowless rooms the lights burned twenty-four hours a day, computers hummed, coffee machines spewed out steady streams of strong black brew, printers, telegraphs and shredding machines clattered and screeched in symphony and, away from the more sensitive equipment, the air conditioning sucked up clouds of cigarette smoke thick enough to set off a sprinkler system on a hot summer day.

As he sat watching the video screen come to life in the room that had once been his office, Robert wondered how he could have lived down here for years. The noise filtering in through the open door was driving him nuts. The air was cold, the lights were cold and he was cold. He missed the warm sunshine, the fresh spring air whispering through the budding trees, and the gentle clap of waves against the side of the moored sloop. He missed Marianne.

Turning back to the screen, he read out loud, "Abu bin Hussein bin Hassan Badrayashi." His deep voice was filled with satisfaction as the long name rolled from his lips. It had taken him two long nights, but he finally had a name.

Tim Dolek, a slim, pale man in his thirties with a thatch of sandy hair, stubbed out his half-finished cigarette and left his own terminal to look over Robert's shoulder. They had been friends for years, long before Tim had taken over Robert's position. Studying the two photos of the man called Major, he said, "I still want to know how you recognized him."

Robert stared from the bushy-bearded man to the fuzzy, but still recognizable, image of the major in army fatigues. Even seen side by side, the two images seemed to have nothing in common. "Marianne said it was his eyes. I first recognized the frown. The rest was gut instinct." Robert's eyes shifted from one face to another and he swore. "With that beard he could stroll through immigration without anyone taking a second look."

"I sure hope you're wrong. We don't want any nasty surprises at the funeral."

Robert frowned. "I don't think so." The church would be searched. And there was only the small walk from the curb into the building. Security would be tight.

Tim shrugged his shoulders. "It's your game. You know the man. Let's see what else we have on him." He sat back down at the next terminal and punched a button. "Are you two getting married again?" he asked, waiting for the screen to roll over, then adding his personal security code sequence for system access.

"If I ever find the time," Robert joked, running a frustrated hand through his hair. *And if she will have me, he* added to himself. He knew that she loved him, even if she wasn't saying it out loud. But she had loved him four years ago and had still walked away.

Tim shot him a sympathetic look. "Things should slow down once that treaty is in the bag." Suddenly he bent forward, whistled and said, "Look at that."

Robert leaned over and read:

Name: Abu bin Hussein bin Hassan Badrayashi
Birthdate: ?/?/1949 (age: 39)
Birthplace: Abadan, Iran
Citizenship: Dual: Iran and Omari
Occupation: Businessman

Robert felt adrenaline pumping through his veins. "What business?"

Tim called up the information. "Import-export. With offices in Beirut, Marseilles and Hamburg, Germany, and, although we can't prove it, that cargo outfit at Kennedy Airport. He's also a suspected arms dealer, but we can't prove that, either."

"He's slick." Reaching for his coffee, Robert leaned back in his chair. "What about military service, family, etc."

While lighting a cigarette, Tim requested the information. "He was an officer in the Shah's imperial forces. His family was killed during the revolution by the Shah's secret police. He fled to Omari with his youngest sister, Selina, left her with his mother's brother, a Sheik Selim—hey, isn't that the guy your friend Jamal has been chasing?" When Robert nodded grimly, Tim continued, "Then he returned to Iran to fight for Khomeini." He pointed at the fuzzy photo on Robert's screen. "That must have been taken about the time he led one of the groups that stormed our embassy. Four years ago he retired and went into business for himself." Tim turned back to Robert, adding, "He must have the Midas touch, or some wealthy silent partners."

Robert rubbed his burning eyes. It all made sense. They had a motive for the hate, an explanation for the military discipline and the major's disparaging yet somewhat protective attitude toward women. Even a link to Muhrad was there. But Robert doubted that he could ever prove Muhrad's involvement beyond a reasonable doubt. "He's a gambler."

A gambler with one last hand to play.

"It takes one to know one," Tim quipped, blowing smoke into the air.

Robert shot him a pointed, amused look. Every man and woman at the division played for high stakes. This was not a place for the timid or the squeamish. Or the old. Although he was but two years older than Tim, he suddenly felt twice his age. "Do you ever feel like folding and cashing in your chips?" he asked, getting to his feet.

"Every night, just about this time," Tim said dryly, pushing his chair back. "But no, I'm not ready yet to quit and settle down." Walking with Robert to the door, he added, "Keep watching your back. I don't like crowds and open places, especially not places with lots of bushes and trees and tombstones."

With his hand on the door, Robert froze. "What do you mean? The service is at the First Methodist Church."

"That was yesterday's plan. The church wouldn't have been big enough." Tim rubbed the back of his neck uneasily. "Besides, Mrs. Dobson insisted on a private family service in their small church. The rest takes place at the cemetery."

"Hell," Robert swore. "If I had known, I would've gone to the funeral alone. Now there's no way I can convince Marianne to go back to Stony Brook."

"I'd feel better if you both stayed here," Tim muttered.

"And let that reporter Splash have the last word? And what about the day after tomorrow? Where do I hide then?" Eyes hard, Robert shook his head. "Just tell your men to keep looking for a man with a beard."

"What makes you so certain that he's coming after you personally?"

Robert's voice was hard, flat and very certain. "I once told him that the world isn't big enough for both of us. My gut feeling is that he feels the same way."

It was long past midnight when Robert let himself into the house. He found Marianne sound asleep on the couch in the den. For a moment he stood in the doorway, looked at her and felt at peace.

All his life he had moved from one game to another, challenging fate and the world, and most of all himself. He was tired of challenges. He had spent his life running, always running to outdistance the past. Now all he wanted was to settle down, to be more than a weekend lover and a once-a-month father. He wanted to put down roots and sink them deep.

But there was still one last game to finish, one last challenge to meet. Softly he walked to the couch.

She stirred when he lifted her into his arms. "I was waiting for you," she said, her voice husky with sleep.

"You should've gone to bed." Robert brushed his lips over her warm, silky skin.

"I didn't know which bed."

"The one with the firm mattress and the cotton sheets," Robert said, carrying her upstairs.

In Jimmy Dobson's hometown, Dallas, Tobias Splash's accusations had not been dismissed as slander but were being repeated out loud as truth. As the convoy of official limousines drove toward the cemetery, Marianne again read the headline of the Dallas newspaper in her lap: State Department Denies Charges Emphatically. But in the smaller print beneath, the question was raised again. "Could Jimmy Dobson's death have been prevented?"

"Don't let it upset you," Gloria Barton said as she gently took the newspaper from Marianne's hand and folded it. "Robert did everything he could."

"I'm more angry than upset." Marianne looked at the beautiful woman in her fifties sitting next to her. Gloria Barton's blond hair was cut short, and her gray suit was fashionably tailored. She was a formidable lady. Earlier, Marianne had watched her silence Senator Colton's chatty and nosy wife with one sharp look from her green eyes. She also had a wry sense of humor that appealed to Marianne.

Gloria Barton nodded. "I know the feeling. I used to see red every time someone pointed a finger at my husband. But when you've lived in Washington as long as I have, you learn to ignore these little puffs of hot air."

"Puffs of hot air?" Smiling, Marianne looked at Robert talking quietly to Howard Barton. "I hope that's all it is," she said. Robert had been curiously tense this morning. Even now his eyes strayed to watch the buildings fly by. Turning back to Gloria Barton, she said, "But I can't help worrying about Mrs. Dobson's reaction."

"I talked to Molly Dobson last night. She assured me that she did not hold Robert responsible in any way. But she would like to speak to him and suggested that we stop at her house before the service. Because of security reasons that's quite out of the question. But after the funeral I'll arrange a few minutes of privacy."

Marianne shot Gloria a look that told her that she wasn't deceived. Perhaps consideration had been given to security, but a meeting between Robert and Mrs. Dobson would be so much more effective out in the open for everyone to see. "A master stroke," she muttered.

Gloria Barton gave her an approving look. "I hope you plan to move to Washington, my dear. We'd get along marvelously."

Minutes later, stepping out of the car, Robert didn't know why he was so certain that the major was there. Considering the tight security precautions, the idea seemed irrational. Agents were sitting in trees, strolling around bushes, patrolling the grounds. The sheriff's office had drawn police lines to keep spectators at a distance. There was no way for the major to get close enough without the risk of being caught. It was a challenge that would appeal to him, Robert guessed, turning to help Marianne from the limousine. He prayed he was dead wrong.

All the hostages had come to pay their last respects. Walking past the chairs, Marianne first spotted Rafe, then Sven Hammond with a tall blond woman at his side. Even Mrs Rafferty had made the trip from nearby Paris, Texas. At the beginning of the row reserved for their own party, Jamal sat with his bodyguard, Hassir. They were surrounded by friends, Marianne thought, feeling her tension ease. The tension left her completely when Molly Dobson thanked them with a faint smile for making the trip. Even with her face hidden by a thin black veil, Marianne recognized her as the woman who had fought to stay with her husband, the one the terrorists had dragged off the plane.

She sat down with Robert at her side, their hands clasped.

As Marianne listened to the speeches from Howard Barton and Senator Colton, she thought about the vagaries of life and death. Being close to death made a person realize the important things. There were no guarantees in life that tomorow would come. She had wasted so much time with evasions and pettiness. What if these were her and Robert's last moments together? She tugged at his hand until he looked at her and whispered softly, "I love you."

For one long moment Robert forgot to breathe. For one long moment he lost himself in the softness of her gray eyes. He read acceptance in their depth, acceptance for what he was, and what he had been. He realized then that it didn't matter to her if he made it to the top or if he fell short. What did matter to her was his happiness. It was the same with him. If she'd ask him tomorrow to leave Washington, to give up his job, he would do so. Hell, he might do it even without her asking. Tomorrow.

Slowly he let out his breath. "I missed you, my love," he whispered hoarsely. The words "I love you" hovered on his lips, when he felt a tap on his shoulder.

"Mr. Sullivan?"

Looking up, Robert recognized one of Tim Dolek's men. With a sigh of resignation he rose to his feet. "We'll talk later," he whispered to Marianne.

The agent introduced himself as Jeff. "We picked up two likely suspects," he explained as they walked away from the service. He was almost as tall as Robert, with sharp brown eyes, wavy dark hair and a young, restless face. Had he ever been that eager and impatient? Robert wondered. He doubted that either of the two men were the major. The man was too cunning to allow himself to be picked up by a rookie. But because he remembered his own youthful mistakes, he didn't mention his doubts.

"Did you pull on his beard?" he asked.

"Sir?" Jeff looked at him as if he'd gone mad.

Robert sighed, praying for patience. "Ten days ago, the man we're looking for had no beard."

Jeff frowned. "Someone forgot to mention that little bit of information when they gave me the mug shot and vital statistics."

"Does either one talk with an accent?"

"The one I caught hiding behind a monument didn't. He insists he's a reporter. And the other one wasn't saying anything."

"And where did you pick him up?"

Jeff grinned. "It was one of those freak accidents. The first guy we caught wasn't very cooperative, so we had to push him along a little. Then, as we were passing the limousines, he fell, and, when I bent down to pick him up, I saw this other guy's foot under the car."

"That could be our man all right." Robert lengthened his stride. It was almost too easy, he thought, but freak accidents did happen. "Did anyone check beneath the car for explosives?" he asked sharply.

"I don't know, sir. I came directly to you," he said, walking up to an unmarked gold Chevy parked diagonally across from the limousines. "But I will do it right away."

One of the agents who were crowding around the vehicle turned at their approach and said, "We let the first one go, sir. His ID checked out. This one has nothing on him. No driver's license, not even a credit card." He stepped aside to allow Robert a look at the man two agents were trying to put into handcuffs.

The gray beard and the gray-streaked hair had given his olive-tinged face a sallow complexion that aged him ten years. Dressed in dirt-streaked corduroys and a blue nylon jacket, he seemed to have shrunk in stature. If he'd met him on a crowded Washington street, he might have walked right past him, Robert thought. But the eyes were the same.

"So we meet again, Abu bin Hussein bin Hassan Badrayashi," he said, taking a step closer.

"I should've killed you when I had the chance," the major snapped.

Robert nodded grimly. "Why didn't you?"

The major shrugged. "I was playing it safe. How do you say it? Keeping the back door open?" His black eyes lit with sudden amusement. "The game isn't over yet, Sullivan. I still have a trump up my sleeve."

Robert's eyes narrowed uneasily. And because he always looked for a catch when things seemed too simple, he had a second of warning. Looking over his shoulder, he saw Jeff kneeling beside the limousine. "Jeff, run," he yelled, turning to pull the young agent from beneath the car. He was tackled from behind and thrown to the ground just before the blast went off.

Acrid smoke filled the air. Screams mingled with the deafening noise. For one moment Robert lay stunned, choking, gasping for breath. The weight pinning him to the ground didn't move. Then he heard the Chevy's motor roar to life. With a tremendous effort, he pushed up on his arms, dislodging the weight above him away from the car's wheels. Twisting, he rolled over, out of its path. The tires passed his shoulder within an inch. When the car shot forward, Robert jumped to his feet. The effort it took to control his balance made him catch his breath. He started coughing again. Covering his mouth, he blindly followed the Chevy, praying the smoke would clear, and would clear soon. He couldn't see a damn thing. His sense of direction was foggy. The Chevy was right in front of him, but it was gathering speed. When his foot hit the curb he froze for an instant, wasting precious seconds. The major, and he was certain it was the major, was racing downhill toward the crowd. He started running, coughing, running faster than he had ever done in his life.

Marianne was also running.

From the moment Robert had left, she had followed him with her eyes. With a mixture of frustration and exasperation she had watched him follow the man past the chairs.

When Robert didn't stop there, but strode up the hill, shivers ran down her spine. She could sense that something was wrong when she watched him join the group of men crowding around a car.

And then the explosion rent the air.

Within split seconds agents surrounded Howard Barton and his wife. Marianne was on her feet, racing into the aisle. The seconds of warning she'd had gave her a head start. She was past the chairs before panic broke out.

There was a white cloud where Robert had been, a white cloud of acrid smoke that drifted down the hill toward her in the mild noon breeze. Within seconds Marianne was lost. Blindly she stumbled on. She tried to cry out Robert's name, but the smoke was choking her. Her eyes were filled with tears, blinding her. She stopped and dried them with the sleeve of her blue-and-white dress. When she heard an engine race, she stopped, trying to determine the car's position. And then she saw the front fender emerge from the cloud, but by then it was too late to jump out of the way. She felt pain sear her side, then she was tossed into the air. She screamed when the ground hurtled toward her at high speed.

The smell of antiseptic hung in the air. Loudspeakers blared out a steady stream of code numbers and names, and nurses rushed past the waiting room on soft-soled shoes. Inside the small area, Jamal, Rafe and Mrs. Rafferty were talking quietly.

Robert preferred to stand in the hall where he could watch the double doors with the sign Surgery. Authorized Personnel Only swing open and close. They had wheeled Marianne through those doors more than an hour ago. There had been some bad moments in his life, especially recently, Robert thought grimly, but none as bad as when he had watched the car bear down on her. If he had been a little faster, only a few seconds faster, he would have reached her in time. Instead, he'd had to watch helplessly as the car hit her and sent her flying through the air.

But she was alive.

Jeff hadn't been that lucky. Robert swallowed at the thought. The rookie had been little more than a kid, only twenty-five years old. Richie, the man who had covered Robert with his body, had been badly cut by flying metal, but he would live. The others had a few cuts, bruises and ringing ears. It was a miracle that no one else had been seriously injured.

The major had been caught. The irony of it was that it had been Marianne who had slowed him down. When she had appeared like a ghost out of the smoke, the bastard had swerved to the right, hitting an oak tree in his path.

He watched another nurse walk through the double doors and he clenched his hands. He felt no satisfaction at the thought that the major would spend the rest of his life behind bars.

"Have some coffee." Jamal held out a steaming cup of the black brew, but Robert refused. "She's going to be fine," Jamal said, laying a hand on Robert's torn sleeve. Jamal's eyes narrowed when he felt something warm and damp touching his skin. Turning his hand over, he saw blood. "Go and have someone look at that arm," he said sharply.

Robert shrugged. "It's only a scratch." What was going on behind those doors? "I should have sent her back to Stony Brook when I had the chance," he said, rubbing his burning eyes.

"She wouldn't have gone," Jamal sipped the coffee. "She refused to remain in the palace the day of the sandstorm." With a ghost of a smile he remembered that night. "The only reason I allowed her to stay at the airport was because I figured she would leave willingly after an hour of tasting sand, but she stayed all day and all night. She's as stubborn as you, Robert.''

A brief smile lit Robert's eyes. "Not quite. But it's a close match.'' The smile vanished abruptly when the door swung open and the surgeon came toward them. Robert pushed himself away from the wall and met him halfway.

"The surgery went without complications,'' Dr. Thompson said as he pulled the green cap off his head. "I had to put a plate in her ankle. It was quite a bad break and it will take some time to heal. Even when the cast comes off she's going to walk with a limp for a while. But she's young and healthy, and I'm confident that in another six months her leg is going to be like new. There are contusions—bruises—but those will heal fast.''

Robert felt light-headed with relief. "What about her concussion?'' he asked hoarsely.

Dr. Thompson turned up his hands. Concussions were tricky. "She seemed to respond well to light. We'll keep her under observation,'' he said evasively.

"When can I see her?''

Dr. Thompson's eyes strayed to Robert's torn sleeve. Pushing back the torn material, he gently probed the two-inch gash. "After you have had that taken care of. It needs stitching. Your wife will be in recovery for another two hours, so you have plenty of time. And get something to eat. Our cafeteria food is actually quite good.''

The food was lousy, Robert thought an hour later, laying down his fork. The roll was stale, the mashed potatoes lumpy and the chicken-fried steak was so greasy it turned his stomach. The others seemed to enjoy it, though. Rafe was already on his second helping, and Jamal's plate was empty.

Impatiently he looked around the table set up for them in the physician's lounge. Howard Barton was discussing arrangements for the flight back to Washington with his security expert. Gloria was writing down Mrs. Rafferty's prized recipe for pecan pie. Jamal was suggesting breeding his new stallion, Sultan, to one of Rafe's mares. They had tried to draw him into their conversations, but he'd never felt less like joining them.

He wanted to be alone for a few minutes. He needed a private place where he could kick something, yell and let go of his rage. Pushing back his chair, he strode from the room.

Halfway down the hall, Howard's voice called him back. "I'm leaving in a few minutes, and I'd like a word with you before I go." Reluctantly Robert turned around.

As was his way with men he felt comfortable with, Howard Barton came straight to the point. "I spoke to Dr. Thompson a few minutes ago to assure myself that Marianne will be all right. He feels that by Friday she will be well enough to fly home." He looked at Robert with a mixture of apology and determination. "I need you in Washington by this weekend. I realize that's a great deal to ask of you at the moment, but we can't delay the negotiations with Omari a second time."

Robert wanted to tell him to send someone else. It was on the tip of his tongue to hand in his resignation right there and then. But discipline was too deeply ingrained. And he owed it to Jimmy Dobson and Jeff to see the deal through. "I'll be there," he promised quietly. Looking over his shoulder, he added, "If there are no complications."

Through the partially open door, Howard took a brief look at his wife. "Of course. I wouldn't leave Gloria, either." Then he added grimly, "With the major in our custody, I don't foresee any more problems and delays. I'm certain Prince Muhrad will withdraw most of his resistance. Things should go quite smoothly."

For a moment, Robert's eyes flared with the need for revenge. Then his tight mouth relaxed, and he allowed a small, dangerous smile. Revenge would be subtle—he could hardly walk up to the prince and knock him down—but he would take great satisfaction in watching Muhrad squirm. "I agree."

Howard Barton hid his relief. For a moment he had been afraid that he had lost one of the few men he trusted, and a good friend at that. Men of Robert's caliber were hard to replace, he thought, holding out his hand. "Give my best wishes to your wife—uh, ex-wife...." He stopped, his gray eyes glinting with exasperation, then added, "Fiancée? Robert, I do hope you plan to straighten out your personal life."

Robert grinned. "I intend to. As soon as Marianne is well enough."

Howard was pleased. "Gloria said she enjoyed Marianne's company." Then he raised one brow. "You mean you haven't talked about it yet?"

Robert shook his head. "There have been a few problems." Dryly, he added, "Lack of time is one of them. Lack of privacy another."

"You have all day tomorrow," Howard said. "I'm afraid I can't remember the last time Gloria and I had a whole day to ourselves."

Her head ached. Her leg was throbbing. Breathing was painful. Waking, Marianne wanted to retreat back into sleep and numbness and keep her eyes closed. She knew where she was. A little while ago a kind voice had told her that she was in recovery, that she had broken her leg and that she would be fine. "I hate hospitals," she said.

At the sudden sound of her voice, Robert turned away from the window and came to her side. "I know," he said soothingly, a tired smile tugging at his lips. Bending over her, he watched her eyes open. Her pupils seemed to contract evenly, he thought. He had worried much more about the concussion than about her leg or the mass of bruises. "Are you in pain?"

She was, but she forgot about her aches at the sight of him. Memory returned instantly. She could hear the bang and the screams. She could almost smell the acrid fumes. "You're not hurt?" Her voice was hoarse and urgent.

"No. Nothing but a scratch." He raised his bandaged right arm to calm her down. It should have been him lying there, he thought, blinking back the moisture in his eyes. It had been his game, his gamble, his fight. And as always before, *he* had walked away with a mere scratch. Lucky Sullivan! That's what he'd always been called. If it hadn't been for him, Marianne would be at home with their son and Jeff would be alive.

"But you were up there, right where the explosion took place."

Later, when she could handle it, he would tell her what had happened, but not now. "I hid behind a car," he said evasively.

She frowned. "The car. It came out of the smoke. I remember it now. It wasn't the driver's fault," she added, her voice suddenly rough with urgency. "I hope no one blamed him for hitting me."

Grimly Robert wondered if anyone had thought of adding charges of hit and run to those of two counts of murder, conspiracy and air piracy. "It doesn't matter, my love," he said hoarsely, bending down to kiss her. This time, because he knew she would feel easier, he told her the truth. "The major was driving that car." When he saw her shudder, he cursed himself for mentioning it. Sitting down on the bed, he leaned over her and brushed her hair back from her face and whispered, "We caught him. He's going to be locked up for life. He's never going to threaten you again."

"It wasn't me he was after. He wanted you. Why?" Convulsively she flung her arms around his neck, clinging to him with all her strength. And then the tears came, part remembered fear, part relief and part just simple joy that they were here, together, safe.

Why? Only the major knew the answer to that, and so far he had refused to talk. Robert, though, had his own suspicions. "Somewhere our paths must have crossed before," he whispered into her hair, holding her tightly. His past was catching up with him, and as for himself, he was too tired to care. But those he loved he would protect and keep safe, he thought, his arms tightening around her.

A few moments later, the nurse came to check on Marianne and sent Robert outside while she gave her a sedative. In the hall, Robert leaned against the wall, feeling almost too drained to stand. He didn't know what to do or where to go. When the nurse allowed him back in the room, he drew a chair near the bed and wearily sat down.

"Did you call Bobby?" Leaning back against the pillow, Marianne shifted her cast.

"Yes. Everyone sends their love."

She was tired and drowsy, but looking at Robert's haunted face, she fought the pull of the medication. "Where are you going to sleep?"

Leaning back, Robert closed his eyes. "Are you throwing me out?" he asked very quietly. He wouldn't blame her if she did.

He looked so weary, she thought, aching to touch his face. His dark blue pants were wrinkled and slightly stained, so unlike his usually immaculate self. The light blue silk shirt was splattered with blood. The bandage on his arm was a white badge of courage against his tan. "No, of course not," she said. "But you need a good night's sleep. Last night you had less than four hours' rest. And today," she swallowed, her voice becoming drowsy, "today was awful."

"Today was hell."

"Promise me you'll sleep?" she asked, her eyes closing and her hand groping for his.

His hand slid over the sheet until it found hers, in a need to touch her. He could feel her fingers tremble in his, and his clasp tightened reassuringly. "I promise," he said quietly, watching her eyes close and her breathing deepen.

She hadn't asked him where he would sleep, so it was an easy promise to keep. Sprawling in the chair with her hand still clasped in his, Robert closed his eyes. But he wondered about the other promise he had made, the one given to Bobby before he had left Stony Brook. He had promised his son a family. How was he going to keep them safe without breaking his word?

Everything should have been beautiful, Marianne thought the following morning, sitting in a wheelchair with her leg raised. The sun was shining. The major had been caught. And last night had added a new dimension to their love. There had been no sexual attraction. No, she and Robert had had a silent sharing of despair, a giving and taking of comfort. She remembered last night's tenderness and love. This morning things looked different.

Robert was very gentle, very patient—and very distant. He hadn't kissed her. He hadn't teased her, either. He hadn't touched her except to help her into the wheelchair.

He had gone out early and had returned with a mountain of presents: nightgowns, robes and ridiculous teddy bear slippers. The new dress hanging in the closet was far too beautiful to wear with a plaster cast. She had enough books to read until the cast came off. He had even thought of a present for Bobby.

At first, when Robert had staggered into the room concealed by boxes, she had smiled. Then she had protested that he had bought too much. And finally she had laughed with happiness. Now she wanted to cry. Because something was very, very wrong.

Her eyes flew to the beautiful arrangement of tiny white, pink and red roses arranged with baby's breath. She had no idea what could have wrought the change, she thought as she looked at Robert reading the Dallas *Tribune*. Early this morning, he'd looked as if he hadn't closed his eyes all night. Now, after a shower and change of clothes at a nearby motel, he looked devastatingly handsome. The gray cotton-knit sweater he had bought molded his broad shoulders, and the charcoal-gray slacks stretched across his thighs. He had pushed back the sleeves, and muscles rippled beneath the hair-roughened skin as he turned the pages. She wanted to reach out and run her hand up his arm, touch him, pull him close, but he was sitting slightly out of reach.

As if sensing her stare, he looked up and met her eyes. "Are you all right?" Outside the sun was shining, its light reflected in his eyes. His voice was solicitous, impersonal, distant.

"Yes." Marianne's fingers clenched around the armrests, and blinked. She rarely cried, but today she seemed to be swinging between laughter and tears.

He folded the newspaper and stood up. "You're in pain. Let me get the nurse."

"I'm not in pain. I don't want another pill or an injection," Marianne snapped. She took a deep breath. Shouting wasn't going to get her anywhere. When she was in control again, she asked quietly, "Robert, what did I do?"

His dark brows rose. "Do? Nothing." Then, seeing the distress she made no effort to hide, his lean face softened a little. "I'm irritated. You're being stubborn about taking medication. I don't like to see you in pain."

She patiently took a deep breath. "I'm not in pain." But she was aching with the need to touch him, to hold him, to kiss him. "At least not that kind of pain."

For a moment his eyes flickered, then his control snapped into place. Staring down at the newspaper in his hand, he asked, "Do I get the nurse or not?"

"No," she snapped, and, unlocking the brakes, pushed the chair forward. When she was on level with him, she flung her arms around his waist and tilted her head back. "Kiss me, please."

He bent down obligingly and brushed cool, dry lips across her cheeks. When he raised his head, she slid her arms around his neck and pulled his mouth down to her. He braced himself on the armrests, but he didn't pull away.

Softly, teasingly, she outlined his mouth with the tip of her tongue. She didn't know what she was going to do if he didn't respond. She loved him so much that she thought her heart would break with the strength of it. Then she felt his jaw harden with taut control. Lightly she ran the tip of her tongue over his teeth, pushing them apart.

It was more than he could bear. He had sworn to himself last night that he was going to take care of her, love her, spoil her for the few days left. But he wasn't going to touch her again.

He had known that his coolness would hurt her. But at least, he had reasoned, she would be safe. But he hadn't counted on her sweet determination. It was killing him not to deepen the kiss. When her tongue entered his mouth, his control finally broke. He knelt at her chair. His arms went around her, hard, desperate, crushing her with his need.

"I love you."

Tears ran down her face and choked her voice. "You have a funny way of showing it," she sobbed.

Kissing her hands, he placed them in her lap. He then walked to the end of the room and faced her across the bed. He chose his words carefully. He had made so many mistakes. Now there was no room for more. "Yes," he said, "you almost were killed last night, because of me."

"I thought it was the major who ran me down," she said quietly. "And if there's any blame, it's mine, not yours. If I had stayed with the others, I wouldn't have a scratch. But I had seen you go up the hill." Her voice shook as badly as her hands, and she took a deep breath. "I didn't think. I just ran." She took another breath and the trembling stilled. "Anyway, that's all in the past. He won't threaten you again."

"There might be others out there or in prison, waiting to be released. I'm not talking about petty thieves, but men with twisted minds, who become more twisted with each day spent behind bars."

Her eyes narrowed and her temper flared. Her nails bit into the palms of her hands as she tried to retain control. "I see. You're being protective in the same way I am when I tell Bobby not to ride his bike out on the street." Her control slipped a little and her voice rose. "I'm not eight years old, you overprotective idiot."

He smiled at those words—a swift, sharp grin that faded almost immediately. He had expected her reaction and had prepared an alternative. "Where do you want to live?"

"What do you mean?"

He ran a hand through his hair. "Do you want to buy a house in Stony Brook, or do you want to live in New York?"

"What's wrong with Washington?" Her eyes snapped. "I refuse to be a weekend wife."

"No. But I'm going to be a retired husband."

Her surge of anger and frustration was so strong that she forgot the cast on her leg. She pushed herself up on the armrests, and the chair tipped forward. Robert moved, but he wasn't fast enough to tilt the contraption back. All he had time for was to cushion her fall and gently lower her to the floor.

It took her only a moment to recover. "That's the stupidest thing you've said so far," she said. "You'd drive me nuts within a week."

Robert leaned back against the chair he had been sitting in earlier and folded his arms across his chest. "I'll keep the house neat," he offered, tongue-in-cheek.

"Then within a week you'll be yelling at me to keep my closets clean." She groaned. And then she saw the laughter in his eyes, the blazing love. "We'll work it all out," she said, reaching for him. When he bent to kiss her, she added determinedly, "In Washington."

*   *   *   *   *

READERS' COMMENTS ON SILHOUETTE INTIMATE MOMENTS:

"About a month ago a friend loaned me my first Silhouette. I was thoroughly surprised as well as totally addicted. Last week I read a Silhouette Intimate Moments and I was even more pleased. They are the best romance series novels I have ever read. They give much more depth to the plot, characters, and the story is fundamentally realistic. They incorporate tasteful sex scenes, which is a must, especially in the 1980's. I only hope you can publish them fast enough."

S.B.*, Lees Summit, MO

"After noticing the attractive covers on the new line of Silhouette Intimate Moments, I decided to read the inside and discovered that this new line was more in the line of books that I like to read. I do want to say I enjoyed the books because they are so realistic and a lot more truthful than so many romance books today."

J.C., Onekama, MI

"I would like to compliment you on your books. I will continue to purchase all of the Silhouette Intimate Moments. They are your best line of books that I have had the pleasure of reading."

S.M., Billings, MT

*names available on request

Silhouette Romance®

AWARD OF EXCELLENCE

LONG, TALL TEXANS

Diana Palmer brings you the second Award of Excellence title

SUTTON'S WAY

In Diana Palmer's bestselling Long, Tall Texans trilogy, you had a mesmerizing glimpse of Quinn Sutton—a mean, lean Wyoming wildcat of a man, with a disposition to match.

Now, in September, Quinn's back with a story of his own. Set in the Wyoming wilderness, he learns a few things about women from snowbound beauty Amanda Callaway—and a lot more about love.

He's a Texan at heart . . . who soon has a Wyoming wedding in mind!

The Award of Excellence is given to one specially selected title per month. Spend September discovering *Sutton's Way* #670 . . . only in Silhouette Romance.

READERS' COMMENTS ON SILHOUETTE ROMANCES:

"The best time of my day is when I put my children to bed at naptime and sit down to read a Silhouette Romance. Keep up the good work."

P.M.*, Allegan, MI

"I am very fond of the quality of your Silhouette Romances. They are so real. I have tried to read some of the other romances, but I always come back to Silhouette."

C.S., Mechanicsburg, PA

"I feel that Silhouette Books offer a wider choice and/or variety than any of the other romance books available."

R.R., Aberdeen, WA

"I have enjoyed reading Silhouette Romances for many years now. They are light and refreshing. You can always put yourself in the main characters' place, feeling alive and beautiful."

J.M.K., San Antonio, TX

"My boyfriend always teases me about Silhouette Books. He asks me, how's my love life and naturally I say terrific, but I tell him that there is always room for a little more romance from Silhouette."

F.N., Ontario, Canada

*names available on request

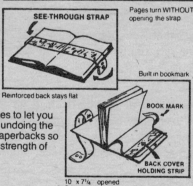

Silhouette Romance®

JOIN TOP-SELLING AUTHOR
EMILIE RICHARDS
FOR A SPECIAL ANNIVERSARY

Only in September, and only in Silhouette Romance, we'll be bringing you Emilie's twentieth Silhouette novel, *Island Glory* (SR #675).

Island Glory brings back Glory Kalia, who made her first—and very memorable—appearance in *Aloha Always* (SR #520). Now she's here with a story—and a hero—of her own. Thrill to warm tropical nights with Glory and Jared Farrell, a man who doesn't want to give any woman his heart but quickly learns that, with Glory, he has no choice.

Join Silhouette Romance now and experience a taste of *Island Glory*.

RS675-1A

SILHOUETTE®

Desire®

ANOTHER BRIDE FOR A BRANIGAN BROTHER!

Branigan's Touch
by Leslie Davis Guccione

Available in October 1989

You've written in asking for more about the Branigan brothers, so we decided to give you Jody's story—from *his* perspective.

Look for Mr. October—*Branigan's Touch*—a *Man of the Month*, coming from Silhouette Desire.

Following #311 *Bittersweet Harvest*, #353 *Still Waters* and #376 *Something in Common*, *Branigan's Touch* still stands on its own. You'll enjoy the warmth and charm of the Branigan clan—and watch the sparks fly when another Branigan man meets his match with an O'Connor woman!